WHAT WILL BE

THE CARMEL SHEEHAN SERIES - BOOK 3

Mary Montoni

JEAN GRAINGER

Dedicated to my mother, who is, and always will be my greatest inspiration, my fiercest defender, my biggest fan and the person who loves me most.

CHAPTER 1

*C*armel sat on the side of the bath trying to breathe normally. Sharif was in the living room watching a documentary about whales, and Nadia was happily surfing the internet on her new tablet. Nadia had decorators in her place, so she was spending a bit more time with Carmel and Sharif to allow the workers to finish the job quickly.

Jen had called Carmel to tell her the exciting news that she was pregnant again. Carmel was thrilled for her sister, of course she was, but why did the news bring stinging tears to her eyes and a pain to the pit of her stomach?

She gazed at her reflection in the mirror over the sink; she looked upset. Sharif would know something was wrong if she came out now. Her naturally blond hair was shiny and sleek as she'd just been to the hairdresser's that day, and she would touch up her make-up, but no matter how she looked, he had a way of seeing past all of it, into her soul.

She'd have to pull herself together. She was forty-one years old, for goodness' sake, she'd had her life transformed in ways she could never have imagined, and she had a home of her own, a caring family, friends and the love of Sharif. So why on earth was she feeling so

1

despondent? She knew the answer, though she didn't want to admit it to herself. She wanted a baby.

'Carmel, do you want some tea?' Sharif tapped gently on the bathroom door. The programme must have ended.

'Eh, yeah, thanks. I'll be out in a minute,' she called.

'Is everything OK? You've been in there a long time...' She heard the concern in his voice.

'Yes, fine. I'm...reading something on my phone,' she lied, reddening, even though there was nobody to see it. She just wanted him to go away for a moment or two, give her a chance to recover.

She tried to keep it together, to not cry.

It was so peculiar, so strong, this longing for a child, and the feeling had taken her totally by surprise. She had never imagined herself as a mother. She'd thought her only chance at motherhood had been her failed attempt with her ex-husband's girls nearly twenty years ago. But even though they were only little when they'd lost their mother to cancer and Carmel and Bill married, the girls had been monopolised by their aunt. There'd been no room for Carmel.

Now that she'd found such happiness with Sharif, she felt frustrated with herself. Why couldn't she just enjoy it? But she couldn't. All she wanted was a child of her own, just one – a boy, a girl, she didn't care.

Being raised in state care in Ireland meant she'd never had a family, never felt part of anything, and now that she was married for love, at long last, things should've been perfect. Sharif was her soulmate, no doubt about it, and his mother, Nadia, had become almost a surrogate mother to Carmel. Nadia had been best friends with Carmel's birth mother, Dolly, for so long that she was able to bring Dolly alive through her stories. Nadia still felt Dolly's loss keenly, and she sometimes expressed frustration at knowing how close they came to reuniting Dolly with Carmel. But it wasn't to be. Dolly died two years before Sharif finally found Carmel on Facebook. He had promised Dolly he wouldn't give up the search, and he was true to his word. Nadia and Sharif had helped Carmel in every way imaginable, giving her a life, a home, helping her connect with Joe, her dad, and

Jen and Luke, his children. She had so much more than she'd ever imagined she could. Nadia and Sharif would have done it all anyway, even if Carmel and Sharif had not fallen in love, but the fact that they had was a happy coincidence.

The hospice they all ran together, Aashna House, was so busy but such a rewarding place to work. Carmel knew she should be content. More than content. She should be doing cartwheels. But here she was crying in the bathroom because her sister, whom she'd only known for less than a year, was pregnant.

Carmel was forty-one and Sharif forty-six, so they were no spring chickens. He didn't have any children. His first wife had died, and afterwards, once he came out of the cloud of grief, he threw himself into creating Aashna. When he and Carmel talked about children, ages ago, he seemed to be under the impression that that ship had sailed, and he was mildly regretful but not sad. He was just so grateful and happy to have found love a second time; that was enough. At the time, Carmel said she'd never envisaged herself as a mother because she was afraid to say what she really wanted. The thoughts swirling around her head at night, as Sharif slept beside her, told her she would probably be hopeless at parenting anyway – she had no experience. What would someone raised in an institution know about being a proper mother? The care workers in Trinity were fine, and even the nuns were all right, but you wouldn't describe any of them as maternal. She wouldn't know where to start to be a mother, she knew that, but nothing would make the yearning disappear.

She was on the pill, and apart from that one conversation with Sharif, the subject was never raised again.

Something had come over his face that day they'd talked about kids, something she couldn't read, and she was afraid to pry. After all, he'd plucked her from her miserable marriage and delivered letters from Dolly, who had spent her life looking for her only child but to no avail. Apparently, the loss of her daughter was the heartache of her life, and the years spent searching and getting nowhere meant she'd died unfulfilled. The thought of it all made Carmel happy and sad in equal measure. She would have loved to meet her and regretted

3

deeply that her mother was unable to find her, but the knowledge that she hadn't been abandoned as a child, discarded like something unwanted, served to heal some of the broken bits inside her.

She took a deep breath and tried to bring herself back to the present. She needed to pull herself together. She was afraid Sharif would think she wasn't happy, or that she was ungrateful. She knew deep down he would think none of those things, but the insecurities she carried, deeply ingrained during twenty-odd years of state care, followed by seventeen years of an empty, cold marriage, were not easily erased.

Before she went back out, she took one more look at herself in the mirror over the sink. The strong spot lighting, ideal for putting on make-up or shaving, hid nothing, and the pain was there in her eyes. Both Sharif and Nadia were very perceptive; she'd have to do a better job of acting like everything was fine.

'Chai or Barry's?' Sharif asked as she emerged.

She smiled. 'Chai, please.'

He handed her a cup of chai, which she'd initially found revolting. At first she'd been afraid to say she hated it because Sharif never drank normal black tea, even though he wouldn't have cared if she did. But after almost a year of living with him, she'd actually come to like chai.

'Are you sure you're OK?' He put his head to one side, his brown eyes looking intently at her.

'Honestly, I'm fine.' She smiled and kissed his cheek. 'Thanks for the tea.' She sipped it.

'Does it still taste like boiled weeds?' He grinned, teasing her about a remark he'd overheard her make to her sister, Jennifer, on the phone months previously. The very next day, he'd gone out and bought her a big box of Barry's tea bags from Ireland.

'Well, aromatic weeds, I'll go that far.'

'So how's Jen?' he asked.

'Good, she's fine. Joe is doing a job for them in the house, and Luke has a new girlfriend, it seems.' She didn't tell him about the pregnancy; she just couldn't get the words out.

She was spared further elaboration when Sharif's beeper went off. He was needed in the hospice. He glanced at it and kissed her cheek. 'I've got to go. I don't know how long I'll be, but text if you need me, OK?'

'Sure.' She hugged him. He was so muscular and smelled of sandalwood and soap. She felt a familiar stirring of attraction.

Something in her embrace caused him to pause and give her a slow smile. 'Mmm, you're so gorgeous. I'll try to be back before you go to bed.' He murmured it all so his mother didn't hear.

'I'll wait up,' she whispered back.

Nadia was so deep in a very animated FaceTime chat in her native Urdu with one of her relatives in Karachi that she wouldn't have heard them even if they spoke normally. Carmel hadn't the faintest idea what Nadia was saying. Sharif could speak Urdu too, as it was the language used in their home as he grew up. Carmel sometimes felt bad that they had to speak English around her all the time so as not to exclude her, but they assured her they were equally comfortable in both languages.

She slipped into their bedroom, leaving Nadia to chat, relieved to be alone. Something made her pick up the phone and call her dad. The discovery that Joe even existed was still new, but in many ways, she felt as if she'd known him all her life. They spoke every day, sometimes several times a day, on the phone. Sometimes just for a minute or two. She knew he wasn't a phone chatter, but he seemed to understand that she needed to have that connection, and to make her feel less needy, he called her as much as she called him.

'Hi, darling, how are you?' He answered on the first ring, his strong Dublin accent immediately soothing her troubled soul.

'I'm OK. You?' She tried to inject some enthusiasm into her voice. She wished he were here in London; she could've really used one of his bear hugs.

'Grand out, pet, flying it. Your cousin Aisling's wedding is taking up everyone's time here, there was some delay with the venue so she was up to ninety, but it's all full steam ahead now anyway. I'm telling you, there was fellas put on the moon with less organisation. I'm

5

staying out of it all as much as I can, but she just rang and asked me to make a sweet cart or something. I thought she was losing her marbles. Like sweets like a child would have, at the wedding reception, only there's no kids going. And I says to her, "Aisling, pet, when people are drinking pints and glasses of wine or whatever, the last thing on their minds are fizzy jellies or smarties or whatever," but she wasn't having a bar of it. 'Tis all the go now, apparently. Sweets, did you ever hear the like? So off with mad old Uncle Joe to the hardware place tomorrow to get the stuff for it. I don't know, more money than sense...'

Carmel chuckled. She loved to hear the stories of the extended McDaid tribe.

'Now, yourself and Sharif and Nadia are still on for the trip, aren't you? I've a great itinerary set up. Come here to me now – you're the very woman for this job. I was talking to Tim earlier, and he was saying he didn't think he'd be able to make it. I didn't like to pry. I know he has some things to sort out over in Mayo with his parents' land and everything, but he was all up for the trip the last time we spoke and now he's backing out. Could you talk to him? See what's going on? He and Brian were very private about their relationship and everything – well, they had to be, on account of Tim's family – and I know Brian was my brother and we were close and everything, but I just don't feel comfortable pressing Tim.

'There's something up, though, I know it, so maybe you could get it out of him? He trusts you. I think it would do him good to come over – it's been decades since he set foot in his native country, and I think it would be to his benefit to lay a few ghosts to rest. Anyway, it's his choice, but you can fly into Dublin and we can all rent the minibus and take off for the West of Ireland, have a proper holiday, not just a weekend for the wedding. Jen, Damien, the baby and Luke are coming as well, so we'll have great craic.'

'Yes, we've the flights booked and everything. Though I can't say I'm looking forward to being back.' Carmel loved that she could be so honest with Joe. Their relationship had started out that way and had continued, no pretence, no saying what she thought he wanted to hear. It was such a departure for her after a lifetime of watching what she said, trying to please, to fit in. 'I'm excited to go to Aisling's wedding, of course, but I just feel happier out of Ireland, you know? Like I escaped. And I'm scared to go back in case I get sucked back in or something. Stupid, I know...'

'Ah, 'tisn't one bit stupid, my love, not a bit of it. But as I'm always telling you, the reason your experience here was so bad, so empty, was because of the behaviours of a few people, not the whole country. You're Irish, Carmel – your mam was Irish and so am I – and no matter what, this place is in your bones. It wouldn't do you any good to build up a big wall between you and it. Like, Sharif is Pakistani. He doesn't live there or anything, but he knows who he is and where he comes from. That's important to the human spirit. I think it is anyway.'

'Maybe you're right. I'm trying just to see it as a holiday, but do me a favour? Keep me away from Ballyshanley, County Offaly, OK?' She smiled.

'Well, I have no notion of going near any town that is home to your ex and his mad witch of a sister, so yes, we're staying out of that part of the country entirely, just in case. But wait till you see where I am taking you – you're going to love it. We need to spend a few days in Westport, to let Tim get things sorted legally with his family farm and all of that, provided of course that you can convince him to come. I'm going to show you all the places I wish I'd been able to show you when you were small, when I could have been a proper dad to you.'

Though his words were tinged with sadness at all the time that was lost, his enthusiasm was infectious, and she felt her mood lighten. 'You're a proper dad now,' she said quietly. 'And I'm so glad to have you.'

'We've a lot of making up to do, Carmel, a lot. Please God we'll have lots of years together. I used to think my job was done, and after Mary died, I was very low. Jen and Luke were reared and doing grand, so I felt like I was only filling in time. But now that you're in my life, I feel like I want to live for years and years to try to make up for all the time lost.'

Carmel felt a rush of love for this man, her dad. She used to dream about her parents when she was small, but she couldn't have dreamed up a better man than Joe McDaid. 'You will. Sure you're fit as a trout, as Sister Kevin used to say. Actually, Sharif was saying the other day that he was at a conference and there's a new drug for the treatment of asthma in trial that is having great effects, so we might both be even healthier in the future.'

'Imagine that.' Joe chuckled.

'Oh, and I'll ring Tim tomorrow, invite him for lunch,' Carmel promised. 'He's finding the days long without Brian, and Christmas was so lonely for him. He doesn't go to his daughter or his son, but I've never raised the question with him. As you said, he's very private, but I'll do my best. I can't think why they are estranged – they could be such a comfort to him now that Brian is gone. It seems such a waste.'

'I know, the poor man. He gave his whole life to my brother. They had a long and happy marriage, even though the state would never recognise it as such, but that's what it was, and his heart is broken – I can hear it in his voice. No wonder himself and his children aren't close. If I had to keep something as big as that – the pain at losing the only person I ever loved – from Luke and Jen and you, I wouldn't be close to you either. The only reason people are close is because they trust each other. If there's no trust, then there can't be anything else either.'

Carmel loved it when he said things like that. As if she was as valid as the son and daughter he'd reared from infancy. 'I know. Maybe he just can't go there now, after all this time. Who knows? I mean, his children must be in their fifties by now. He was only married for a short time when he was very young. I'll try to bring it up with him anyway, or at least figure out why he's backing out.'

'Sure that's all you can do.'

'Well, we're going to be a right motley crew on this bus trip you've planned, but we'll have a laugh, I'm sure.'

'We sure will. Now, pet, I'm going to have to love you and leave you. There's a meeting in the parish hall about trying to do something about the homelessness situation. It's awful, you know, families living in hotels and the whole city full of empty properties. I'm volunteering to get them into habitable shape.'

'Sure you are a marvel, you do know that? Give me a call tomorrow if you get a chance.'

'Will do, pet. Night-night.'

Carmel ended the call and realised that talking to her dad had made her feel better. She wondered if she ever might confide in him about her baby dreams. She doubted it. Despite all the love and family and everything she'd been gifted with, she still felt separate and alone sometimes.

CHAPTER 2

'It is quite impossible. I mean, honestly, what am I going to do?' Nadia fumed as she paced around Carmel and Sharif's kitchen the next day. 'I didn't even invite her, and she just announced she was coming. Booked flights and everything without a word! Who does that? I can't have her – she will drive me insane!'

'Maybe it won't be so bad. After all, her husband isn't long dead. Maybe she just needs to spend some time with her sister...' Carmel was trying to be supportive; she knew how much Nadia's sister, Zeinab, irritated her.

'And what about our trip to Ireland? Her so-called visit is right in the middle of it. It is as if she knew the very worst time and picked it on purpose.'

Carmel tried to suppress a smile as Sharif grinned behind his newspaper. 'She could come with us,' Carmel suggested. 'I'm sure Joe won't mind.'

Sharif winked at Carmel – he knew how her suggestion would go down with his mother.

'Come? Come to Ireland? Have you lost your mind? All of us stuck in a little bus with Zeinab and her ailments and her complaining and her snobbery? It would be hell, absolute hell. No, I'll just have to cancel. There's no other way.' Nadia was clearly devastated.

Carmel knew how much she was looking forward to the trip. She and Joe got along so well, and at one stage, Carmel had even thought there might have been a spark of romance there – but no, they just really had fun together.

'She will come over here and complain and criticise and tell me how my house is too small, my bottom is too big, my *gajar ka halwa* is too dry – I can't bear it. There is a reason I live 5,000 miles from my older sister.' Nadia's tiny frame was almost quivering with frustration. Her normally serene brown eyes glittered.

Sharif sighed and put down the paper. He stood and rested his hands on his mother's shoulders. His bulk dwarfed her. '*Ammi*, you're making this worse by getting yourself into such a state. If you won't contact her and say not to come – which you are perfectly entitled to do, by the way – then you'll have to come up with a way of not letting her get under your skin. You have to come to Ireland. You've been looking forward to it, and now it's all set up. Carmel's right. We'll just take her with us. I think Zeinab might actually enjoy Ireland, and she'll have Joe, me, Tim, Luke and Damien, not to mention little Ruari, to fawn over. You always said she's an old flirt and behaves much better around men, so maybe it's the best idea.'

Carmel smiled as Nadia calmed down. Sharif had that effect on people. Somehow he managed to make people realise that nothing was ever as bad as it seemed.

Nadia sighed and relaxed a little. 'Ah, Sharif, why does she do this? Always the same. Remember the time she came over to help when your father was ill? Dolly and she nearly came to blows, and I was so stressed, trying to keep her away from poor Khalid. The man was dying, and still on and on she would talk, jabbering away incessantly about people we don't know, always this one and that one from Karachi society. It was all to show off how well connected she and Tariq were, as if Khalid gave a hoot about that... Even if we did ask her to come to Ireland with us, she would find some reason not to. She would refuse simply because she would know I want to go.'

Carmel was incredibly fond of her mother-in-law and hated to see her so wound up. Sharif adored his mother too but sometimes thought she was inclined to be a bit melodramatic. She was just a really animated person, the kind who talked with her hands and told great stories. Carmel, after years of people being guarded and detached with her, loved Nadia's spontaneity and how she wore her heart on her sleeve.

Carmel had an idea. 'Look, why doesn't Sharif call her? He can explain that we're all planning a trip to Ireland, about my cousin's wedding and all of that and how we can't change it at this stage, so if she wants to visit, then she'll have to come to Ireland with us. You said yourself she idolises Sharif and would never refuse him anything.'

Carmel tried to quell her own anxiety. Since she'd never experienced them before, confrontation and outbursts of emotion unsettled her and sometimes confused her, though she was trying to learn that they were a normal part of human interaction. One Friday, when her friend Zane had described an argument he'd had with his sister, Carmel had been horrified and really worried about him all weekend. But when he came back to work on Monday, he was full of how he and his sister had had such a laugh at a wine tasting on Sunday. And the first time Carmel had an argument with Sharif, over something silly, she'd convinced herself the relationship was over. But he'd come home and they'd talked and solved it.

Carmel had confided her fears to him, and he'd explained that people who loved each other sometimes fell out – it was no big deal. She was trying to be more relaxed about conflict, along with about a million other life adjustments she had to make every day.

But Nadia seemed genuinely distressed at the prospect of her sister's arrival. Maybe the trip to Ireland wasn't such a good idea after all. Carmel didn't really want to go back, Tim was backing out as well, and now Zeinab was arriving.

The holiday had been mooted as an idea by Joe last year before she and Sharif were married, as a way of helping Tim go back to Mayo and sort out his family affairs, as well as giving Carmel some time with family and to see the sights of her country she'd never experienced before.

Carmel wondered why Tim was suddenly reluctant. He'd told her his story briefly, how as a young man, he had been found kissing one of the local lads in the barn by his father and was told to get out and never come back, that he never again wanted to see his son. Tim had taken his father at his word and had only returned once since the old man died, for his mother's funeral. Tim moved to England and married in London, as was expected, but of course the marriage was a disaster. So one day his wife confronted him with her suspicions and left, taking their little son and daughter with her. Tim met Joe's brother Brian – or perhaps he knew him before the marriage broke up, Carmel never asked – and they'd lived happily and quietly together until Brian's death last year.

The idea of going back to Ireland, even with Sharif and all of her new family, made Carmel nauseous, so maybe Tim felt the same. She was convinced there was nothing there for her any more. The shy, insecure, lonely woman she was still lurked inside somewhere, but she was stronger now than she could have ever imagined. A big part of her believed that strength would disappear the minute she set foot on Irish soil.

'Carmel is right,' Nadia said with a sigh. 'Perhaps if you speak to her, Sharif… She is not so difficult with you.'

Sharif gave his mother a squeeze with one arm. 'That's the spirit. It will be fine – I'll call her this afternoon and smooth it all over. Now don't you have to meet with the family of Juliette Binchet?'

Nadia glanced at her watch. 'Yes, and I'm late. She was a difficult woman too, and her daughter and son are now at loggerheads about the funeral, mainly because the daughter wants a very flashy affair to show off to her friends and he doesn't want to spend the money.'

Carmel smiled at Nadia. 'You'll sort everything out beautifully to everyone's satisfaction, like you always do.'

'We'll see. These two would try the patience of a saint, as Dolly used to say. Anyway, see you two later.' She gave them each a quick kiss on the cheek and was gone.

Once they were alone, Sharif put his arms around Carmel, his eyes searching her face. She loved how his eyes crinkled when he smiled.

'OK, I've tried waiting for you to tell me what's wrong, but you won't, so I see I'm going to have to extract it.'

He led her to the courtyard of their apartment. The plants she had sown last summer, when she arrived, were blooming in profusion, and the fragrance of the lilac and sweet pea was heady.

'If we have to sit here till tonight, I want to know what's up. You've been distracted for the last few days, and sometimes I watch you and you're a million miles away. Judging by the look on your face, it's not somewhere pleasant, so I'm worried.' His voice was soothing and gentle as always. 'Remember, we agreed – no secrets, no keeping things in. We say what we feel.'

Carmel sighed. 'OK...I don't want to go to Ireland.'

'OK.' He paused. 'The first thing is, you're a grown adult...'

'I know, I know.' She finished his mantra. 'I'm a grown adult who can make her own decisions.'

For her first forty years, she'd never had any autonomy. Everyone else had decided what would happen, and she was expected to fall in with it. Sharif was gradually trying to give her back that independence.

'But my dad has gone to so much trouble, and he loves Ireland so much, and he hates that I just don't feel the same way about the place. If I back out, I'd feel like I was letting him down – I *would* be letting him down – and they've all done so much, been so welcoming, especially considering a year ago he didn't even know I existed.

'I know it's not too much to ask to go on a little holiday with my family. And, of course, the wedding. It will be the first time I meet all these cousins and aunts and uncles, and I know he's dying for me to meet them. I longed for a family for most of my life, but it just all feels...I don't know, overwhelming? And then there's Tim. He's getting cold feet as well, apparently, for different reasons maybe – I don't know. I told Dad I'd speak to him. And now Nadia needs some way to cope with your auntie, which is a further complication. To be honest, I'm happier here than I've ever been anywhere, and I just don't want to go back.'

'All right, now tell me exactly why you hate the thought of it so much.' Sharif held her hand, making small circles on her palm with his thumb, which she found strangely relaxing.

Carmel thought for a moment. 'Because I think – and I know this is mad – but I'm afraid I'll be that person, the woman I was when you met me first, if I go back. My independence, the courage I've got, is all to do with moving away from all of that, and going back, well, it feels…terrifying, if I'm honest. Back there, I didn't know about my mother, my father, nothing. I was nobody.' She tried to keep the tremor out of her voice. 'Here, in Aashna, I'm not nobody. I'm Carmel the events manager, Carmel the friend, Carmel the daughter. Here, I'm your wife. Things I never dreamed I could be.'

He drew her into his arms and held her tight. 'What would Dolly say?'

Carmel didn't answer.

'I'll tell you, shall I?' He took her phone from her pocket, scrolled to her videos, and selected the one of Dolly's last birthday party, in Aashna, a few months before she died. Carmel watched the video every day.

There her mother was, in a wheelchair, wearing jeans and a white silk shirt and red lipstick, a bright turquoise scarf tied pirate-style around her head. She sang in her unmistakable Dublin accent. 'When I was just a little girl, I asked my mother, what will I be? Will I be pretty? Will I be rich? Here's what she said to me. Que sera, sera, whatever will be, will be. The future's not ours to see, que sera, sera.'

Sharif paused the video before Dolly gave her speech and looked down into Carmel's eyes. 'When *you* were a little girl, she moved heaven and earth to find you, but your grandfather made sure she never could. If she were here now, she'd say, "What will be, will be, Carmel, my love, but go forward, face the future with bravery." You are one of the bravest people I've ever met, and I know it must be scary, but you're a different person now. You're stronger and you can do this. You might even enjoy it. But in this, just like everything else, we're a team. If you decide you can't or you really don't want to go, then I've got your back, one hundred percent. Always.'

She thought about bringing up the other thing, the pregnancy – or lack of it – but didn't. 'Thanks. I know you have, and I really appreciate it. It'll be fine, I suppose, and I'll have everyone with me, and Joe assures me we're not going near Ballyshanley, County Offaly.'

'I don't know, maybe Julia would invite us all for tea?' Sharif teased.

'Unless you wanted it laced with arsenic, I wouldn't be drinking anything she made you.' Carmel didn't need to remind him of the lengths her ex-husband's sister was willing to go to hurt them. She'd tried to destroy Aashna last year, colluding with a criminal to bring a malpractice suit against Sharif. In the end, Carmel had to visit Bill in Ballyshanley to get him to call her off. Carmel swore that day she would never go back to Ireland – the day she left Bill and the lonely farm for good – and yet here she was, making plans to return to the country of her birth.

CHAPTER 3

*C*armel strained to hear the announcement over the tinny PA system of the airport. The screen said the flight from Karachi was due to land in forty-five minutes, and she and Nadia were sitting in a coffee shop killing time. Nadia stirred her coffee so much it was as if she were trying to wear through the cup. She drummed her fingers and fidgeted constantly.

'Nadia, can you just try to relax? If you meet her like this, then it's going to start off on the wrong foot and that's only going to upset you.'

Nadia had been up since dawn trying to identify and rectify anything with which Zeinab could find fault. Sharif couldn't accompany her to the airport as he was in meetings all morning, so Carmel offered her services as a chauffeur.

'I know, I just wish...'

They both knew what she wished: that Zeinab hadn't decided to soothe her allegedly broken heart in London with her only sister.

Nadia had seemed unusually silent every time Zeinab went on about her 'darling Tariq' when they spoke on the phone. Whenever Carmel tried to talk to Nadia about her sister in the weeks leading up to the visit, it had ended with Nadia listing all the reasons the idea of Zeinab visiting was so terrible.

Eventually, after much gentle probing on Carmel's part, Nadia told her the story of how she and Zeinab grew up together in Karachi's Garden East area, called so because it was surrounded by the Karachi Zoological Gardens. Carmel loved to hear stories of life in Pakistan, and Sharif promised her they would visit his home country just as soon as they got some time. It all sounded so exotic and magical.

Interestingly, up to then, Nadia's stories about their childhoods had always showed Zeinab in a good light. This time, though, Nadia explained how Zeinab had married Tariq, a man older than her but with excellent credentials, a business associate of their father's. Nadia confided in Carmel how she and Zeinab used to make fun of Tariq when he came to the house to discuss business. When their parents sat her older sister down and told her that Tariq had asked for her hand in marriage, Nadia laughed uproariously at such a suggestion, but Zeinab agreed, much to her sister's horrified bewilderment.

From Nadia's point of view, the match made no sense whatsoever, but their parents were traditional, and arranged marriages were the norm, though Nadia was quick to point out that they were more enlightened than many of their friends and would never have forced their daughters into a marriage they didn't want.

Nadia tried to talk her sister out of it. Tariq was as old as the hills, she claimed, and had hairy ears, and was too short, and his breath smelled bad. Despite her giving Zeinab any number of other reasons she should not marry Tariq, Zeinab was determined. Tariq had a fabulous apartment in Clifton, overlooking the beach. He had lots of staff, so his new wife would not need to lift a finger, and all the international designer stores were on their doorstep.

Even the night before the wedding, Nadia begged her sister to reconsider, trying to make her see that money and status were no substitute for love, but Zeinab accused her of being jealous and naive. Things were never the same between the sisters after that.

Two years later, Nadia married Khalid Khan, a man her family didn't really approve of because he wasn't from the right neighbour-hood and his family were not wealthy. They finally agreed to the match because they saw how much the young people meant to each other. Nadia often told Carmel the story of the day she met the man she would marry, when her scarf blew away in a sudden gust of wind and this young man ran to retrieve it. He walked beside her all the way home, telling her stories and making her laugh. It was not the done thing for young ladies from respectable backgrounds to be seen walking with strange men, but Nadia was so taken with him, she didn't rush away. He begged to meet her again, and she slipped out to the market the following day, claiming she needed something, just to see Khalid. After weeks of secret meetings, where they would get together for a few moments of conversation, he asked to meet her family. He professed his love and his desire to marry her before they'd even held hands.

It was a topic Nadia loved to talk about, so Carmel thought it might be a good way to pass some time now in the airport. 'Tell me again about the night your parents met Khalid. I love that story.'

Nadia smiled. 'I know what you're doing, and I appreciate it, Carmel, but I'm not yet an old lady in a nursing home telling the same story over and over, you know!'

A young couple with a toddler and a baby and a huge amount of luggage squeezed past them into the café. Carmel noted the baby sleeping in a sling on the woman's chest, and she felt a longing so intense it almost took her breath away. She tried to focus on Nadia; such thoughts were not helping her at all.

She smiled and placed her hand on Nadia's. 'I know you're not, but I never had any stories like this when I was a kid, so I like hearing them now. It makes me feel more connected or something, so go on.' Carmel made a funny expression, and Nadia grinned and began to tell the story. Carmel wondered at the glow that came over the older woman's face as she recounted her own personal love story.

She began as she always did, with the first night he came to their house, when she was so nervous she threw up. If her parents were not seduced by Khalid Khan's charm, the marriage would be forbidden. He had no fortune, and his father had only a small shoe shop in Orangi Town, not the most fashionable of areas.

When she asked if he could come, both her parents were horrified – firstly, that she would suggest a man not of their choosing, and secondly, that this was someone she had clearly lied to them about in order to meet. He was not connected to their circle in any way, so they knew she must have had unchaperoned and unsanctioned visits with this man. It wasn't the best of starts.

As the crowds milled around, waiting for the flights coming from places Carmel had never even thought about, Nadia reminisced. 'Oh, Carmel, the fear. My father was a gentle, kind man, but he was a proud Pakistani and a Muslim, and this was just not how things were done. It was a testament to how much he loved me that he even considered meeting Khalid. My mother said nothing, but I knew she didn't approve either. Khalid arrived, bless him, in his best suit and in a pair of shoes I later realised had been handed in to his father's shop for repair. He brought my mother flowers from his mother – in our culture, it isn't appropriate for a male visitor to give a female a gift unless it came from another female. Then he and my father withdrew to the study.'

Carmel smiled at how the other woman's eyes shone with love for this young shoemaker's son, even now, all these years later. 'So obviously it worked – he charmed them?' Carmel asked.

'Yes, it worked. My father saw a bright young man, who, though he may not have come from money or status, was a very hard worker, and he knew Khalid would take care of me. It was a great leap of faith for someone like my father, but he took it and agreed to the marriage. Zeinab told our parents they were being foolish to allow it, and that they were always too soft when it came to me. She always said that, that they were harder on her, but I don't think that's true.

'She said there was no way she could associate with me if I insisted on marrying someone so far beneath us in social status. On and on she went about how embarrassing it was for her and Tariq, what would people say and all of that rubbish. Where Tariq was heavyset and short, with a gruff attitude and terrible table manners, Khalid was tall and handsome and funny, and everyone who met him fell under his spell. I think she was just envious. Tariq gave her a lovely lifestyle, true enough, but he was constantly unfaithful.'

Carmel was surprised. This part of the story was new to her.

'Oh, yes, that's one of the strange things about some people in our culture. Not everyone, of course, but a significant cohort of Pakistani men, back there anyway, enjoy a forgiving society when it comes to extramarital affairs. Sometimes faithfulness is not expected, and society would not condemn a man for cheating, often not even the wife. Of course for women, no such understanding is shown. Tariq was discreet, spending time in clubs where women were available and such, but never in public. He would have considered that the height of consideration for Zeinab, almost like she should be grateful he was being so considerate. Some other men in his circle would have made no secret of their mistresses, which is humiliating for the wife. Zeinab knew about his affairs, as he didn't try that hard to hide them, but she never confronted him or even admitted she knew.'

'How awful for her,' Carmel murmured.

'That's not the half of it. One evening, soon after Khalid and I were engaged, Tariq came to our house. I was in the kitchen helping our mother, and she was called away to deal with something. When she left, he came in and made a pass at me. I was horrified and reacted angrily – he really was a horrid old goat – but Zeinab arrived just as I was giving him a good dressing down. I was not the typical demure Pakistani girl, even then.' She gave a deep, throaty chuckle.

'Oh my God, did Zeinab realise what had happened?'

'Yes, and she was mortified, but instead of taking it out on her awful, lecherous husband, she blamed me. She accused me of flirting with him – as if I would – and we had a terrible fight.'

'Oh, no,' Carmel gasped.

'Over the years, things mellowed a little, and we got on up to a point, though she never stops criticising. The only reason there hasn't been a huge blowup between us is because I live here and she stayed in Karachi. Whenever we've visited over the years, it has been tense, and we've spent as little time together as possible. So why she is now coming here, after everything, is a total mystery.'

'But she likes Sharif?' Carmel asked.

'Oh, yes, she loves him, and she loved Khalid too, in the end. He was relentlessly charming, long after he needed to be. It was just his way. But she never really forgave me. Our lives were in such sharp contrast. Khalid never would cheat on me. He treated me wonderfully, and I was his whole world. Even though, as far as she sees it, I married beneath me in terms of class, I got to marry for love, to a man who adored me. And to add even more insult to injury, I had a son. She never had children, and I think it made her so sad. I heard that Tariq had two children with one of his mistresses, but that might just be gossip. That's why it is so complicated between us. I feel sorry for her, of course I do – who wouldn't? But she makes it so difficult to like her.'

'She must have felt like you got it all,' Carmel said. 'That must be hard.'

'Yes, exactly, and on top of it all, she was jealous of Dolly. Your mother was much more of a sister to me than Zeinab ever was. Any time they met, they knocked sparks off each other. Zeinab accused me of confiding in Dolly more than her, of loving Dolly more than her, and of course she was right. That's the sad thing. She was absolutely right.' Nadia stared at the table, lost in thought.

Carmel thought back to the secret Sharif had shared with her about his father. On his deathbed, Khalid confessed to his son that he had been unfaithful to Nadia years earlier, but that it meant nothing and that it was just once. It was with a woman he had known years earlier in Karachi. She'd come to London and they'd had a few weeks together. She returned to Pakistan, never to make contact again. Sharif told Carmel how he was so appalled and accused his father of keeping quiet not to protect his family but to protect himself. Sharif had stormed out of the hospital, horrified that his beloved father would betray his mother in that way. Sharif spoke to Dolly about it at the time, knowing he could trust her, and he'd told Carmel he would never forget the answer she gave him.

Apparently, Dolly claimed that the truth was totally overrated. She calmed Sharif and explained that if Khalid had admitted it to Nadia, the marriage would have been over. She would never have taken him back. Nadia, unlike her sister, was not one of those who would turn a blind eye to a philandering husband. And so by bearing the guilt alone all those years, Khalid saved his wife the heartache of betrayal and spared his son a broken home. According to Sharif, Dolly had a way of explaining things that made the most incomprehensible things seem simple.

For the millionth time, Carmel wished Sharif had found her just a few years earlier. She would have given anything for just ten minutes with her mother.

Carmel dismissed the futile dream and returned to the matter at hand. Nadia never knew her darling husband was unfaithful to her, and she never would.

'Poor Zeinab. Of course she resented my mother,' Carmel said gently. 'I mean, I know she can be a pain, but she's had a lot to deal with too. Look, we'll get through this, I promise you. Sharif and I will be there a lot. If it gets to be too much, you can come round to ours and scream or punch things. And if we can convince her to come to Ireland with us, then the McDaids will charm her for sure.'

Nadia smiled and sat back, thinking for a moment. 'When it became evident that I was only going to have one child, I convinced myself Sharif was all anyone could want. And he is – I adore him, as you know – but it is so nice to have a daughter. Your mother and I talked about you a lot, never knowing where you were, how you were getting along. We would look at women out shopping with their little girls, and we both felt it, a little pang. I feel like we're getting the chance now, not just me, but Dolly too.'

Carmel swallowed the lump in her throat as a tear threatened to spill. She couldn't speak but squeezed Nadia's hand.

They hadn't much more time for chat as the flight had landed, so they made their way to the arrivals area. And eventually, behind a stack of suitcases manoeuvred by an airline staff member, Zeinab appeared, being pushed in a wheelchair.

They watched as the large woman wearing the most beautiful lilac and gold *shalwar kameez* – the loose-legged trousers and tunic top synonymous with Pakistan – tipped the young man fifty pounds. He could hardly believe his luck, the usual tip being closer to five.

'Thank you, my dear.' Zeinab waved regally as he handed her over to Carmel and Nadia.

'Zeinab, what happened? Did you hurt yourself? You never said!' Nadia was clearly shocked to see her sister in a wheelchair.

Zeinab ignored the question, launching straight into criticism. 'Oh my word, Nadia, it is so cold! How can you endure it? And look at you – not enough clothes on.' She turned to Carmel. 'You must be darling Sharif's new wife! I saw the photos of the wedding, even if I wasn't invited. It looked like a big affair.'

Though the words were delivered with a sweet smile, Carmel felt the barbs. Nadia had insisted that Zeinab would ruin the wedding, and anyway, at the time, Tariq was dying, so if she had been asked, she would have said they were being insensitive. According to Nadia, you just couldn't win with Zeinab.

'Hello, Zeinab, how nice to meet you. Nadia's told me all about you. I'm so sorry you missed our wedding. It was quite small, actually. Nadia and Sharif didn't want to add to your pressures, as you were caring for Tariq, God rest his soul.' Carmel began to manoeuvre the heavy wheelchair as Nadia struggled with the trolley and Zeinab's four large suitcases, two duty-free bags and an enormous jewelled handbag. Nadia shot her a grateful glance, and Carmel had a moment of exhilaration at how well she'd handled the situation. The old Carmel would just have reddened and muttered something apologetic.

Once they were at the car, Zeinab calmly got out of the wheelchair, walked to the passenger door and sat into the front seat, regally allowing Carmel and Nadia to load up her many bags and return the wheelchair.

The two women exchanged a glance that expressed more than words could ever say. Nadia was gritting her teeth in frustration already, and Carmel stifled a grin. This Zeinab, clearly perfectly healthy, was certainly a piece of work.

Carmel sat into the driver's seat and tried to look confident. She hadn't been driving long, but she had passed her test first time and Sharif bought her a gorgeous Renault Kadjar as a wedding present. She was determined not to look incompetent in front of his aunt.

Nadia said nothing but seethed in the back as Carmel switched on the satnav.

'Do you not know how to get home?' Zeinab asked incredulously, looking in distaste at the screen.

'Well, I'm not from London – I've only been living here less than two years – and it's a huge city, so I'd get lost without the satnav.' Carmel tried to keep the frustration out of her voice. Nadia wasn't wrong, though – Zeinab was a bit of a weapon all right. That said, she couldn't be any worse than Bill's sister, Julia, and Carmel had managed her for seventeen years so she was sure she could cope with Zeinab for a month. 'I imagine Karachi is the same?'

'Oh, I rarely leave the house, and when I do, I have a driver, so I wouldn't know,' she answered imperiously. 'London is very run-down, is it not?' Zeinab gave a running commentary as they drove, criticising everything: the congestion, the buildings, the jaywalkers… And as they came closer to Aashna House, she ramped it up. 'I'm surprised Sharif did not act on my suggestion for gold gates for this place. At the moment, anyone can just drive in. It doesn't give the right impression. And also those cars in the car park, they are so small! Surely he has a separate staff car parking area? What will people think? If you come to Aashna House, it is for the exclusive treatment by my nephew and his team. You don't want to have to park your Mercedes beside some old dirty *Japanese* car.'

Carmel smiled. Zeinab had Sharif so wrong. He wanted patients, families and staff to realise the place was open to all and that money didn't matter. Those who could pay did, but many more did not.

They drove through the grounds, where verdant lawns stretched either side of the avenue and a tinkling fountain sparkled in the sun. Aashna House itself was an old stately home, so the main building was protected, but behind it, Sharif had built so many wonderful spaces for the patients and their families to enjoy. The one thing he was adamant about was that it should neither look nor smell like a hospital.

The Aashna restaurant, which specialised in organic locally sourced food, was used by everyone in the locality and housed in a huge glass building along with yoga studios, classrooms for all sorts of things, therapy suites and a pool. On the other side of that building was a beautiful garden full of trees, flowers and shrubs, cared for in the main by the patients and anyone else who wanted to get stuck in. There were gardeners for the heavy lifting, but they really only encouraged and supported anyone interested in getting their hands dirty. Carmel had been delighted to discover she too had a love of plants, having never grown anything before. Bill would not have seen the point in wasting grazing land, and in Trinity House where she grew up, there was just a yard.

She felt a surge of pride as they drove slowly past the main house to the apartments at the back of the property, where she and Sharif, Nadia and other staff members lived. She waved at the children from the local primary school who would come in and help the patients with the garden. There was even a group from a young offenders rehab place coming twice a week, and they were teaching some of the older people who were interested how to use the internet. The patients seemed to love them. Initially, she and Nadia had been reluctant when Sharif suggested it, but she had to admit it was working out great. Though if Zeinab saw any of them with their tattoos and earrings, she would probably run away shrieking.

They pulled up outside Nadia's apartment, on the other side of the staff complex from Carmel and Sharif's place.

Zeinab demanded her handbag from Nadia, who was sitting on

the back seat being crushed by suitcases. Nadia shoved the enormous Michael Kors bag forward with a heave. Zeinab took it without a word of thanks and extracted her huge Versace sunglasses. 'The sun in England is much too glary,' she announced.

Carmel caught Nadia's eye in the rear-view mirror. It was going to be a long month. It was with a sigh of relief she left the sisters to it, inviting them both over later.

CHAPTER 4

$\mathcal{N}$adia and Zeinab came by before Sharif finished work. When he arrived, barely in the door, he found himself enveloped in the voluminous embrace of his aunt before he even had time to register her arrival. Carmel marvelled at the transformation in Zeinab.

Though Carmel had invited them for dinner, Nadia said she would bring something, not because she didn't love Carmel's cooking – she did – but because she would hate for her daughter-in-law to get the full inevitable lash of Zeinab's tongue on day one. Nadia had been cooking feverishly all week to prepare for the welcome dinner, and Carmel remarked to Sharif how it was touching that even though Nadia exclaimed how annoying her sister was, she was going to such lengths to impress her.

'My darling boy, look at you! You are so handsome and so fit, I cannot believe some Pakistani beauty did not snap you up, though of course it is impossible to replace dear Jamilla! Oh, what a lady she was. You must miss her terribly to this very day.' She laid her hand on his cheek.

Both he and Nadia spoke of Jamilla often, but never in a way that made Carmel feel inferior or left out, which was exactly Zeinab's intention.

'Hello, *Khala* Zeinab,' Sharif answered, extricating himself from her hug. 'It's nice to see you.' He crossed the room and put his arm around Carmel protectively. 'Hi, darling, how did you get on with the traffic?' He knew she'd been nervous about driving to Heathrow.

'She did wonderfully, like a pro.' Nadia smiled while she chopped coriander, and her son kissed her cheek and gave her a quick squeeze.

'How are you, Zeinab? You must be lonely, finding it hard to adapt to life without Tariq?' Sharif had a way of being both direct and gentle. Carmel had seen it many times with the patients who came to Aashna to die. He never used fluffy words or euphemisms, but he was so empathetic, people seemed to be able to take it. Not only that, but she had seen the trust in his patients' eyes. When everyone else would skirt around the realities and refuse to tell the person in the last phase of life the truth, they knew Dr Khan would be honest.

'Oh, I am finding it very hard. He was my world, my whole world, and life without my dear Tariq is just hopeless.' She sniffed for dramatic effect.

'Well, hopefully you will find some peace and joy here with us, even if just for a while. Company is good, even if you don't feel like it, especially in the early days.' He smiled kindly. 'Be gentle with yourself. It will get better even if it doesn't feel like it now.'

Zeinab replied in Urdu, which caused Nadia to roll her eyes and Sharif to say, 'I'm sorry, Zeinab, Carmel doesn't speak Urdu, so we use English. But if there's something you don't know, then of course I'm happy to translate. Now I haven't eaten yet today, so I'm really looking forward to whatever *Ammi* is working on in there.' He grinned to lighten the mood after his gentle reprimand.

'Your mother has been making something in there, though I don't recognise the smell.' Zeinab dismissed all Nadia's hard work with a wave of her jewelled hand. 'I feared at first we would not be eating properly. Tariq and I always found the food in England dreadful whenever we visited in the past, despite only staying in five-star hotels. All fish and chips and boiled vegetables. But I'm sure Nadia won't poison us.' She had a horrible, tinkly laugh. 'Tell me, Carmel, can you cook? I hope so. If nothing else, you'll need to be a good cook to keep this handsome nephew of mine at home!' The implication was clear: Carmel did not appear to be in possession of any other traits that might keep her husband by her side.

'I love cooking, Zeinab,' Carmel replied smoothly, 'and I've learned a lot about Pakistani cuisine from Nadia and Sharif, so we eat half Pakistani, half Irish, I would say.' She smiled, marvelling at her ability to take Zeinab head-on. The Carmel raised to be quiet and grateful for any small kindness because she had no entitlement was not gone, but she was definitely on the back foot.

'Irish? Oh, dear me.' That laugh again. It was really grating on Carmel's nerves.

Zeinab was oblivious to the insult and carried on. 'I suppose they eat the same as the British but insist on calling it something else. The Irish are a total mystery to me. I mean, where is the gratitude? They don't seem to realise, as we in Pakistan did, that without the British Empire's civilising care, they would still be savages. Instead, all they do is try to create havoc, for a reason nobody understands, not even the Irish themselves, I dare say.'

Carmel understood it was now or never. She'd bitten her tongue often that afternoon, but she knew if Zeinab was allowed to speak to her like this at the outset, it would never change. 'Well, Zeinab, we Irish understand the whole situation perfectly. And we don't see it like that. The British never cared for us, as you put it. They invaded and subjugated us, stole from us, terrorised us, and over the centuries eroded our most basic human rights, such as the right to speak our language, or practice our religion, or own our own land. We were ruled from Westminster with an iron fist, and woe betide anyone who dared to object. So no, we are not *grateful*. We got rid of them through force of arms, the only language they understood at the time, after eight hundred years. That is something Irish people, me and my family included, are very proud of. I would have thought you, as a Pakistani, would appreciate that, given your country's long history as a colony of Britain also.'

Silence descended on the room as Nadia studiously chopped and Sharif grinned, giving Carmel a squeeze and a kiss on the top of her head. 'You'd better be careful what you say to my wife, Zeinab. They are feisty, these Irish ladies.'

Zeinab tried to appear nonchalant, but Carmel knew she had thrown down the gauntlet.

Zeinab looked her up and down as if she was not worth her attention. 'I recall that Irish woman – what was her name – who worked for you. She was very outspoken as well,' Zeinab replied haughtily. She was clearly fuming that Carmel would speak to her like that but dared not say anything further.

Carmel watched her reaction carefully. She might've been a snob and a pain in the neck, but she wasn't stupid. She'd taken in the situation and realised that Sharif wouldn't stand for anyone coming in and upsetting either Carmel or his mother, so Zeinab realised she would have to tread more carefully than when the women were alone together.

'Dolly,' Sharif said. 'She was –'

'Dolly was my mother,' Carmel finished. 'I never met her, though it was my dearest wish, and still is, to have even a few moments with her. But Nadia and Sharif have kept her alive for me.'

Zeinab could not hide her shock. She opened her mouth to speak and closed it again. 'Well, I must say I am' – she noted Sharif's warning gaze – '*surprised*. You never mentioned this before, Nadia.' Zeinab turned on her sister.

'It wasn't relevant. Sharif and Carmel fell in love, and I'm thrilled, as I'm sure Dolly would be if she were here. Dolly loved Sharif, and she spent her life looking for Carmel. I think the whole thing has a nice symmetry to it, don't you?' Nadia smiled a genuine smile, clearly willing Zeinab to keep her nasty thoughts about Dolly to herself.

'Oh, yes, I can see a resemblance now that you mention it.' There was no doubt in anyone's mind that Zeinab did not see that as a good thing, but Nadia only sighed – it could have been much worse.

Dinner was served and was so deliciously tasty. They washed it down with a lovely bottle of Merlot. Initially, as Sharif went to pour some wine for his mother, she placed her hand over the glass, refusing. 'I'll just have water,' she murmured. Drinking alcohol was frowned upon by polite Pakistani society.

'But you love this one – I got it specially.' Sharif smiled innocently, but he knew perfectly well what he was doing. If she refused a drink now, Nadia would not have one for the entire month her sister was there, and while Nadia wasn't a heavy drinker, she loved to unwind with a glass over dinner. Sharif was clearly not going to have his mother deprived of her pleasure because of Zeinab.

'Can I tempt you, Zeinab?' he offered.

She looked at him like he had ten heads. 'I don't drink alcohol, I never have, so no, thank you, Sharif. I was not brought up that way.' She looked pointedly at her younger sister, who was now sheepishly sipping her wine.

Carmel could empathise perfectly with Nadia. Though she was a very capable and confident person, something about being back with the people of childhood makes one revert to who they were then. Nadia was intimidated by Zeinab, and who could blame her? Zeinab was twice Nadia's size and dressed so ostentatiously, complete with an arm full of very expensive bangles, both hands adorned with jewelled rings and a hand-embroidered *dupatta* covering her head. Though she looked in no way like Carmel's ex-sister-in-law, Julia Sheehan, Carmel realised there were lots of similarities. Both women were only happy when they were undermining someone else or pressing their own advantage.

'Well, maybe you should start.' Sharif cheerfully topped up Carmel's glass. 'It is a wonderful way to relax, and we have a glass of wine most evenings, so if you change your mind...'

'I don't think I will, Sharif, but thank you,' Zeinab said primly and went on eating, and even had seconds, without ever once complimenting the cook.

'So have you ladies filled Zeinab in on the surprise we have planned?' Sharif asked.

Neither Carmel nor Nadia responded.

'A surprise for me?' Zeinab beamed. Clearly she thought that this was more like it.

'Yes, a really special one, actually,' Sharif said enthusiastically. 'As you know, Dolly, our family friend, was Irish, and when she gave birth to Carmel, she was forced to give her up for what she thought would be adoption. For a variety of reasons that I won't go into, Carmel never was adopted and therefore was raised in state care. When I eventually found her, as I promised her mother I would, she was married to someone else, but it was not a happy marriage, so she left and came over here.'

Carmel kicked him under the table. This was excruciating. Nadia had deliberately kept the details very scant in her communications with her sister.

'So you are a *divorcee*?' Zeinab's eyes bored into Carmel.

'Y…yes,' Carmel admitted, all previous courage seemingly having deserted her.

'Well, you must consider yourself very lucky indeed then, to have snapped up a man such as my nephew. He could have had anyone.' She rested her jewelled hand on Sharif's proprietarily, but he removed his immediately.

'Oh, I'm the lucky one, Zeinab, not Carmel, make no mistake about that.' His voice was quiet but firm. This dinner was excruciating, but they needed to get everything out in the open. He went on. 'Anyway, in that process, and through a connection we have over here, Carmel was reunited with her father, Joe McDaid. He is a lovely man, and he has a daughter and a son besides Carmel, so she not only found her dad but got two siblings into the bargain. The connection we have with him is through two friends of Dolly's, a gay couple, Brian and Tim. Brian died last year, but he was Joe's brother.'

Sharif carried on despite the look on Zeinab's face, horrified at the mention of illegitimate children, long-lost parents and now homosexual men. 'Anyway, his surviving partner, Tim O'Flaherty, needs to return to Ireland to attend to some legal affairs there, regarding his family land. Carmel's father has arranged that we all go and take a tour of the West of Ireland. Tim hasn't been back to Ireland for years, and since the trip is to take place while you're here, we've checked with Joe and we have room for one more. Isn't that exciting?'

Zeinab looked like she would rather have a root canal than go on a trip with those awful people. She was clearly appalled but managed to recover her composure. She clearly longed for Sharif's approval almost as much as she wanted to undermine Carmel and Nadia. Carmel glanced quickly at her husband. He was suppressing a smile; he seemed to enjoy scandalising his aunt.

'Well, it will be lovely to spend some quality time with you. You've always been so busy when Tariq and I visited before. And I have never been to Ireland. I hear it is very…er…green?' This last was addressed to Carmel, with the most fake smile she had ever seen.

'Oh, yes, very green indeed, and lovely.' Carmel smiled. 'It's a special place. You're going to love it.' She hoped her parents would've been proud of her defence of her homeland.

CHAPTER 5

'Would you mind horribly if I pulled out?' Tim asked as he percolated the coffee in the bright, sunny kitchen he had lovingly decorated with Brian. Carmel had rung earlier to see if he was free, and he'd been delighted. They'd enjoyed a lovely lunch together, and Carmel felt she'd cheered him up a little. Brian's death had taken so much out of Tim, and he seemed suddenly much older than he had when Brian was alive.

'The right thing to say is "of course not"' – she grinned and made a silly face to make him smile – 'but the truth is, yes, I would. Look, Tim, I don't want to pressure you, though I kind of am, I know, but you being there was going to make this trip easier for me. So selfishly, I do really want you to come. I was dreading it too – well, I still am, I suppose – but to be honest, of late I've not had much time to think about it, what with Nadia's sister being here. And now that she's coming to Ireland with us… Well, you'll see for yourself, but she's a handful.'

Tim stopped and looked at her. 'I made one last attempt to speak to Rosemary and Charles last week.'

Carmel waited. He never really discussed his son and daughter; Carmel just knew they were estranged.

'I thought now that Brian is gone, they might... Anyway, they made it very clear they still want nothing to do with me, not now nor at any time in the future.' The pain was written all over his face.

'Why not?'

He poured her coffee. 'I approached them a few years ago. I never said anything about Brian or anything at that stage, but they were not willing to even meet me. Then, soon after Brian died...I don't know, I just wanted to see them, to explain things in my own way, not the version they would have got from Marjorie, so I convinced them to meet me in a hotel bar. I told them everything. I mean, they are middle-aged people now. But they said that as far as they were concerned, I had abandoned them when they were very young, they'd grown up without me, and they didn't need me. They are very bitter at how I deserted their mother, as they see it. The realisation that I am gay seemed to be something they found disgusting, by the way they reacted, but it changed nothing. In fact, it made things even worse. So I left that day, devastated, but there was nothing I could do. Now that I have this land in Ireland, I was going to offer them each a fifty-percent share – call it bribery if you like – and so I wrote to them both and made the offer. I got this last week.' He pushed a letter towards her.

Carmel took it out of the envelope and unfolded the thick cream paper. It was a solicitor's letter threatening a barring order if Tim ever tried to make contact with either Rosemary Taylor or her brother or any member of their family in the future.

'Oh, Tim, I'm so sorry.' She wanted to hug him but resisted. He stood tall and erect, his white hair brushed back from his high fore-head. He wore a shirt and tie every day of his life, and while he wasn't forbidding exactly, he was somewhat private and a little bit aloof. She knew he'd told nobody except her about his life, his loss of Brian or his children, and she was profoundly touched.

'So that's that. I never had a relationship with them to lose, but any hope of a reconciliation is truly dead in the water now, isn't it?' He shrugged.

Carmel nodded. There was no point in giving false hope. 'We are a lot alike, you and I,' she said. He nodded slowly. 'We're both a bit outside of the world...a bit, I don't know, separate. Others seem to interact more easily with society.'

'They had normal upbringings by people who loved them. I think that's the difference.' Tim sighed. 'But yes, we have a lot in common.'

'So this is the reason you won't come to Ireland?' Carmel asked, glancing at the envelope with the solicitor's letter.

'There seems no point. There's a young couple renting the place, farming it – their family and mine have been neighbours for generations. I have enough money, my needs are few these days, so I just haven't the heart for it.'

Carmel knew going back to Westport would be hard for him, but she believed it would ultimately do him good, as it would her. Bury the ghosts, as it were. 'Please reconsider, Tim. We are your friends, and Joe and the McDaids are Brian's family, which makes them yours too. My dad was only saying the other night that you and Brian had a long and happy marriage, and that makes you a McDaid too. Sure, neither of us exactly fits the bill, but they are offering us their hospitality, their homes and hearts, and maybe we should take it. To hell with your children – they've made their choice. Let's go over to Ireland, to Brian's family, and tell them who you really are. Claim him as yours after all these years. Let them know their uncle was loved and had a full life, a happy life. You can let them know how much their Uncle Brian meant to you, be authentic for maybe the first time. I know you probably think I'm begging you for selfish reasons, and I am to a certain extent, but I really do think it would do you good as well.'

She saw the impact her words had on Tim. He wasn't able to speak for a second. Then he said, 'Maybe you're right. It would feel good to be honest, especially with people who loved Brian too. I hated sneaking around. I always wanted to reassure him that it wasn't because I was ashamed of him or of what we had, but because I promised Marjorie I wouldn't ever reveal what I was. She felt it was the least I could do for her after treating her so badly...' He had only the hint of an Irish accent after over half a century in the UK. 'And now the thought of going back... Dublin would be OK, but Mayo... I don't know if I can. I was forcing myself to go as it was, thinking if it would fix things with Charles and Rosemary, but now that it won't...'

'Are you not even a bit curious to go back, to be in the house where you grew up?' Carmel hoped she wasn't being insensitive, but the idea of having a home and having no interest in it was a hard one for her to grasp.

'No,' he said firmly. 'I've no happy memories there. It wasn't a particularly happy house, even before my father threw me out. My mother was fervently religious, to the point of obsession, actually, and my father was a bigot. They were well matched. I never fitted in, and back then, nobody spoke about anything. Really, they didn't. Farming, the price of things, the neighbours – that was all they talked about. I knew there was something wrong with me from a very young age, but I could never tell anyone. I didn't even know what it was to be honest. But when the local lads were chasing after the local farmers' daughters, driven on by lust and greed for land, I just didn't get it. I definitely lacked the lust part, and the idea of farming even more land filled me with horror. I didn't want to farm the land I had, but as an only child, my future seemed set in stone.

'One girl, Kitty Lynch, was my friend. She seemed to just like me for me and didn't make any demands. She was the one that got me into gardening, actually – her parents' garden was the talk of the town. Brian took over the garden here, but he was into all the exotic plants. I love wild flowers. When I lived back in Westport, I planted a wild flower garden in some waste ground at the back of the house. Mam could see it when she was at the kitchen sink, and she said it cheered her up no end to see the different flowers coming at different times. I think it was the only time in my life that I pleased her. My father thought it was ridiculous, of course, that a young fella would be planting flowers when there was farming to be done, but he ignored me most of the time anyway. Just more proof that I wasn't what he wanted in a son, I suppose. All through my late teens, and up to the time they threw me out really, Kitty and I would pal around, getting wild flower roots in the hedgerows all around. Everyone thought we were the makings of a match, though we were never more than friends. If it wasn't for her, I'd have cracked up. I left without a word to her. I've always regretted that.'

'Is she still there?' Carmel asked.

'I've no idea, though I doubt it. She'd be seventy odd years old now. She didn't come to my mother's funeral, so I'm assuming she's either dead or has moved away. I wouldn't blame her, getting out of that godforsaken place.' He sighed heavily.

'Were you never tempted to go back after your father died? See if you could patch things up with your mother at least?' The idea of having a mother, knowing she was there and still choosing not to have anything to do with her was strange to Carmel.

'No, never. That night when my father found me in the barn with Noel Togher, well, it wasn't pleasant. Noel was married the previous summer, but he was gay. He and I sought each other out almost intuitively, but there was no relationship – we never talked, we just met occasionally. And, well, it was the release valve we both needed, I suppose. I hated myself, and in a way, I hated him too. It was complicated. I was so screwed up, as they say nowadays. My father came into the barn – I think he might have seen us go in – and he was armed with a big shovel. He clouted Noel across the back of the head, knocked him out, drew blood and everything, and then he beat me up. I let him, even though I was bigger than him by that stage. I don't know, maybe I felt I deserved it or something, but he really tore into me. Blood, broken ribs, the whole lot. He called me all the names he could think of, and then he told me to get the hell off his farm and to never darken his door again. So I didn't. I left that day. I didn't even stop to say goodbye to Kitty. I felt terrible, but I was in such a state after the beating my father gave me, I would have frightened the life out of her, and anyway, I couldn't face her. I was so ashamed.'

Carmel sat in silence. Tim had given her the outline of the story before, but this was the first time she'd heard the details.

'The only place I could get to was England,' he went on. 'I had no

39

money, no real skills, no friends… I was so lonely at first over here. I wrote to my mother. She replied, care of a priest I knew down in Cricklewood. I don't know if my father told her why he threw me out, but I don't think he did because she didn't mention it. All I got back was a short note, all about saying my prayers and going to Mass and all of that, but nothing more. She wrote again, later, to tell me my father had died. He got cancer.' He paused. 'I didn't go back. The next time I had anything to do with her was arranging her funeral. I lived up on the Kilburn High Road at that time. I'll never forget the feeling, turning the key in the lock of my flat when I came home after burying my mother, the emptiness, the loneliness. I'll take that feeling to the grave with me.'

'Is that why you married?' Carmel asked gently. 'Because you were lonely?'

'I suppose so. I thought if I could just ignore the part of me that was attracted to men, then everything would work out. Marjorie was nice. She was a well-brought-up girl who wouldn't dream of having relations before marriage or anything, so I was off the hook on that front for the entire courtship. She would say how lucky she was to have met someone so respectful, when her friends' boyfriends were forever trying to grope them in the back row of the pictures. She was nice, and she used to bring me home to her parents' house for tea. It felt so comforting to be in a proper home. I was living in that flat in Kilburn – that's where all the Irish were – and I'd got a job in Lloyds Bank. Just a clerk to start with, but I was making progress, so from Marjorie's perspective, I was a good, safe bet. I didn't drink or smoke or go with women. I was steady and likely to be able to provide for her. So she angled for a ring, and eventually, when I could think of no more excuses, I proposed marriage.'

Carmel was confused. 'But you surely didn't think it would work out?'

Tim sighed and sat back in his chair, the home he and Brian had built together all around him, clearly giving him comfort. 'I don't know. I just thought maybe I could deny that part of me. I'd never had any relationships with men after the Noel experience, and that wasn't a relationship at all. Marjorie was going to break it off if I didn't propose, so I asked her. I know to someone of your generation, it seems mad, but I can't tell you how different things were then, not like now, where homosexuality is fine, no problems. It wasn't like that then. Back in Ireland, you could be arrested, put in prison, made to take chemical castration drugs. It was terrifying, and even in London, society was not accepting. Marjorie and a nice safe life was a much more appealing prospect.'

'So you married, and then what?' Carmel was intrigued.

'Well, we married, and she had the children, Charles first, then Rosemary. I managed that much, though I doubt it was much fun for her, and for me, well, it was awful. And then, once the children were born, she announced that she was more or less done with the sex thing. Lots of women of her generation felt that way, I'm told, that it was a nasty but necessary business, and once you had your children, you could happily dispense with it all. That suited me perfectly, and you know, Carmel, we kind of rubbed along together fine for a while. The children were lovely, and I was promoted in the bank. We had a nice house, played tennis, went to drinks parties – it was all fine.'

Tim stopped, and Carmel wondered if he was finished with his confidences. Even though she'd known him almost a year, this intimacy was new.

'I'm sorry, this must be boring you to tears, listening to my tale of woe.' He went to gather the cups.

'No, quite the opposite, actually. It's so interesting. What happened between you and Marjorie if everything was going along fine?'

'Brian happened.'

She could hear the pain of losing Brian McDaid in Tim's voice, as raw as the night she came to tell him Brian was dead. He died in Aashna with her and Sharif beside him, and she'd wanted to be the one to break the news to Tim. They'd said their goodbyes, and Brian didn't want to put Tim through watching him die, so he asked Sharif not to tell Tim that the end was as close as it was.

'I met him through a work thing. He was in insurance. I was in banking – not exactly rock and roll, or what you'd imagine two young

41

men in the mid seventies to be like. Films and so on always present that time in London as all Carnaby Street and flares and outrageous behaviour, but we were so conservative. Suits every day, churchgoers, neither of us drank in those days. But when we met, I don't know, something just clicked. We played tennis together, a perfectly reasonable activity for two young men, and we even took up golf. We were both hopeless, but it allowed us to spend time together without arousing suspicion. I – well, *we*, I suppose – we fell in love, and for me, it was the first time. For him too, I discovered, and we just couldn't get enough of each other. He'd heard about places down in Soho where men would go to be together, so one night we arranged to meet, and down we went.'

Carmel tried to visualise Tim and Brian, terrified but excited to go somewhere they could relax together. Life was so hard for gay people then compared to now. She thought of her friend Zane, the care assistant at Aashna, with his endless swiping left or right on Grindr, the gay dating app. 'How did it go?' She was almost afraid to ask.

'It was…marvellous, really, an eye-opener, no doubt about that. We must have stuck out like sore thumbs. The scene was so very camp, even then. Lots of sequins and colour. We got two beers and sat at the bar, another first for us, and just took it all in. It was the first time in my life I didn't feel like a freak of nature.'

'Did Marjorie find out? Is that what ended it?' Carmel was hanging on every word.

'Yes and no. She didn't like Brian – she was very racist against the Irish. A lot of people were. Signs up on digs: no Blacks, no dogs, no Irish. It was rampant, and even though I was Irish, she always complimented me on having lost my accent completely. I never spoke about Ireland, never wanted to go back, so as far as she was concerned, that was fine. I suppose I lost my accent on purpose, immediately after I landed here, but Brian, as you know, was a pure Dub, and there was no getting rid of his Dublin accent. Marjorie hated that. Maybe on some level she knew, sensed something. Who knows? Anyway, she said she didn't like him and didn't trust him and that she didn't want me seeing him any more, like I was a child. We fought, and she demanded to know why I was so determined to go against her wishes. So I just blurted it out. I think I actually wanted something to happen. I didn't like sneaking around with Brian while simultaneously playing happy family with Marjorie and the children.'

'So you just told her you were gay?' Carmel was incredulous, trying to picture the scene.

'Well, I told her I loved Brian. The word gay wasn't used in those days. Temperamental, theatrical were the kinder words, but there were others, and to my horrified amazement, she knew them all. I never saw such venom and hatred. The vitriol just poured out of her. It was truly shocking to me, this mild-mannered girl, in a twinset and pearls, screaming all sorts of profanities at me. And so I found myself banished from my home, once again, for being who I am. She said that I could never see her or the children again, that it was more bearable to be seen as a deserted wife than the wife of an unnatural beast. She even said she feared I would interfere sexually with the children.' The raw anguish of the reminiscence was etched on his face. 'She made me promise to leave and never contact her again, nor was I to flaunt my disgusting habits around London in case any of her family or friends found out what I really was. There was a threat in there, I suppose, that she'd report me to the bank, to my colleagues. She wanted me to remain a closet homosexual all my life to spare her, and so I agreed. I felt so guilty, I suppose...'

'But wasn't it legalised in the late sixties?'

'Yes, but *legally allowed* and *socially acceptable* are two very different things. I'd have lost my job, so would Brian. We'd have been pariahs. And I wanted to try to make it up to her. It was stupid, I know.'

'I don't think it was stupid at all. I think it was too much to ask, but the fact that you kept your promise all these years, well, it means something. Brian understood, and he loved you for it.' Carmel leaned over and covered his hand with hers.

Tim allowed the tears to fall, and for a long time they just sat in the bright kitchen. Eventually Tim spoke. 'So we're doing this, are we? The pair of Irish misfits going back home, not knowing what awaits us?' He managed a weak smile.

'It's going to be OK.' Carmel found herself reassuring him, though she was also filled with trepidation. 'We'll all be together, and there's strength in numbers. I'm nervous too, but we'll stick together and we'll be grand. To be honest, I think we'll have our hands too full with the infamous Zeinab to be dwelling on our own issues.'

'OK, I'll come. For you, and for Brian.'

CHAPTER 6

*C*armel waited in line in the local Boots pharmacy for her contraceptive pill prescription. Beside her on the shelf were a whole lot of different pregnancy testing kits. What she wouldn't give to be buying one of those instead.

She'd never had occasion to buy one when she was married to Bill since they never had sex, but she could just imagine the horror of walking into Quigley's Pharmacy in the square in Ballyshanley and asking for a pregnancy test. She doubted they even stocked such a thing, and if they did, all it would take is for one of the locals to walk in behind you and your business would be all over the town within the hour. She was still getting used to the indifference, in a good way, of the British. Nobody really cared what anyone else did, or who they did it with. Sharif thought it was funny when she asked, 'What will people say?' about particular things, and he always responded with, 'What people?'

Life here, though only an hour away by plane from Ireland, was light years away in virtually every other way. Well, the way Jen and Luke described Dublin, it was probably more like London, with everyone going about their business without the crippling fear of what the neighbours would have to say about anything, but her experience was of a town in the Midlands, where people had very definite opinions about the business of others.

For example, she was fascinated by Zane's openness about his sexuality. He was gay and proud, and she'd admit to having been a little shocked at his antics at first. Or how Oscar, the yoga teacher at Aashna, dressed in baggy trousers and tie-dyed t-shirts and wore beads around his neck and wrists and probably never thought he looked a little odd. And over here, he didn't, but any man wearing clothes like that or bangles and beads in Ballyshanley would definitely have been on the gossip radar. Ivanka, the occupational therapist, had explained nonchalantly one day how she did a pole-dancing class for exercise and loved it, not even considering for one second how her choice of exercise looked to anyone else.

When Carmel brought it up with Sharif, he was circumspect.

'I, and I suspect most people here, only care what the people they love think. If you or my mother thought I was being ridiculous, or doing something stupid, then I would take notice. But as for anyone else, people I don't know or barely know, why would their opinion have any impact on my choices? I don't care what they do – it's nothing to do with me – and they presumably feel the same way about me.'

She knew he was right, but it was still hard to shake the feelings of a lifetime.

She paid for the pills and smiled her thanks at the Sikh man with the saffron-coloured turban who served her. She buried the little purple oblong box of pills, in its paper bag, in the bottom of her handbag. Her period was due tomorrow.

She went into the bakery section of Waitrose and bought herself a Danish pastry and a takeaway coffee. As she sat in the lovely public park, munching her snack and drinking her latte, she smiled. There was no way on earth she'd have been seen eating a pastry in the castle grounds in Ballyshanley. Public eating was another taboo. She could picture the mothers, taking their kids on the swings, whispering to each other, 'No wonder she's got a muffin top, eating cakes all day long.' Both the muffin top and the gossipers of Ballyshanley were long gone from Carmel's life, but sometimes she had to remind herself of that.

Many's the long discussion she and Joe had about her perceptions of Ireland. He was of the opinion that she was ridiculously negative and that people were not as she imagined them to be at all. Maybe he was right; maybe the women in the park in Ballyshanley would care nothing about whether she ate a bun or not, or maybe they'd think to themselves, *That looks delicious. I think I'll pop in and get some for myself on the way home.* It was hard to know. Her life there had been one of isolation.

Despite living in the town as a respectable married woman, her husband a reasonably wealthy farmer, and the sister-in-law of the formidable Miss Sheehan, local school principal, Carmel had not been part of the community in any meaningful way. Partly it was the fault of those around her, but she'd been forced to admit that some of it was because she didn't try to connect. She'd been insecure and worried people wouldn't like her because of her background, but she may have come across as standoffish.

She sat on the bench, watching life go on around her. A man was teaching a little boy how to ride a bike on the path beside the bench where she sat. Two old ladies were walking their chihuahuas around the lily pond, chatting animatedly as their little dogs pranced along on their tartan leads. A young couple lay on the grass to her left, studying and testing each other.

Carmel marvelled at how she now felt part of this world, not like an outsider looking in, unsure of how to enter this community of living people. She knew it was crazy – she'd evolved so much as a person since leaving Bill and Ireland and the person she was – but she was still afraid to go back.

She checked her watch; it was time for her appointment. The first meeting she'd had with the counsellor, Nora, she'd felt so intim-idated, but now that she'd been a few times, it was actually some-thing she looked forward to. Seeing someone had been Oscar's suggestion, and initially she'd been hurt when he mentioned it. She was of the belief that only people who were mentally ill went to counsellors. She remembered Donie Kinsella in Ballyshanley, who was convinced that Sheila Moriarty who worked in the post office was, in fact, Saint Seraphina, to whom he had great devotion. Nothing would convince him otherwise, even a punch from Mr Moriarty one day when his wife was driven to distraction from Donie saying prayers to her and trying to touch her cardigan every time she came out of the post office for a cigarette. Eventually Donie was admitted to the county home, where a psychiatrist, and presumably some heavy medication, cured him. He was reintroduced to Ballyshanley society after about a year, and he always scurried sheepishly past the post office. The poor man was mortified, and nobody ever forgot his obsession.

Carmel had resisted Oscar's suggestion of talking to someone more than once, until one day Oscar cornered her. He said he understood her concerns, but he went on to explain. 'Carmel, I'm only thinking how hard it has been for you. There's been so much to process, and we all need to take a time out sometimes, to talk to someone who has no emotional investment in us, someplace safe. When I flipped out, lost a ton of my clients' money and was a demon to my ex-wife and kids, spun out of control, I went for counselling, and it really helped.

'Now, you're not like I was, but everyone you confide in – Sharif, Nadia, me, or Zane, or Ivanka, your family in Ireland – we all want what's best for you, but we all have ideas about how you should cope that's all loaded with our own agendas. And how you react, well, that's loaded too. You don't want Sharif to get sad, so you temper the stories of your childhood. You don't want to seem ungrateful, so you don't tell Nadia the things that bother you. You want your friends to like you, and they do, but you hide bits of yourself that you think are less attractive. We all do it. That's why speaking to someone outside of your life, where you can be totally honest, is so cathartic. Just go once, and if you hate it, well, fair enough, but I'm confident you won't.'

He had given her the number, and one day, she made the call.

She'd told Sharif that night, and to her surprise, he thought it was a great idea. He echoed Oscar's thoughts, and she felt better about it.

'Hi, Carmel, how are you doing?' Nora took her jacket, and Carmel sat in her usual seat, opposite the counsellor.

The room was lovely, in the attic space of an old house, full of light coming through the two enormous skylights. The walls were covered with bookshelves, and multicoloured rag rugs covered the polished rosewood floor. Nora had told her she often burned sage, an ancient Native American and also Celtic custom for clearing a space of negative energy, and the aroma lingered in the air.

'Fine, thanks.' The first few minutes were always a bit awkward. Carmel never knew whether to launch into chit-chat about the weather, stay silent or get straight to the issues.

Nora was so still, the most serene person Carmel had ever met, yet she also had a wicked sense of humour, and Carmel liked her enormously.

'How was your week?' Nora asked. 'Last week you were telling me you were all waiting on the arrival of your husband's aunt?'

'Oh, yes, Zeinab. Well, it turns out Nadia wasn't exaggerating – she is a handful. She doesn't think much of me, nor anyone from my country, it seems, so our upcoming trip to Ireland will be interesting, I'm sure.' Carmel smiled.

'And does it bother you that she doesn't think much of you?' Something about Nora's gentle voice made Carmel feel safe.

'Well, it shouldn't, I know that, but I suppose it does, and I'm nervous that she'll be rude to Joe or the others. Sharif says he'll have a word with her before we go, and he'll warn my family not to take any notice if she says something racist or offensive, but I'm dreading it.'

'Is Zeinab the only reason you're dreading it?'

Carmel went on to explain just why she hated the thought of returning to Ireland, of slipping back into who she was.

'That won't happen, Carmel. Who you are now is who you are. You've grown so much, you're your own person, and while the emotions you experience are going to be challenging sometimes, you must remember that the person you have become, that's the real Carmel. Do you understand that?'

Carmel nodded, not trusting herself to speak. After a pause, she blurted, 'I want a baby.' She had not intended to just say it like that, no warning, no build-up.

'Are you pregnant?' Nora asked.

'No. My period is due tomorrow, but I just can't stop thinking about what if I did...' Tears stung her eyes.

'Have a child?' Nora probed gently.

'Yes. I'd love to have a baby with Sharif, but I think I'm too old, or maybe I'm infertile or something. We haven't really discussed it.' She reddened. 'Anyway, I'm on the pill.'

She began to cry, unsure why, but Nora just sat in her chair and allowed Carmel to let it out. Eventually, the sobs subsided.

'Why have you not spoken to Sharif about your dreams to be a mother, do you think?' Nora asked.

Carmel took a breath to steady herself. She'd wondered this herself. She could talk to Sharif about anything...but this, for some reason. He and his first wife, Jamilla, hadn't had children, but Carmel assumed it was because Jamilla was ill. A shadow of grief crossed Sharif's face when he spoke about her still, so Carmel didn't bring it up for fear of upsetting him. But Sharif was so gentle, so approachable. Maybe there was another reason Carmel couldn't bring it up.

'I'm not sure,' she said slowly. 'I think he still misses his wife, and the way she died...and so young... They didn't have a family, but I imagine they would have wanted to, and I don't want to make him talk about it, I suppose.' She paused. 'Or maybe I'm just hiding behind that. Maybe I'm afraid of sounding ungrateful? Or perhaps I'm afraid he would think someone like me, with no experience of being a parent – or indeed, being parented – wouldn't be up to the huge task of rearing a child. I try not to air such thoughts because it hurts Sharif. He never says it, but he gets upset when he hears me think so little of myself.'

She went on, and it felt good to be honest about her feelings without having to consider the effect her words had on the other person. 'He gets it on one level, that no matter how confident and secure I seem now, during the important years, and so many of them, I was disregarded. A lifetime of that can't be erased in a year, no matter how much a person is loved. Maybe it never can be.' Tears stung her eyes, and she wiped them away, embarrassed. She was so unused to being open and honest about how she felt, it was difficult – but surprisingly cathartic. Now, at least, she could express all those feelings of inadequacy to Nora and be spared seeing the fleeting hurt in Sharif's or a friend's eyes.

'Carmel, your emotions are not a reason to feel ashamed. You feel what you feel, and you don't need to apologise for it. Own your emotions instead of trying to stifle them. Why do you think the prospect of not becoming a mother upsets you so much?'

Carmel thought for a moment. 'I want someone of my own to love and for them to love me,' she whispered.

'But you have lots of love in your life now. How would a child change that?' Nora sat forward, shortening the space between them.

'I never knew my mother. And my father – and I'm not even sure he *is* my father – has only been in my life for less than a year. Sharif and I, we love each other, but he could leave, he could die, anything could happen. I suppose I want a baby because that boy or girl would be mine and I'd be theirs or something. I don't know. It's mad.'

'Why are you not sure your father is your father?'

Carmel sighed. If she was to go forward with this and really heal all the years of pain, she'd have to be upfront and honest with Nora. The story of her conception was one that hurt her deeply, and she'd never spoken about it with Nora, even though this was her third session. She took a deep breath to steady herself.

'My mother used to go out with the man I call my father, Joe McDaid. They grew up together in Dublin. She and Joe were sleeping together and intended to get married. Joe hated his father – he was a bully and violent and all of that, terrorised his wife and children. So one night, to stop his father attacking his mother, Joe got into a fight with him. He beat him up and put him in hospital, but more than that, everyone now knew what the old man was like. He was holier-than-thou, you see, reading at Mass and being the real Catholic on the outside but a demon at home. Anyway, he knew how Joe felt about my mother, and so to punish Joe for exposing him, he dragged my mother, Dolly, into a wooded area one night and raped her.' Carmel shuddered.

She took a drink of water to steady herself and went on. 'My mother discovered she was pregnant, and in a panic, she told Joe's father. She didn't know which of them was the father. He arranged for her to be put into a place run by nuns for girls who got pregnant outside of marriage. What he did then, he never told Dolly. He paid the nuns handsomely, I'm sure, but he lied to the Reverend Mother. He said he'd been foolish and had a relationship with Dolly but he was a married man. He told the nun he was going to try to convince his wife to take the child – me – when she got over the shock of him having an affair. He never said *rape*, of course, called it a little mistake, flattered by the attentions of a lovely young woman, all of that. Dolly was never consulted.

'Anyway, he insisted to that end that I never be adopted, and so I was never even eligible for adoption. I was born in a mother-and-baby home and immediately transferred to Trinity House on the other side of the city. I used to hope and pray that someone would come for me. I saw other children adopted over the years, but nobody ever showed the slightest interest in me. I assumed I wasn't pretty enough or something. I didn't know why they didn't want me – I just knew they didn't. I spent my whole life there. In fact, I outstayed my welcome. We were supposed to leave at eighteen, but I had nowhere to go so the nuns let me stay on for a bit. If they were found out, they would have been in trouble, so when one day the letter came from Bill, enquiring if there was anyone who wanted to get married to a widower with two little girls, it seemed perfect. Even the nuns thought I was insane, but I agreed to meet him. And he seemed OK, very quiet but not mad or anything, even though he was much older than me. The idea of having two little daughters to love, well, that sealed the deal for me.'

'And how did you learn all of this if your mother died before you could meet her?' Nora asked.

'Sharif. My husband. He found me. Dolly spent her whole life looking for me, but she'd been told I was adopted and so contact was impossible. Dolly and Nadia, Sharif's mother, were best friends. Dolly was a kind of other mother to Sharif, and he promised her, on her deathbed, that he wouldn't give up. And he didn't, so here I am.'

'And he introduced you to Joe?' Nora asked.

'Well, Dolly had known Joe's brother Brian here in London. They were reunited after years and years completely by chance, and she told him the story of what happened from her end – what their father had done to her, and to me. Brian wanted Dolly to contact Joe, but she refused. She said she didn't want to disrupt his life and too much time had passed.

'Later, I met Joe at Brian's funeral. We met, and instantly I liked him. He knows the truth now, but he thinks he's my dad and so do I. He left it up to me, and I decided against a DNA test, because what good would it do? I can't bear the thought that the man I see as my father is actually my brother and my grandfather is my father. It's all too horrible. So as far as both of us are concerned, Joe is my dad, and we're leaving it at that.'

Carmel stopped speaking, and Nora just waited. The silence wasn't awkward; if anything, it was soothing.

'Our time is nearly up, but this week I'd like you to give some thought to this. Why are you not telling Sharif about wanting a child? Maybe do some of those guided meditations I gave you. Stillness can clarify our thoughts.'

Carmel nodded as she put on her jacket. She had a lot to think about.

CHAPTER 7

*C*armel was counting down with dread the time before the trip to Ireland. She knew she was being ridiculous. It was just a holiday, she was a grown woman, and they weren't going anywhere near Ballyshanley or Bill or Julia. She needed to get a grip.

She'd slammed her computer shut the previous day when she heard Sharif's key in the lock because she'd been looking at pictures of newborn babies. She knew she should talk it out with him, but something was stopping her. Besides, he had so much to organise in order to get away. He would never pry; she'd have to tell him. He didn't ever interrogate her about the counselling, and at the beginning, she'd felt she should tell him how things were going with Nora. But over dinner the first night after Carmel started seeing her, he'd said, 'I know this therapy is a process, because when Jamilla died, I found it so hard – not just her loss, but the fact that I was a doctor who could help others but could do nothing for her. I just sat there, watching her fade away in front of my eyes. In the end, I went to speak to someone, a therapist, and it helped. I was against it at first – doctors are terrible patients – but in the end, my grief, depression, whatever you want to call it, was taking over my life. The man I saw was great, and he gave me good advice. He said not to talk to people about what happened there, not to let the work that was done in the therapist's office spill out into my life, and he was right. Deal with it in there, say what you need to say, and then get on with your life. Sometimes when we are working through issues, we feel a need to share it with those around us and then, afterwards, regret it.

'In the months after Jamilla died, sometimes I talked incessantly about her, then other times I didn't mention her name for weeks. It was weird. After a while, George explained that I needed to get things clear in my own head first, and so at his suggestion, I told my parents that I would speak to them when the time was right. I asked them if they could just accept that I was dealing with it my own way and give me the space to do that. They understood, and though they were worried about me, they never pried. And in due time, we got to talking about her again. I want you to have that same space, so I won't be badgering you to tell me how you're getting on. Talk to me any time you want, of course, but only when you decide.'

He was so understanding, so emotionally evolved, that sometimes he intimidated Carmel. He never lost his temper, or got frustrated or upset. He really was a very calm person, very mindful. But sometimes she wished he could be a bit more flawed. Immediately after she thought it, she felt a pang of guilt. She'd had years and years of marriage to an emotionally stunted man, totally incapable of even the most perfunctory of human interaction, and now here she was with Sharif and she wished he was different. It wasn't even that she wanted him to be different – he was funny and charming and handsome and kind, everything you'd want in a husband – but she felt inadequate beside him, no matter how often he told her that in the eyes of the world, they were equals, that only she saw all her hang-ups and imagined shortcomings.

Carmel pottered about the apartment, taking a rare day off. Sharif was very busy at the clinic that day, but he checked in by text whenever he got a moment. She'd gone out for sushi with Zane and Ivanka the previous night and woke at three in the morning, vomiting. She thought the sushi had tasted off, but since she'd never had it before, she didn't want to appear gauche in front of her friends and ate it. Sharif gave her an injection to stop the nausea and left her with strict instructions to stay in bed and take it easy. Though she felt like death warmed up, he assured her it was a mild case of food poisoning – Ivanka and Zane were off with the same complaint.

She had stayed in bed for an hour, but a lifetime of early rising was ingrained, so eventually she got up. She thought she might as well pack her bag for the trip. She was a bit early, but she liked to be ready and anyway couldn't venture too far from the bathroom. In the bottom of the wardrobe lay her little brown suitcase; it looked like the one Paddington Bear carried, Sharif had joked. The idea that she had fitted everything she owned in that just a year ago astounded her as she surveyed her walk-in wardrobe with the long shoe rack. She still didn't spend much, and lots of things she picked up in charity shops or in the sales, but still her wardrobe was so much more diverse and glamorous than it used to be.

She was choosing which jumpers to bring – even though it was summer, the evenings got chilly – when the doorbell rang. Sharif was working, and anyway, he had a key and so did Nadia, though she never really called unannounced.

Carmel went to the door, her heart sinking as she saw the colourful bulk through the opaque glass. She opened it with a fake smile on her face. This really was the last thing she needed. 'Zeinab, how nice to see you. Is Nadia not with you?' Carmel desperately looked behind Zeinab in the hope of seeing her mother-in-law. She'd never had to deal with Zeinab alone before, and she was nervous.

'No, she is not my keeper, Carmel. Can I not visit my nephew's house without a chaperone?' The way she pronounced Carmel's name seemed to leave out the middle R, sounding more like 'Camel'. Carmel was sure it was deliberate.

'Of...of course... Please come in.' Carmel moved aside to allow Zeinab to enter.

The other woman swept imperially into the apartment, perfectly able-bodied despite the incessant complaints about her knees and her hip and her back that drove Nadia up the walls. 'This really is such a small place, considering Sharif owns this entire complex.' Zeinab glanced around their lovely home dismissively. 'Why does he live so modestly, do you think?'

'Er...well, we like it here. And we don't need much space.' Carmel wished she could be more forceful and tell this old bat where to get off, but she didn't dare.

'Well, I expect that for you it must seem like a palace, after all you've been through?' The tone was sickly-sweet, but the words cut Carmel. She didn't need sympathy, and anyway, what Zeinab was offering wasn't sympathy – it was condescension.

'Actually, the house I grew up in was very large, lots of rooms, so this is nice and cosy.' She tried to inject some brightness into her voice. Zeinab reminded her of those predators she and Sharif had watched on Planet Earth on the BBC, David Attenborough explaining how they sat and waited, sensing fear, and then pounced on their prey.

'Yes, an orphanage, Nadia said. And then you were sold into some kind of arranged Catholic marriage or something?'

Carmel swallowed the lump of hurt. She was fairly sure Nadia would never have spoken about her like that. This was Zeinab twisting the knife, trying to belittle her. 'Well, it was a children's home, not an orphanage, and my first marriage wasn't arranged. It just didn't work out, that's all, and now...well, now...' She had started well but faltered.

'Now you're happily installed here, married to my very wealthy nephew. How nice for you. It must be a relief to live so comfortably after years of uncertainty.' Zeinab smiled, but it never reached her eyes. She was eagle-eyed as her gaze rested on photographs and the few special items Carmel and Sharif had chosen to decorate their home. She went on. 'I was looking at the property pages this morning. There really are some lovely homes to be had around here. Not of the standard you'd find in Karachi – space is at such a premium here in

London, so people have to forego the extensive grounds and so on that we enjoy in Pakistan – but very nice homes nonetheless.'

Carmel had no idea where this was going, but she was convinced it was going somewhere.

'Have you ever looked at those?' Zeinab asked, and produced that smile again. It gave Carmel the shudders.

'Er…well, I've seen some houses for sale when I go for a walk sometimes, but I can't say I've taken too much notice, to be honest.' Carmel tried to steer the conversation into less bewildering waters. 'Would you like a drink?'

She tried to quell another sudden wave of nausea. The injection Sharif had given her had stopped the vomiting, thankfully, but she still felt very queasy.

'Yes, tea.' Zeinab sat herself down on the sofa and took up the framed wedding photo on the side table; Carmel and Sharif were laughing in it. Zane had taken the picture on his phone the day they got married. Though they'd had an official photographer and his album was really lovely, this was the photo they liked best. Carmel would always remember the moment it was taken. A very disgruntled Ivy, one of the cleaners at Aashna, had just returned from the ladies', where, she explained, the cast-iron guaranteed-to-have-no-spare-tyre slip she was wearing beneath her dress had rolled up from the bottom and down from the top and had been attempting for the entire wedding ceremony to cut her in half around the middle. Her descriptions of the struggle to get the cursed thing off in the bathroom had the entire table in stitches.

'I must say, I was surprised to hear Sharif had remarried. He so loved dear Jamilla.' Zeinab interrupted the happy memory. 'She was such a wonderful girl, an angel. I never thought he would get over it. Then I suppose one never truly recovers from the loss of a spouse. A love like they had, well, it only comes along once in a lifetime, if you're lucky.' She accepted the cup of tea from Carmel.

'He often talks about her,' Carmel said, trying to ignore the jibe. 'She sounded like a wonderful person. I know they were very happy together.'

'Oh, yes, she really was. She was a nurse, such a kind, caring girl, and her family are very well respected. Her uncle runs a lovely country club just outside Karachi, and her mother's people are very wealthy, property tycoons really, you could say. I remember how she came to my house when I hurt my back years ago – oh, she was so knowledgeable, so gentle, but you just felt like she was so competent. I begged her to go back to Sharif once I was able to get around, but she insisted on staying until I was totally better. Oh, and my Tariq, he adored her. Well, everyone did really.'

'She went to care for you in Karachi?' Carmel tried not to sound incredulous. The idea that anyone would leave Sharif to spend time with this old bat mystified Carmel.

'Yes.' The normally verbose Zeinab was surprisingly tight-lipped. She gazed at Carmel, her dark eyes scheming, and then she spoke. 'She needed some time, after all she'd been through.' She sipped her chai.

'With the cancer?' Carmel asked, not out of curiosity as much as not wanting to appear unfeeling.

'No... Well, yes, among other things. I'm sure Sharif has explained.' She smiled sweetly.

Carmel had no clue what she was going on about but was determined not to show her ignorance of such a huge part of Sharif's life. 'He's told me a lot about the life he and Jamilla shared. They were lucky to have known such love.' She didn't really know what else to say. She'd never felt threatened by his dead wife before now, not like she had with Bill and the huge wedding photo in the living room of his dear departed Gretta. Bill was not free, that was the fact. It seemed so obvious now, but she'd wasted all those years trying to get him to feel something for her. His rejection merely confirmed what she'd known all her life: that she was unlovable. She was trying so hard to foster feelings of compassion for her younger self. It wasn't that she was unadoptable – her grandfather had ensured nobody could adopt her. Likewise, Bill didn't reject her because of anything she was or wasn't – he'd just never got over losing Gretta. Carmel had to keep reminding herself of these facts.

Sharif, on the other hand, acknowledged that he and Jamilla had been good together but it was in the past. She was gone and they were here, and he was convinced she would want him to move on and be happy.

But Zeinab droned on. 'Yes. Everyone loved Jamilla. Especially Khalid, Sharif's father. Oh, he adored her, and she him. And of course, Nadia, Tariq and I – she had everyone under her spell. Now tell me more about you. As I said, I was so surprised to hear Sharif was remarrying, but I suppose men, they have needs, and Sharif is not the sort to just have a string of romances behind him. Still, there must have been something special about you?' Her tone suggested that Carmel being remarkable in any way was most unlikely.

Carmel resented this cross-examination, the feeling that she had to make the case for her and Sharif's marriage, and on top of that, she got the distinct impression there was something Sharif hadn't told her about him and Jamilla, something everyone else in the Khan family knew. They were normally so open and honest with each other, it hurt her to think there was something important he had kept from her.

'I don't know, really. We just met and sort of clicked, I suppose. He said I remind him of my mother, and he was very fond of her. She was almost like another mother to him...' That was definitely the wrong thing to say, judging by the look on Zeinab's face.

'Really? I thought she just worked for Nadia. I know she and Khalid gave Dolly – was that her name? – some support, financially, I mean, but I thought that was simply because she was a loyal employee of Nadia's business.'

Carmel gritted her teeth. Zeinab knew well the relationship between her mother and Sharif's family, but she was trying to unsettle Carmel. 'No, Nadia and my mother were partners in the dressmaking business, and she certainly was more to the Khan family than just that. She and Nadia were best friends, and she helped nurse Khalid in his final months. It was because she meant so much to him that Sharif found me. He promised her that he wouldn't stop looking.'

Zeinab seemed to be enjoying getting rise out of Carmel, as they said in Ireland. She barely suppressed a smirk. 'So you are Dolly's daughter, and your father – I know you've met him and his family? – was married to someone else?' Her brow furrowed dramatically. She was making it sound like Carmel's family was not only highly distasteful but also utterly confusing.

How dare she? Carmel was seething now. Normally, she was very open about her story – well, the part about her mother and father anyway. Very few people knew her true story, the reason she was never adopted, and she did not care to enlighten them. She prayed Nadia hadn't inadvertently let something slip.

'Oh, Joe is wonderful. I love him dearly. Yes, after he and my mother parted ways, he married a lovely lady called Mary and they had two children, Luke and Jennifer. You'll meet them. Sadly, Mary died a few years ago.'

'And does he live alone?'

Carmel was thrown by the question. Everything Zeinab said was heavily loaded, so this was a bit of a random enquiry. She wondered what was behind it. She longed to chuck the nosy old biddy out, but she was Sharif's aunt and Nadia's sister, so Carmel didn't dare. 'Er... yes. Jennifer lives close by with her husband and little boy, and Luke has an apartment in the city. My sister, Jennifer, is a stay-at-home mum at the moment, looking after my nephew, Ruari, and my brother, Luke, is a detective in the Irish police.' She felt the familiar surge of pride at saying the words 'my brother' and 'my sister'.

'How interesting that they would consider themselves your siblings though you were a stranger up until recently. It must take some adjusting to suddenly find yourself at the centre of a big family when for so long you were alone?'

How did Zeinab manage to make everything she said sound mean, when those words from anyone else's lips wouldn't be seen as such? Carmel berated herself – she was being too sensitive. Zeinab was trying to rile her, and Carmel was damned if she would allow it. 'Yes, it is a bit different, but I'm loving it.' Carmel smiled serenely.

'And your father lives alone? Is he fit and healthy?'

'Yes, he's in great shape. He loves DIY and all of that, so he's always doing something.' Carmel glanced at the clock. Sharif wouldn't be back for ages, and she could think of no other way of ending this audience with Zeinab, but she wasn't going to spend her whole afternoon talking pointlessly with her.

'Well, when someone is fit and healthy, then it is fine, I suppose. I was never alone, thankfully. I always had Tariq, bless his soul. But now that I'm older and not as agile as I was, well, it is different. So many of my friends are lucky to have children to take care of them, but Tariq and I were never blessed with a family. It is a struggle to keep going, I can tell you.'

Nadia had told Carmel that Zeinab had all kinds of help in the house and that she got out and about all the time. She had a chauffeur, and a maid and a gardener. As they said in Ireland, there was no fear of her, but she was angling, no doubt about it. 'But don't you have a lot of staff back in Karachi?' Carmel asked.

'Oh, yes, paid employees. Not the same as family, though. Nothing like family. In our culture, Carmel, care of the elders, respect for them, is very important. It is part of what we are, the way we take care of our older generations, visit them, spend time with them. Many of my friends now live with their children, or even nieces or nephews. Take my friend Amal, for example. She held out in her own house for as long as she could, of course, but in the end, her children were so upset at the thought of their elderly mother living alone that they insisted she come and stay with them. She was sad to leave her home, of course, but she is so lucky. I don't have anyone to do that for me. Nobody at all.' She sighed heavily.

Carmel fought the urge to either panic or laugh. Was Zeinab seriously angling for an invitation to come and live with her and Sharif? *She must be off her rocker if she thinks we'll agree.* 'But, Zeinab, you're still a young woman. You're fit and healthy, and as you said, you have lots of friends. I know it is hard to cope without Tariq' – Carmel managed to make it sound sincere despite what she knew about the creepy man – 'but if you can, try to see it as a transition phase in your life. You will need to grieve for all you have lost, but certainly it is not advisable to make any big changes so soon after a bereavement.'

Zeinab gazed at her, clearly weighing up how best to proceed. 'Yes, I am sure you are right.' Her tone could've cut glass. 'Now I must go. Thank you for the chai.' And with remarkable agility for one supposed to be so infirm, she left, leaving Carmel standing in the middle of her kitchen wondering what on earth had just happened.

CHAPTER 8

'Hi, Jen!' Carmel accepted a FaceTime call from her sister in Dublin the next day. She was back at work and feeling better, though not one hundred percent yet, as she still had some stomach cramps. Ivanka was still off, and Zane was thrilled the impromptu food poisoning meant he'd lost five pounds. He was thin as a rail anyway but incredibly vain, so he threatened to go back there again for another dose any time his impossibly skinny trousers felt tight. Carmel couldn't help but laugh, though she would never again darken the door of the Sushi Palace.

'Hi! Is it a good time or are you busy?' Jennifer asked. She was always conscious that Carmel could be dealing with anything when she called. 'I've just got Ruari down for a nap, so I can talk in peace for five minutes!'

'No, it's great. Let me just get a coffee and I'll go into my office and we can have a proper chat.' She filled her cup from the fancy new coffee machine in reception, donated by the family of a grateful patient.

'Now,' Carmel said, settling into her chair, 'tell me all your news.'

Carmel had got used to the idea of Jen being pregnant again and felt fine speaking to her about it. That initial wave of longing seemed to have dulled to an ache, and she knew she could hide it successfully. If living as she did for the first forty-plus years of her life had taught her anything, it was how to cover up her true feelings.

'Oh, I've no news really. My social life is zero these days, in bed by eight, dozing when Damien gets home and can take Ruari for an hour, not cooking at all, you know yourself.' Jen, with her blooming complexion, grinned at Carmel from the screen of her iPhone.

Carmel wished she did know herself but dismissed the thought immediately.

'Actually, Dad's on his way over here,' Jennifer said. 'We're going to put on an extension out the back. Dad reckons himself and Damien will be able to do it, with a bit of help from Luke, but I'm not sure. I'd rather get proper builders.' Jen chuckled. 'Y'know, the kind that are actually qualified?'

Carmel smiled. 'But think of the money you'll save, and Joe has done loads of that sort of thing before, hasn't he? I'm sure it will be gorgeous.' Carmel sipped her latte. 'What are you building anyway?'

'Well, you'll see when you come over! I can't believe you haven't been here – it feels like you've been in the family forever. Anyway, yeah, we're building another bedroom. We're going to need it when this little one arrives.' Jen's smile said it all as she placed her hand on her belly. 'Apart from the fact that I need somewhere for my sister to stay when she comes to visit.'

Carmel nailed a smile to her face, ignoring the maelstrom of emotion churning inside her. 'Well, Joe is determined to get us over for the wedding and this big road trip he's planned, so I'll be there, all right. Now tell me, how are you feeling? I've heard the first three months can often be the toughest?'

'Not too bad, actually. Exhausted, but I'm that way anyway running around after Ruari all the time. He's got the energy of five kids, I swear. But all in all, I'm doing well. I hate coffee now – I was the same when I was expecting Ruari. I can't even bear the smell of it, and I used to be a five-cup-a-day girl. But apart from a little nausea now and again, I'm grand.'

'I'll send you some of this amazing tea Sharif gets. I never had it before coming here, but he recommends it for people who feel a little nauseous after chemo. It really perks you up, but it's made just from flowers and roots or something. I know it's safe in pregnancy because he gave it to a patient's daughter who was pregnant, and she said she felt much better after it.'

'Thanks, sounds good. I'm just really happy, so all that small stuff doesn't matter really. We were waiting ages for Ruari – I told you that. I didn't know if there was something wrong or what, but when I finally got pregnant after two years of trying, well, we weren't sure if we'd ever get lucky again. But it seems we hit the jackpot again, so we're over the moon.'

'Of course you are! It's wonderful news. Joe must be delighted at the prospect of another grandchild.'

'He was. He got kind of emotional, actually, which isn't like him. I'd told Luke already and he's thrilled. He's on some big drugs case in Madrid, an Interpol case involving loads of countries, but the culprits are Irish, wouldn't you know, so he's out there. He comes home most weekends though and goes back out on Mondays.'

Carmel had spoken to Luke last Monday morning as he waited to board a flight back to Spain. 'Would it not be easier for him just to stay there?'

'Well, that's the other bit of news. Don't say I said it – I'm not even supposed to know – but our Lukie is seeing a girl and he seems to be very into it. She's the reason he's on a flight every Friday. Otherwise, boy wonder would be chilling out with the tapas and the *señoritas* at the weekends in sunny Spain. But no, back he comes to rainy Dublin, sure as anything. He's being very cagey about it, though. Hasn't said a word to anyone, not even Dad, and he tells him everything.'

'So how do you know?' Carmel was intrigued and really hoped it was someone nice. Luke was such a sweet guy; she'd hate for anyone to hurt him. For all his messing and joking around, he was a sensitive soul.

'Well, because Dublin is a village really, and you can't do anything without the whole place knowing your business. Aisling works for Aer Lingus, so she saw him in arrivals at the airport. Real romcom stuff – this girl was waiting for him at the gates, then running into his arms kinda thing. He didn't see Ais, so she let him off, but we were all wondering what he was up to. He's been very secretive of late. Sometimes he gets like that when he's on a big case, so we thought it was that, but no. Love is in the air, apparently.'

'Ah, I hope it works out for him. He hasn't had a serious girlfriend before, has he?'

'Oh, he did – God, what a tale of woe that was. She was Italian, gorgeous, tiny, all brown eyes and shiny hair and talking with her hands...' Jen rolled her eyes.

Carmel chuckled. 'I'm sensing some resentment there, Jen.'

'Yeah, well, wait till you hear. He was weak for her, stone mad about her, and she was a right little princess. Anyway, she went home to Verona for her mother's birthday or something. Luke was supposed to go but had to work, so she went alone. They were together over a year, and he just idolised her. And anyway, what does my lady do? Only send him a text – a text, can you believe it? – to say she was staying in Italy, she had fallen in love with some Marco or Pietro or Franco or whatever, like in four days or something, and basically told poor Luke to send on her stuff, that she wasn't coming back. He was gutted, absolutely devastated, and I wanted to rip her stupid Barbie doll head off of course. But anyway, it ended and that was that.'

'Oh no, poor Luke. That's awful.'

'Yeah, he was months getting over it. I'm half afraid this is another Italian and that's why he's being so secretive. Or maybe he just doesn't want us all having opinions. It's one of the downsides of a big family, Carmel – everyone's an expert!'

Carmel laughed. 'I can't wait to meet everyone at the wedding.'

'Oh, you'll be like Kim Kardashian! You'll be photographed to death, and everyone will want to hear your story from the horse's mouth. You've given the family no end of gossip fodder. I never really knew about your mam – thankfully Dad didn't go on about it – but now that you've reappeared in our lives, it seems like everyone knew Dolly was the great love of his life.'

Carmel detected a sadness in her sister, and she was anxious to alleviate any misgivings. 'Joe's told me so often how much he loved your mam, Jen, genuinely loved her, not as a consolation prize or whatever. They had a great marriage. I'd hate to think me turning up was destroying the real memory of that. And even though I never got to meet my mother, I think she would have been very upset too if that happened. She knew your dad was happy with Mary, and that's why she never went back.'

'Ah, I know that. It's a bit stupid, and I'm really happy we found you, so happy about that... But yeah, in a way, it does make me sad that everyone is going on about the thing my dad had with Dolly. Not to mention being forced to face the fact that my dad had a physical relationship with someone other than my mam. It's not something anyone likes to dwell on, I know, and we never had to until now, so yeah, it's not always easy. I mean, they always say, "Oh, but he had a great marriage with Mary too", but almost like a side point or something. Luke and I got a bit odd with our aunt the other day when we met her and she started with it again...'

Carmel loved the honesty that existed between them. From the very first meeting with her sister, there had been no pretence. They both just said things as they felt them.

'I can imagine how hard that must be,' Carmel said gently. 'I wish I could do something to stop it. I know that's not how Joe sees it anyway, and that's what really matters.'

'Yeah, exactly. We'll just have to stick together and put up with a bit of tongue wagging.'

'Always. I'm one hundred percent behind you and Luke. You could have told me to buzz off and that you wanted nothing to do with me, and nobody would've blamed you, but you didn't. I owe you both big time, so you'll always have my loyalty.'

Jen smiled; her eyes were suspiciously bright. 'Don't mind me, it's all the hormones. Damien says I'm mental these days, laughing one minute, crying the next. It's this little trickster in here I blame.' She placed her hand on her belly again.

'So speaking of which, is it a boy or a girl, do you think?' Carmel asked.

Jen smiled. 'I don't honestly know, though either will be great. My mam used to say boys wreck your house and girls wreck your head, so either way, destruction is in my future!'

'You must miss her, especially now,' Carmel said quietly.

'I do, so much. But – and I'm not just saying this, Carmel – I love having you as a sister. I know you don't have kids, but it's nice to have a woman in the family to talk to. Dad's great and everything, but he's my dad, y'know? And I think every time I mention the pregnancy, Luke changes the subject for fear I'm going to give him too much information on my internal workings.'

Carmel felt a flood of warmth engulf her. To go from nobody loving her to this new life full of family and friendship threatened to overwhelm her sometimes, but to hear Jen talk like this always soothed her troubled spirit.

They chatted about the impending arrival for a few more minutes, until Ruari woke from his nap and Jen had to go.

Once she ended the call, Carmel sat in her chair and, try as she might, couldn't prevent the tears. She was really happy for Jennifer, of course she was, but that didn't stop her feeling sad. She didn't know where this sudden longing for a child of her own was coming from, but now it seemed all-pervasive. She was becoming obsessed, constantly looking at babies in the park, in cafés, and imagining having one of her very own. She'd even bought some Johnson's baby powder the other day, just to imagine what having a baby would smell like. If anyone saw her, they'd think she'd lost her marbles.

Since the peculiar conversation with Zeinab, she'd suspected there was something Sharif hadn't told her. Zeinab was definitely stirring, though why, she didn't know yet. Probably just her fondness for causing dissension.

Carmel pulled herself together, fixed her face and went about her business. She was going to have to talk to Sharif. Maybe they could go out to dinner later, have a chat uninterrupted. Between the new extension being built to the main building and the demands of the patients, it was hard to get quality time together, but she knew if she told him she wanted to talk, he'd organise cover. Still, she felt bad asking for his attention at the moment; he didn't often take vacation, and the preparation for his absence was very time-consuming. Patients and their families panicked when they heard Dr Khan wasn't going to be around for a few weeks, so he was anxious to help them build up trust with Dr Benedict Cruz and the locum team who were covering his holiday.

She could put it off, she supposed, but once they were in Ireland, the whole family would be there and it would be even harder to get time alone. She'd have to try before they left.

Part of her wanted to run scared from the conversation, but she had lived too many years of her life in silence, not daring to have a point of view. Then Sharif had come and changed all of that. He would want her to speak her mind.

CHAPTER 9

'You look lovely.' Sharif smiled, his head to one side, admiring her as the waiter grinned and gave her the menu.

One of the many things that surprised her when she and Sharif first got together was the compliments and how he didn't care who was listening when he gave them. She would get embarrassed and wish he wouldn't, but she was getting used to it.

'Thanks. So do you.' She smiled, and it made him laugh.

'You always say that. I love it. Most women just accept the compliment, as if giving them is a one-way street, men to women. You don't do that.'

'I suppose there have to be some advantages to having an emotionally delayed, inexperienced wife?' She winked to take the self-pity from her words. 'I haven't a clue what's normal.'

'Well, don't ever change.'

They were at a lovely Thai place near Aashna; they liked the food and the ambiance. Sharif had figured out quickly that very fancy places made Carmel feel on edge – she hated the sensation of being a VIP – so they tended to go more low-key with socialising. The Siam Orchid was lovely, and Carmel adored their fresh, spiced food. The

71

staff knew them and were friendly without being overbearing. And just last year, the grandmother of the family who owned it died peacefully and happily in Aashna, so they always made an extra-special effort to make Sharif and Carmel feel welcome. The place was quite busy, and the general hubbub of chatter and low background music meant they could talk without being overheard.

After giving their selections for dinner, they ordered a bottle of red wine and were sipping in companionable silence when Sharif spoke again. 'So what did you want to talk to me about? Anything in particular?'

Carmel put down her glass and swallowed. It was stupid to be nervous around him, but she was.

The food arrived, and it gave her a chance to gather her thoughts. Once all the dishes were on the table, Sharif raised his eyebrows questioningly. 'Well? Out with it.' He grinned.

'I…I don't know really where to start. I…I'd love to have a baby.'

There. It was out. She knew she should stop now, allow him to digest it, but she babbled on. 'I know I'm probably too old, and you may not want to anyway, what with Aashna and everything, and even if we could, like, I have no experience of being in a family, let alone being a mother, and…then Zeinab said something…about you and Jamilla. She assumed you'd told me, but she wouldn't elaborate.'

Sharif leaned over and put his hand on hers. She stopped talking.

Something in him had changed. Gone was his twinkly smile; the roguish grin had been replaced by something else, something she couldn't read. He put his chopsticks down and sighed.

The silence was frightening. Maybe she shouldn't have said anything. She had no right to demand more, to pry into his past. If he wanted to tell her, if he wanted a child, he would have said so. The insecurities and fear raced around in her brain.

It wasn't like him to be speechless. He was always the one who soothed her, made her feel everything was going to be OK. Seeing the pain and confusion on his face now was so hard.

Eventually, he spoke, and even his voice sounded different. 'Carmel, I don't even know where to start.' He sighed again and took a sip of his wine. 'I haven't been honest with you. I should have been. I wanted to be so often, and even my mother asked me if I'd told you, but I just... I don't know... It was in the past, and I didn't want to go through it all again. We should have talked about this, about children and all of that, your wishes, your expectations, but to be honest, I hoped it would just go away. I didn't want to deal with it. Too afraid, I suppose.'

He withdrew his hand, and it was as if he was pulling back from her. She cursed herself for bringing it up. Everything was fine – why did she have to go and ruin everything?

'It doesn't matter. You don't have to do anything, Sharif,' she said, trying to turn the clock back. 'Forget I mentioned it.'

'No, Carmel, no. Secrets are bad. I should know that better than most. I've seen so many people when they're dying, regretting keeping secrets.'

He took a breath, and she panicked. Had she ruined everything? Was he going to end it? She forced herself to be calm. Everything was going to be OK. He wouldn't leave her because she told him the truth. She knew he wouldn't.

'There is something,' he said. 'It's a sad story, but I should have told you before. I'm sorry.'

Carmel could hardly bear to see the distress on the face of the man she loved.

'I wish Zeinab had not said anything. I should have been the one to do that. But since she has opened that can of worms, I want to tell you now.'

'OK,' she said quietly, and placed her hand on the table, hoping he would take it once more.

He did, and then he began. 'Jamilla and I knew each other all our lives. You knew that. We grew up together, her family and mine emigrating from Pakistan at the same time. Though Zeinab likes to go on about Jamilla's family being wealthy, and one or two of them did do well, her parents were poor immigrants just like we were. And when we got married, well, it wasn't arranged, exactly. If either of us hadn't wanted it, then we could have pulled out. But both families were pleased. She was a nurse, and I was in my final year of medicine. We were happy.

'Despite lots of hints from our extended family, we decided to put off having a family until I finished my exams. She probably wanted to start trying to get pregnant right after we got married, but she waited because when we spoke about it, I told her I felt we would have more money, be able to get a house suitable for a child, once I was actually working. Jamilla must have been more upset about it than I thought, because she told her mother. Then her father came and offered me money to tide us over until I was earning a proper wage. And I...well, I'm a proud man, and I refused – rudely, I must admit – and I got really cross with her. We fell out. I told her that what happened between us should stay between us and not involve her family. But that's not how Pakistani families work, I'm afraid.'

Carmel stared at the uneaten food in front of them, hoping the staff didn't interrupt their conversation to check everything was OK.

'So,' he went on, 'we fought, and there were tears and everything, but eventually I got my way and we waited. It was a long road, with lots more study, and many more years of experience needed, but I felt I could do it. And so again I asked Jamilla to wait. I was working crazy hours, sixteen- and seventeen-hour days. I thought we had all the time in the world. She was working too, but she was happy as a staff nurse and had no aspirations for further study or career advancement. But she understood that I did. So she agreed to wait, but not before extracting a promise that we would have a family within five years. I agreed, and it seemed like everything was going to plan. She deflected all the nosy aunties with their questions about babies and was totally loyal to me.'

Carmel gave his hand a squeeze as he spoke. He glanced down at that and gave a weak smile. Though it clearly hurt him to tell the story, he kept going.

'Eventually, I qualified, and we stopped using contraception. Jamilla was pregnant quickly, and we were all over the moon. We'd moved to a little house with a garden, and while I still worked long hours, at least now I could support her and the baby financially, so she could stay at home.'

He took a deep breath and then sipped his wine again. 'The early weeks of pregnancy were tough. She was exhausted all the time, she felt nauseous, and she'd feel full after just a mouthful or two of food. But we thought nothing of those symptoms. In fact, her mother and all the aunties were delighted – those were symptoms of a good, healthy pregnancy. So we weren't worried.

'But when we went for the first scan, I saw the tumour right away on the screen. Jamilla knew by my face that something was wrong. The radiographer and I exchanged a glance, and she left the room. I knew her well, because Jamilla was attending the hospital where I worked.' His voice cracked, and his breath was ragged.

'Jamilla turned and examined the screen. Of course, she was a nurse, and she could read the scan for herself. We were both fairly sure what we were looking at, though we had to have it confirmed. There was a slight chance it was just a cyst, but we both knew the more likely thing was much worse. She had ovarian cancer.

'We were referred that day to a colleague of mine, who told us that it was bad, about as bad as it could be, actually. The foetus was at thirteen weeks' gestation, and Jamilla would need immediate treatment. Usually cancer is only at stage 1 when found in pregnancy, and there are a number of options, but in her case, it was stage 2. The cancer had spread into the fallopian tubes and the uterus, and so there was only one way to save her life, and that was to remove the womb completely, which of course meant terminating the pregnancy.'

Carmel could barely hear him; each word clearly hurt him so much to say.

'Of course, as a doctor and her husband, no matter how horrible the prospect, I was in favour of that course. But she wanted to wait. She wanted the baby so badly. There was a fighting chance of saving Jamilla's life, but time was against us. Both I and her consultant convinced her to make the hardest decision any woman could ever have to make. I know you might be thinking I should not have pressured her, it was her decision, but I just couldn't bear to lose her.

Losing the baby was going to be horrific, but my darling girl… I just couldn't let her sacrifice herself like that. She finally agreed to the surgery, and it was the hardest day of our lives. I felt guilt, pain, fear… We clung to each other in the hours before she went to theatre, and I cursed myself for asking her to wait. If we'd gone ahead and had a family when she wanted to, maybe none of it would have happened. That thought has tortured me for my whole life, Carmel.'

She blinked back tears, all thoughts of eating forgotten.

'Afterwards, I lay beside my wife, held her in my arms and cried with her for our lost baby.'

A tear ran down his cheek, and Carmel leaned over and wiped it away with her thumb. 'If it's too hard…' she began, barely able to speak herself.

'No, I'm fine.' He took a drink of water. 'Anyway, the operation was done. Afterwards, she grieved and I worked. The more pain I felt, the angrier I was, the harder I worked. I tried to be there for Jamilla as much as I could. She was in constant treatment and almost full-time in the hospital. I would do my shift and then go to her room and sit with her. We even got a double bed put in her room so I could sleep there in the hospital with her.'

Carmel could hardly bear to see the pain etched on his face. She wanted him to stop, for his own sake, to go back to the smiling, jokey Sharif he'd been half an hour before, but it was impossible. He needed to finish.

'After the hysterectomy, she had chemotherapy, and once she was finished with that round of treatment, she went to Pakistan for a visit. She knew on some deep level that the treatment wasn't going to work long-term. I think she knew it from the start, actually. At that point, she was in good enough health and her spirits were high, and she wanted to go home one last time. She loved Pakistan in a way that I don't really. I wanted to go with her, but she asked me not to. It broke my heart to let her go, but she went back with her parents and wanted to spend the time with them on their own. They never said anything, but I know they blamed me as well for making her wait. They felt that if we'd had a family right away like normal people, then the cancer would have either never happened or been picked up at a very early stage. Jamilla loved her parents dearly, and she loved me too, but knowing how they felt about me was just going to add to her stress if I went. Very reluctantly, I let her go.

'She looked well, considering how sick she was. She didn't even lose her hair after that first round – not everyone does. We didn't tell anyone – only her parents and I knew about the cancer. She hated fuss, and if there's one thing an extended Pakistani family excel at, it is fuss. She said she wanted to keep things as normal as possible for as long as possible. So she went back, met up with all the family and all of that, and pretended everything was fine.'

'Oh, Sharif, I'm so sorry.' Carmel's heart was breaking for him. 'What a terrible story.'

He nodded sadly. 'They stayed there for a few weeks, and then she was due back for more treatment. She called me every day, telling me about all the places they visited, places from her childhood, and the people they caught up with. She missed me, I know, but she was happy too. And she knew the goodbyes to everyone in Karachi were forever.

'I worked day and night. I would come home from the hospital after a fifteen-hour shift and start researching alternative medicines. As a clinician, I would have dismissed almost all of that stuff when patients suggested it to me, but now that it was my own wife, well, I'd try anything. I was exhausted, overwrought and blinded with grief and pain.

'The tests when she came back were our worst nightmare. The chemo hadn't worked, the cancer had spread, and while the ovaries had been the primary, there were secondary tumours everywhere. They scheduled one more round of chemo, more to keep it at bay than cure it, but the cancer was so aggressive it was pointless. She was so sick. She lost her beautiful hair and just faded away in front of my eyes. Palliative care was all that was available. Back then, hospices were everything Aashna is not, all candles and whispers and people trying hard to make the environment peaceful. But Jamilla was too full of life for any of those places, so I took her home. We spent the last months together. We realised there was no time for anything but love. I took a leave of absence indefinitely, and the hospital were understanding. I looked after her, and we listened to music, watched films, slept, ate, everything together. She loved Elvis Presley, not really my thing, but I must have listened to "Can't Help Falling in Love" about a thousand times in those months.

'The day she died, she was actually brighter than she'd been for days, and we talked about my future. She told me to live after she was gone, not to just work all the time but to actually get out and live life. That's what it's for. She wanted me to meet someone, to have a family, all of that. The next morning, a Tuesday – I'll never forget it. We'd been up late the night before watching a Bollywood thing. She loved them – in so many ways, she was more Pakistani than I was – and she fell asleep in my arms. Normally she woke early, needing pain meds, but that day I woke up and looked at my watch – Jamilla's head was on my chest – and realised it was after ten. She'd died in her sleep. I lay there for over an hour, holding her, not wanting to move, not able to face that day.

'But eventually I got up and called the doctor. He came, and the whole thing after that is a blur. Relatives, friends, the funeral, food... It was like I was watching it all underwater or something. I couldn't even think of living the way she wanted me to, so I threw myself into creating Aashna. I didn't really fulfil her wishes until I met you.'

Carmel smiled weakly. 'You always said, when I thanked you for rescuing me, that I rescued you as well. Nadia says it too, but I never understood how.'

'Well, now you do. I'm sorry I didn't tell you all of this before.'

'It's OK. I understand. It is so hard to talk about it, I can't imagine, and we kind of bury the past, don't we? But I'm glad you told me.'

'So when we never spoke about a family, I was relieved, I suppose. I'm afraid of going back to that time in my life, afraid of you getting pregnant. That's the truth. I know it's irrational. I of all people should understand that. But pregnancy can be complicated...'

'And I am over forty.' She smiled. 'It's OK, Sharif, you can say it.'

'I just couldn't bear to lose you. I know you and Jamilla are two different people, totally different circumstances, all of that, and I hate even the sound of myself saying the words, but...I don't know, Carmel. The thought of it terrifies me.'

'We don't have to do anything you don't want.' She heard the words, but even to her, they sounded hollow. She felt for him – of course she did, what a horrible experience – but her overriding emotion was one of bitter disappointment. She would never be a mother.

Sharif nodded and squeezed her hand. The food had gone cold, but neither of them was hungry. Carmel stood and went to Punyaa, the owner.

'It's been a really hard day,' she said. 'Do you mind if we just settle up and go? It's nothing to do with the food, but we just can't tonight...' She took out her card to pay, but he waved her away.

'Of course. We will box it for you. Heat it tomorrow. You and Dr Khan and everyone in Aashna do lot good. Sometime is hard,' he said in halting English. 'Do good for my mother. Please, no money, you go, good sleep, no money tonight.'

Within moments, the food was boxed up and handed to her in a paper bag.

She smiled. There really were such good people in the world. 'Thanks, Punyaa. I appreciate that. We'll see you soon.'

Sharif was outside on the pavement waiting for her. She linked her arm with his, and for the first time in her life, she felt like the strong one.

CHAPTER 10

'*L*et's take a day off.' Sharif was up on his elbow, looking down into Carmel's sleepy face.

'What?' She struggled to wake up.

'Today, you and me, let's take a day off and just go somewhere.'

She opened her eyes, the events of last night slowly coming back to her. They'd walked home from the restaurant and gone straight to bed. And even though they were both exhausted, they'd made love, and afterwards, Sharif had cried, the first time she'd ever seen him do that. She'd held him in her arms until he fell asleep.

'But aren't the architect and engineer coming to go through the snag list with the builders today?' She hated to be the voice of reason.

'They are, but I asked *Ammi* to supervise it. They are more scared of her than me anyway. I just texted her, and she said it was fine. It will do Benedict good to have a day on his own in charge before we go away.' He smiled. 'What do you say?'

'Well, you're the boss, so I suppose if the boss tells me I have to take a day off…'

'Great.' He lay back down and drew her head onto his shoulder. 'Thanks for last night.' He spoke the words to the ceiling, suddenly serious, and she heard the rumble of them in his chest, along with the beating of his heart.

'No need. I love you, Sharif.' She kissed his neck and put her hand on his chest. 'How are you today?'

'Better. I should have told you the whole story ages ago. I just… well, I couldn't. But you're right – we need to take out those buried feelings every now and then, no matter how painful, and take another look at them. I was so scared to even go back to those days, I buried it so deep. But now I feel so much better having got it all out. I just wish it hadn't been precipitated by Zeinab. But maybe if she wasn't stirring it up, you wouldn't have raised it and I would never have got the guts to tell you. Maybe I should be grateful to her.' He chuckled.

'Well, gratitude is fine, but not so much you let her move in with us, OK?' Carmel snuggled closer to him.

'Oh, did I not say? We're buying a huge mansion on St Andrews Park, nine bedrooms, loads of staff, dressing in black tie for dinner every evening, and Zeinab is coming with us. You're going to love it. Ow!' He yelped as she slapped him sharply.

'Not even as a joke, Sharif! I swear, I think she was deadly serious the other day.'

'Let me think, how would my life be improved by having my aunt move in with us? I'd be adored, but then I'm adored already. I'd be well fed, but I've got to like Irish cooking so I don't need her for that. I get to curl up on the couch every evening in my pyjama bottoms with the most gorgeous woman on earth, and Zeinab would definitely not approve. And we get to make as much noise as we like together, whatever the activity, so again, I can't see Zeinab going big on that. So on balance, there's nothing in it for either of us. Therefore, it won't be happening.'

'Promise?' Carmel wanted one hundred percent assurance.

'Cross my heart and hope to die. I'd hate it, you'd hate it, *Ammi* would hate it, so no, my love, it will never happen.' With a smile, he asked, 'So what will we do today?'

Carmel thought for a moment. 'Now you can say no if you don't want to, but how about we bring some flowers to Jamilla's grave together? I've never been there, and I'd like to say a prayer and just show her that you're OK and happy...'

She tried to quell the familiar feeling of panic that came whenever he was silent, the feeling that she had no right to make such an intrusion into his life.

'I'd love that.' His voice was barely a whisper. 'Thank you.'

The subject of her wanting a baby was like an elephant in the room. She felt like she should say something, tell him she didn't mind, but the thing was, she did mind. His fears were irrational. Jamilla was a different person, in a different place and time. But he was worried, and Carmel was older. A fleeting thought appeared: Maybe his saying he was worried about her was just an excuse; maybe he just didn't want to have a child with her because he didn't think she was up to it.

She went to get up, but he stopped her. 'I know we haven't talked about the reason you wanted to talk to me last night,' he said gently. 'It all became about me and the past and everything, and I know I mustn't have sounded very logical. We will talk about it, I promise. I just need some time. I'm sorry, Carmel. I want to be able to give you everything your heart desires, but this whole thing is so tangled up for me...'

Carmel felt a surge of hope. Maybe all was not lost. 'It's OK. We'll talk again. I get it, I swear I do. Life can seem overwhelming sometimes, and you need to take it in small chunks just to get through each day. You've been so patient and kind, and I'm sure all my insecurities and craziness have tested you. But you've given me the space and time to figure it out, so I'm going to do the same for you, OK?'

'I love you, Carmel Khan.' He held her in his arms, and she felt safe. Whatever happened, they would be fine.

After a light breakfast, they got up and on the road. As they drove, Sharif told her more about his life before she knew him, the things he and Jamilla had enjoyed, the experiences they had. Carmel felt she finally knew Jamilla more as a person than as just a woman who'd died. All the stories, reminiscences and pain were unleashed, and Sharif talked and talked. She was happy just to listen and let him relive that part of his life.

As they sped along the motorway, she felt this new information had kind of balanced things up a bit. He wasn't perfect, he didn't get things right all the time, and he was a vulnerable, flawed human like the rest of the world. He would have always said he was anyway, but Carmel realised she had put him on a pedestal of perfection that was hard to live up to. Now things felt a bit more even, and she felt herself growing a little more confidence. He needed her as much as she needed him. He always said as much, but she'd never believed it until now.

They came off the motorway and stopped to buy some flowers in a small garden centre. Carmel didn't consult Sharif but made her own selection.

The Muslim cemetery was part of a large interdenominational one. Sharif led her to Jamilla's grave. On it was a black marble head-stone with a crescent moon and star and an inscription. Sharif explained that the inscription was in Urdu but read 'Jamilla Khan, 1971–2000. Beloved wife and daughter.'

Carmel laid a beautiful wreath of yellow rosebuds and baby's breath, because she remembered Nadia telling her Jamilla loved roses.

As they stood there at her grave, Sharif spoke quietly. 'Jamilla, this is Carmel. She's Dolly's daughter, who we searched so long to find. After you died, I could not keep my promise to live on. I'm sorry, but I just couldn't. But then I met this wonderful person. I love Carmel and she loves me, and we are really happy together. Sleep well, my darling sweet girl.' He wiped his eye with the back of his hand, and Carmel linked her arm through his.

When she spoke, her voice was husky with emotion. 'I'll look after him, Jamilla, I promise. We were both so lost, and now we're finding peace at last. I hope you have too, and your lovely little baby. Say hello to my mam if you ever see her. I know she looks after us, and I think you do too. Rest in peace, Jamilla.'

They stood together in silence for a few minutes, each lost in their own thoughts, before leaving, hand in hand.

They went for a pub lunch in a lovely place with a garden on a canal, and the sun was shining. A family were sitting beside them, the kids throwing bread to the ducks that paddled along the canal. Just as their food arrived, the mobile phone on the next table started ringing. The couple were at the water's edge with the kids, but the ringtone caused both Sharif and Carmel to smile amazedly. Elvis was crooning 'Can't Help Falling in Love' as the man dashed up from the canal bank to answer it.

'Our loved ones have a habit of doing that.' Carmel grinned. Her mother's song was 'Que Sera, Sera,' and she'd heard it coming from a pub the first night she met Sharif. And then on the first night she went out with Joe, an old lady used the phrase in a conversation with them. Carmel knew some people would say it was mere coincidence, but she knew it wasn't. Just as her mother communicated with her through a song, Jamilla was sending her blessing to them. She was sure of it, and she knew Sharif believed it too. He always said that nobody who had seen as many people die as he had could ever doubt the existence of life beyond the grave.

As they munched on delicious sandwiches and tea, Sharif seemed so much more relaxed.

'You look like you're on holiday already,' she said.

'It's strange... I can't explain it, but I feel like a weight has been lifted, one I didn't even know I was carrying. I would have said last week that I was blissfully happy, and I was, but since we talked and after visiting Jamilla today, I don't know... I'm just glad we did it.'

'Me too.' She watched the mother hold the toddler's hand as she led him up from the canal bank to the table where their food had arrived.

'We can try if you want.' Sharif's words were gentle.

'We'd both have to want to, though,' she said, never taking her eyes off the family.

He put his hands on her shoulders and gently turned her to face him. 'I won't lie to you, Carmel. I've been thinking about this. I could say nothing, just go along with it, but I'm going to be straight with you. Having a child isn't something I have a burning desire for, especially now, as I'm getting older. My only experience of fatherhood was so heartbreaking. I'm worried about you, and your health, and all of that. But I want you to be happy. More than anything, I want that. So if having a baby would make you happy, then I'm happy to give it a go.'

Carmel thought for a moment. Was that enough? That he'd do it for her but not because he really wanted a baby? She knew what it was to be an unwanted child, and while if she managed to get pregnant, she would want that child with all of her heart, what if Sharif didn't?

She knew that he would love the child, if she managed to have one, but what if he resented the baby for how it disrupted his life? What if he resented her? Was it better to leave well enough alone? They were happy, they wanted for nothing, and they lived fulfilled, satisfying days doing good in the world for people at the end of their lives. Did she have the right to bring a baby into all of that just because it was what she wanted?

She needed time to work this out. It had been such an emotional roller coaster these last few days; she needed time to process. She still didn't trust her own instincts, and even though she was getting better at it, she was unused to giving her emotions credit. Allowing herself to feel things without dismissing them as stupid was an exercise set by Nora. This was one of those times to practice it.

'Let's just see how it goes, OK?' She smiled. 'We won't do anything for now, and let's just go to Ireland and get that over with, and we'll talk again when we get home.'

'Of course, whatever you want.'

Did she detect a hint of relief in his smile?

CHAPTER 11

*C*armel, Tim and Nadia were bundled into the back of Sharif's SUV; he and Zeinab took their seats in front. Zeinab had made to open the passenger door and Sharif was just about to shepherd her into the back, catching Carmel's eye as he did so, but Carmel gave a slight shake of her head. One thing she'd learned was to choose battles wisely. Zeinab was going to be a trial, but they could not go to war on every tiny thing.

Already there had been words when he saw the size of her suitcases.

'Zeinab, we are going to Ireland for ten days, not to the South Pole on an expedition. There's no way I can fit all of that in the car. You'll have to go through it and leave most of that stuff here.' He was firm, and Carmel heard the frustration in his voice.

Nadia and Tim were already in the car, their modest-sized baggage in the boot. Zeinab had looked traumatised, but Sharif was adamant. She emerged from the house twenty minutes later with still by far the biggest of all the cases – but at least there was only one of them.

'What on earth was in them anyway?' Sharif asked as they pulled away from the kerb.

'Well, I don't know what it is like there, do I? I've never been somewhere so…well, somewhere so primitive. I was just trying to be prepared.' She looked like a scolded child.

'Ha!' Sharif scoffed. 'Zeinab, that's so funny. You come from Pakistan to Ireland, and you think Ireland will be primitive? I guarantee you won't see the kinds of sights you would witness any day in Karachi. Extreme poverty, dangerous electricity wires, mayhem traffic, human life in all its rawness is to be seen in Karachi, and well you know it. We love it, of course we do – it's home and there is nowhere like it – but I think you'll be very pleasantly surprised at Ireland. It's very beautiful and totally First World.'

Carmel could see Zeinab was fuming; Sharif's aunt was well aware of the social divide between the haves and the have-nots in her country, but because she inhabited a beautiful home with lots of servants, she tried to block the rest of it out. Sharif reminding her, especially in front of Tim and Carmel, was clearly infuriating.

'I've been to India. Brian and I went there a few years ago,' Tim said, trying to mollify her. 'It's a marvellous place. The colours and the culture were fascinating.'

'India and Pakistan are two entirely different places,' Zeinab snapped. 'India is filthy and corrupt, and they are no better than they should be.' She then caught Sharif's eye, and his look clearly told her to rein it in or she would not be happy with the consequences.

Carmel glanced at Nadia beside her. This was going to be a long trip, and they weren't even at the airport yet.

'So, Tim, tell us about County Mayo,' Nadia said, trying to restore peace. 'It is very different from Dublin, I believe?'

'To be honest, Nadia, I haven't been there for so long, I doubt I'd recognise the place. I went online a few days ago to look at photos of the town I grew up in, Westport, and I was stunned. It looks so bright and colourful and full of prosperous businesses and lots of tourists milling about. It looks gorgeous, so I'm sure we'll all enjoy visiting, but it looks nothing like it did fifty years ago, and that's the truth.'

'Well, nowhere does, I suppose,' Nadia said. 'The Karachi I grew up in is so different now, so much busier, so many more people, but time is a funny thing – it plays tricks on us. I'm really looking forward to this trip, though. Khalid and I came to Dublin once with Dolly, on one of her quests to find you, Carmel, but it was just going to fruitless meetings with religious orders and state officials and we saw very little really. We had thought of spending a few days, but Dolly was so distraught at the lack of progress, we just took her back to London. It was like that every time. She went over every year at least, sometimes twice a year, but never with any success. She would come back and lock herself in her little flat for a few days, and then she'd emerge ready to start again. She never gave up.'

'It is amazing how, with all the effort Dolly seems to have put in, she couldn't find you, Carmel,' Zeinab said. 'And then Sharif does some internet search and there you are, ready and waiting to be rescued like a princess in a tower.' She smiled beatifically.

Sharif interjected, a slight steel in his tone. 'The technology just wasn't there, I suppose. It was really a fluke. I found her through a Facebook group, and I'm not even on Facebook. It was set up when the late Dr Wayne Dyer came to speak at Aashna. Carmel was a fan of his so she was on it. IrishCarmel. It was a total long shot that it was the same Carmel, but it was. I did some investigating, some research on her based on her Facebook posts, and hey, presto! It was wonderful.'

Everyone agreed how amazingly fortuitous the finding of Carmel had been, but Zeinab's mouth was set in a hard line. Carmel was convinced Zeinab saw her marriage to Sharif as the only obstacle to her living happily ever after with her nephew. She was totally deluded, but deluded or not, Carmel was, from Zeinab's perspective, a horrible Irish fly in the ointment.

The trip to the airport passed relatively calmly, and then Sharif and Tim fawned a bit over Zeinab, just to ease the whole thing through the security gates. The last thing anyone wanted was a scene. Sharif had heard about the wheelchair when she landed from Karachi, but she didn't request one this time, happy instead to have Tim and Sharif carry her luggage while Nadia and Carmel managed their own.

The previous night, Nadia told Carmel about a stunt Zeinab had pulled a few years earlier. She had been telling her sister, and everyone else too, that she'd had heart trouble and had a pacemaker fitted. Everyone rallied round, and even though Khalid and Nadia were not inclined to, they visited her in Karachi. She really went to town on the convalescence, apparently unable to lift a finger. She had minions running all over the city getting her obscure treats, and she nearly drove everyone daft. Any time it was suggested that she do something herself, or she wasn't getting her own way, her 'heart' would start playing up. It turned out, several years later, when she was travelling to London, Tariq told the security staff at the airport that his wife had a pacemaker. They needed to see the paperwork to allow her to avoid the X-ray machine, and that's when the truth came out. There had been no heart surgery, no pacemaker – the whole thing was a fabrication to garner sympathy. Apparently, Tariq was fuming when he arrived and told Nadia, Khalid and Sharif the whole story, much to the embarrassment of his wife.

It had never been brought up since, but airport security was now a thorny issue. While Carmel could see Zeinab pulling a stunt that ridiculous, there was something very sad about it too. All she'd wanted was for her husband to pay her a bit of attention, but instead he told everyone the story, humiliating her. Carmel felt a pang of sympathy.

The whole procedure went as smoothly as it could go, and soon they found themselves sitting on the Aer Lingus plane to Dublin.

'*Cead mile failte a dhaoine usaile, ar an turas seo go Baile Atha Cliath,*' the glamorous air host began.

'What on earth is she saying?' Zeinab asked in a loud voice.

Carmel was seated beside her, and Tim on her other side. 'It's Irish, the Irish language. She's just welcoming everyone aboard,' Carmel explained.

'Oh, for goodness' sake, everyone speaks English here. Why must we listen to that gobbledygook?'

'*Fágamid siud mar atá sé.*' Tim smiled as he spoke.

Carmel's Irish was rusty, but she remembered what he meant: *Leave well enough alone.* It was a well-used phrase in Irish. She realised that brushing up on her native language skills could be quite useful.

Sharif and Nadia couldn't speak it, obviously, but the rest of the gang could, and more importantly, to Zeinab, it was gobbledygook. That could prove very handy indeed.

Carmel texted Joe, who was meeting them at the airport. *Just boarding now x*

The wedding was in ten days' time, at the end of the trip, so once they landed, they were taking to the open road in the minibus he had hired.

Brilliant. I'll leave in ten minutes so I'll be waiting for you all. Can't wait to see you, pet. Dad xxx

She smiled. He always signed his texts 'Dad', even though she knew who they were from. It was like he wanted her to know how much finding her meant to him. She recalled the conversation they'd had last night, when she'd warned him just how difficult Zeinab could be. But he'd put her mind at rest.

'I'm well used to dealing with females of a certain age and disposition – I've been doing it all my life,' he said. 'Don't worry your head about it, my love. We'll manage Zeinab grand. She'll be eating out of my hand by tomorrow night, just you watch!'

Carmel had felt a little better after speaking to him, but she was still nervous. It was the first time she would meet her full extended family. Several McDaids had come over for Brian's funeral last year, but they didn't know at that stage who she really was, so this was going to be what Luke jokingly called the 'Carmel Launch'. And the last thing she wanted was mad old Zeinab upsetting anyone. She was so racist about Ireland already, based on zero experience of anyone or anything Irish, apart from Dolly.

Carmel knew whoever Sharif had married, Zeinab probably wouldn't have approved, but the fact that she was Dolly's daughter was certainly not helping. Zeinab was jealous of Dolly's relationship with Nadia, and any time Dolly was mentioned, Zeinab did a kind of irritating sniff. It drove Nadia mad. Carmel was dreading being associated with Zeinab in front of the McDaids. Joe's siblings remembered Dolly and were sure to want to talk about her. Carmel wanted so much to savour these titbits of information to further fill in her mental picture of her mother, but the thought of Zeinab sniffing disapprovingly every time the subject was raised was just mortifying.

Sharif had offered to stay right beside his aunt for the whole wedding to intervene before anything got too humiliating, but Carmel needed him at her side more. And Nadia seemed to exacerbate the situation unwittingly, Zeinab always trying to outdo her younger sister, reducing the normally able Nadia to a little mouse. Perhaps Tim could manage her? It was a lot to ask – she really was a tyrant in silks. She could be charm itself, or she could be a menace. The problem was she was so fickle, they never knew what they were going to get.

Carmel gazed appreciatively out the window as the horseshoe of Dublin Bay, ringed by the purple mountains, came into view. The countryside beyond the city was a patchwork of green, and the Irish Sea glittered azure as the cabin crew instructed everyone to prepare for landing. She wished she was sitting with Sharif; she needed his reassurance. But when she glanced across to where he was sitting with his mother, she found him looking over at her, smiling, and she relaxed. Everything was going to be OK.

She had not been back since the time she came to beg Bill to call off his horrible sister, who was trying to ruin Aashna and Sharif. Amazingly, she and Bill had talked more that day than in the seventeen years of marriage they endured before that. She had been dreading meeting him – things had ended so badly with her just running out and leaving him – but the conversation was actually very cathartic. He apologised for being a terrible husband, admitted that he still loved his first wife and that he should never have remarried and said he understood why she left. All those years of being nothing more than a housekeeper, dusting the Waterford Crystal framed photo of him and Gretta on their wedding day, seemed to fade away that day and, with it, some of the pain of rejection. She'd wanted it to work, but she was so naive, thinking a girl raised in a children's home, without a family or a bean to her name, could just slot into Gretta's shoes and be Bill's wife and Niamh and Sinead's mother. It was never going to work.

Bill did as she asked, though, and Julia was called off. And what's more, he signed all the divorce papers when the time came. Carmel didn't want a penny, or any bit of his precious farm, and that helped smooth things over. Still, she was surprised the morning she married Sharif to find a special delivery of a lovely Waterford Crystal frame from Bill, along with a card wishing them well and a note saying the frame was for their wedding picture. It was a sad life she'd had with him, but it ended as well as it could have.

She'd had no contact with him since that day. The divorce was handled by solicitors; she didn't even need to turn up. And so ended her association with Bill Sheehan, Ballyshanley, County Offaly, and she thought with Ireland forever. And yet here she was, looking down on the land of her birth, preparing to meet her father's family. Life was very strange sometimes.

CHAPTER 12

*A*s she looked down on the country that was her home for so long, Carmel saw Tim doing the same thing out of the corner of her eye. They were both going back, and though the circumstances were different, it was going to be a complicated trip for both of them. She hoped he'd be OK, that the legal business with the farm would go smoothly and nothing bad happened. He looked so distinguished, so tall and together, but she knew that inside he was in turmoil. Brian had been the stronger of the two in some respects, and Tim missed him immeasurably.

She caught his eye, and he smiled. 'Well, here goes. We'll stick together, Carmel, and we'll be grand.'

She would have liked to hold his hand as the plane touched down on Irish soil, but Zeinab was snoring loudly between them and they didn't dare wake her. They needn't have worried, as the slight jolt of touchdown roused her anyway, and she self-consciously dusted the crumbs from the two ham-and-cheese croissants she'd had on the plane from the front of her top.

'That was a nice easy landing,' she remarked. 'Sometimes they are so bumpy.'

'Oh, that's the Irish pilots – they are very well trained,' Tim quipped, winking at Carmel over Zeinab's stooped head as she bent to retrieve her unfeasibly huge handbag.

Sharif, with Tim's help, managed to gather all of the luggage, and soon they found themselves in the arrivals area smothered in hugs and kisses. Carmel beamed as she saw not just Joe but Jennifer and baby Ruari, Luke and some of the other McDaids she recognised from Brian's funeral. They had all made the trip to the airport to meet them.

'Welcome home, darling.' Joe grinned, embracing her warmly. All available hands grabbed suitcases as they made their way to the bus in the car park, the noisy chatter causing other travellers to look up in surprise.

'I got a sixteen-seater, so I thought we might all go for lunch. I've arranged a kind of buffet lunch, since we're so many, at a hotel on the Galway road. This gang of relatives wanted to catch up with you before the wedding, so they'll come for lunch too, and we can strike off afterwards on the big adventure. How does that sound?'

'Wonderful.' Carmel smiled up at her dad as he walked with his arm protectively around her shoulders.

Her cousin Aisling was all chat, and Carmel asked her about the upcoming wedding.

'Ah sure, they all think I'm being a right bridezilla, but you know how it is. If I left it to anyone else, 'twould be a total train crash, so if you want something done, do it yourself. My sister is taking the flower girls to get their shoes this morning, and there's going to be a stand-off because my eldest niece doesn't want baby shoes, but I told Aoife just to put them in something that kind of matches – after that I don't care.'

Carmel grinned. 'So how many in the bridal party?'

Aisling caught her Uncle Joe's eye, and she playfully thumped him on the shoulder. 'Oi, you, what would you know about weddings? Keep your opinions to yourself.'

He chuckled. 'I never said a word.'

'You didn't have to.' Aisling rolled her eyes and turned back to Carmel. 'Well, there was to be ten bridesmaids and seven flower girls, and then ten groomsmen, but we only have five little boys so we only have that many page boys, but then one of my bridesmaids went off and got herself pregnant, which was very inconsiderate...' She deliberately spoke loudly enough to include Jennifer in the conversation.

'I had to take extreme measures to get out of wearing that horrific dress you picked out. Honestly, I looked like a demented flamingo, all peach and feathers. So even though me and Damien don't want another kid, I had to do something.' Jen laughed.

Aisling looked mock outraged. 'Don't mind her, Carmel. She wouldn't know fashion if it came up and bit her on her ever-widening arse! She's a mammy these days, so it's all tracksuit pants and greasy hair.'

Carmel marvelled at the way the two women hurled insults at each other in such a jovial way. They were almost the same age, and Carmel had often talked about Aisling with Jen. They were best friends as well as cousins. Everyone was thrilled for Aisling that she was finally having the wedding of her dreams despite the slagging she got from her uncles. Aisling had been engaged before, but her fiancée was killed in a road accident; she took years to get over it. Her soon-to-be husband was a lovely guy and didn't mind a bit that the wedding was a match for Prince William and Kate Middleton's bash.

Joe chuckled too, used to the two of them knocking sparks off each other.

Sharif was deep in conversation with Luke. Nadia and Tim were being escorted by presumably another cousin, who was also pushing Ruari in his stroller. Only Zeinab seemed unaccompanied.

Carmel stopped and allowed her to catch up. 'Dad, this is Zeinab, Nadia's sister who is visiting from Pakistan. Zeinab, this is my dad, Joe McDaid.'

Joe stopped, released Carmel and gave Zeinab his full attention. 'Well, Zeinab, it's my pleasure to meet you. Carmel has been telling me all about you, and I want to say how sorry I was to hear about your husband's death. My own wife, Mary, died five years ago, and I miss her every day. All I can tell you is that it does get easier, but those early days were just a fog, to be honest. We won't expect too much from you, and I hope the trip just helps you to get through these early days some kind of way.'

He offered her his arm to link, and she took it. Carmel watched in amazement as Zeinab seemed to fall totally under his spell. Her cranky expression had changed to one of contentment, and she basked in the glow of Joe's attention.

Living in England for a year, Carmel had forgotten some of the subtle differences between the English and Irish. In England, people were very conscious of the need for privacy, and nobody would dream of discussing someone's recent bereavement so openly, but in Ireland, people were much more forthright. It was refreshing, but somewhat scary too, as she had no idea how Zeinab would react. She needn't have worried; the woman clearly was enthralled with Joe. Then Carmel remembered how Sharif always said Irish and Pakistani culture was similar in that way – people were quite direct and emotions were allowed.

'Thank you, Joe. It's a relief to speak to someone who understands how hard it is to lose a loved one,' Zeinab fawned with a saccharin smile. 'Tariq was my life, and I was his. We did everything together, and we were so united. Life without him, well, it just seems so bleak...'

Carmel was glad Nadia was out of earshot. Zeinab spoke as if Nadia hadn't lost Khalid, and the way the lecherous Tariq was being eulogised after his demise was enough to drive poor Nadia up the walls. While Zeinab was playing the distraught widow, they knew the reality: Tariq had an apartment in the Central Business District of Karachi, hardly ever visiting his wife in the Clifton house.

That Nadia knew was one of the many reasons Zeinab resented her. She spun her tale of the devoted Tariq regardless to all and sundry, but she hated that Nadia understood the truth.

'Tell me, Joe, do you live alone?'

Here we go, thought Carmel.

'I do, Zeinab, but to be honest, I've such a huge family, there's always someone on the doorstep or someplace to be. And my daughter Jennifer – that's her over there with the dark hair – lives very nearby with her husband, Damien, and little Ruari. And of course, there's another on the way, so we'll all be kept very busy, I'm sure. And then my son, that's him' – he pointed with pride at Luke – 'he lives in town, and I see him very often too, so I'm very lucky. After Mary died, I was inclined to stay at home, but they kind of made me get out and about, even when I didn't feel like it. And you know, 'twas the best thing for me. It doesn't do you any good, moping around the house, so I'm happy you're here with us.'

'Well, thank you for inviting me. I was delighted when dear Sharif mentioned it. I've always wanted to visit Ireland, such a fascinating country, so rich in culture and language and everything. I can't wait to learn more about it, and I'm sure you're a wonderful teacher, Joe.'

Carmel couldn't believe her ears. Zeinab really was a piece of work. All that stuff about the Irish being backwards and ungrateful and only speaking gobbledygook was out the window, and suddenly Ireland was a cultural kingdom? The woman was something else. Now she was squeezing Joe's arm and giggling up at him like a teenager.

Oh, great, Carmel thought. *Zeinab is flirting with my father.*

They boarded the bus, and Sharif sat beside Carmel. 'OK?' he asked, giving her hand a gentle squeeze. 'They love you. It's going to be fun.'

'I know it is. I'm not nervous really, and amazingly, Zeinab seems to be behaving herself so far, so barring any unforeseen disasters, it should all go fine.' She took a deep breath to steady herself.

'Don't worry about Zeinab. Between *Ammi* and Tim, they'll keep her on a tight leash, and anyway, as you say, she's behaving well. In fact, I think she has a thing for your father.'

'Did you notice that too? Oh my God, I hoped I was imagining it. I can't think of anything worse than Zeinab trying to get her claws into Joe. Do you think he noticed?'

'He's a man, and I know we are not always the most perceptive of creatures, but Zeinab isn't exactly subtle. She was practically salivating at the prospect!'

'Oh no, should we warn him?' Carmel didn't know whether to be amused or horrified. She was a little of both.

Sharif chuckled. 'I think Joe is a big boy. He'll manage Zeinab just fine. Now let's go on this mad Irish adventure and enjoy ourselves, OK?'

'OK, let's do it.'

CHAPTER 13

*T*he lunch was a noisy, fun-filled affair, and everyone mingled and chatted happily. Carmel was introduced to yet more cousins, and they seemed to have taken the news that Joe had a daughter with another woman before he was married to Mary in their stride. She felt welcome and like she'd always known them. Her cousin Tadhg, Aisling's brother, even teased her about getting an English accent. There was no formality; it was just straight into laughing, talking and good-natured banter. It was amazing.

Several times she looked up from a conversation to find either Joe or Sharif watching her protectively, and she basked in the warm glow of their love. She thought of all those years in Trinity House, watching families on the street, or in the park where the care workers took them sometimes. She would wonder if her cousins were among those children playing, or if those mothers and fathers holding their kids' hands on Grafton Street at Christmastime were her aunts or uncles.

Maybe she passed these very people on the street and never knew her blood ran in their veins. She allowed herself to feel that loss; Nora was working hard with her to allow her to feel her emotions. The idea that this huge extended family of hers had lived in the same city all through her childhood but she never knew them made her immeasurably sad, but she tried to focus on the positive: It had all turned out OK in the end.

After a longer lunch than anyone had anticipated, Joe finally herded everyone onto the bus. Nadia was glowing, possibly helped by the brandy Joe had insisted she try, and Zeinab was laughing happily while clinging like a limpet to Joe at every opportunity. Tim talked with Joe's brother Colm, and Carmel was so happy for him, to get to meet another of Brian's brothers and have him accept Tim for what he was to Brian. With Tim's permission, Joe had told the whole family a few months ago that Brian was gay and Tim was his partner. The tenderness and respect they'd all showed to Tim since he arrived was heart-warming.

The bus was loaded and everyone was buckled up when Joe slid into the driver's seat and announced, 'Now, I'm not claiming to be an expert of anything, but I've been swotting up and I think I'm going to do OK as a tour guide. But you'll have to bear with me. If you have any questions, feel free to ask. If I don't know the answer, sure I can make something up, all right?'

'And he will,' Luke teased from the back seat. 'We've been victims of his Irish tours since we were kids. I ended up failing history in the Leaving Cert because of all the claptrap he told us!'

Jennifer was sitting in front with Ruari strapped into a car seat that Joe had made sure was safely installed. Damien and Luke had started out across the aisle from Jen and the baby, until Zeinab announced that she was very unused to buses so the front seat was the best place for her. Carmel suspected she just wanted to be behind Joe. Tim, Sharif and Carmel had taken their seats. The bus was big for their little group, but the extra space allowed them to spread out, and luckily Joe had a bus driving licence – one of his many jobs back in the day, he explained.

They were just pulling out of the hotel car park when Luke jumped up and called, 'Stop, Dad, stop a sec!'

Bewildered, Joe opened the door to allow his son out. The group on the bus watched in bemusement as an ethereally beautiful, tall, willowy young woman with long dark hair threw herself into Luke's arms. She was absolutely stunning, all silky hair and toned abs, though she was dressed a little optimistically for Ireland, in teeny-tiny denim shorts showing off her slim, tanned legs that went on for days and a tie-dyed t-shirt that said 'Woodstock Forever' on the front. Carmel guessed it was probably meant for ages five to six because it barely covered the young woman's rib cage. Her bare abdomen was adorned with a glittering belly-button ring. She had a pull-along case beside her.

Luke, who seemed thrilled to see her, kissed her fully before grabbing the case with one hand – and her with the other – and helping her up the steps of the bus.

'Everyone, this is Carrie,' he announced. 'She wasn't sure if she'd make it, so I didn't say anything, but here she is!'

Carmel melted; he looked thrilled. But since nobody had even known about the existence of Carrie – though Jen had some inkling – the welcome was somewhat delayed.

Jen recovered first. 'So you're joining us for the whole trip, Carrie?' she asked, and Carmel sensed the reticence in her voice, though her tone was friendly enough.

'Ya, like, I totally want to see, like, Ireland, and, like, the culture and stuff. Like, it's all so green and so historical, and I'm really psyched about the Wild Atlantic Way, so when Lukie said I could come, I was totally, like, psyched.' She smiled sweetly.

Sharif glanced at Carmel, and she suppressed a giggle.

'So are you American?' Joe asked innocently.

She laughed, and everyone started. She sounded like a braying donkey. Her speaking voice was husky, seductive almost, but her laugh... It was straight off the stage.

'Like American from the US?' she asked.

'Yes,' Jennifer said slowly. 'From the United States of America?'

'No, like, not really, like, but I watch a lot of vloggers? That's video bloggers, like on the internet? Y'know, stateside, but I'm not actually from there.' She smiled sweetly, glad she was able to explain the concept of the cyberworld to these hopeless cases. She had that highly irritating habit young Irish people seemed to have developed of late, of upwardly inflecting every sentence so all statements sounded like questions.

Luke saw the direction things were taking and shuffled her into a seat, clearly delighted she'd made it.

Carmel caught Jen's eye and tried not to react. Carmel knew Jennifer was not amused. The young woman hadn't made a great first impression with her fake American accent, condescending attitude and barely there clothing, and Jen worried about her brother, especially after last time. But Carmel just wanted Luke to be happy, and this Carrie seemed to put a very genuine smile on his face. If she was good to him, what difference did her accent make?

'Right. Sure we'll get going so, I suppose.' Joe grinned as he sat back into the driver's seat.

'Joe, it is wonderful how you can drive such a big machine. How ever did you learn such a skill?' Zeinab was bordering on simpering, which made Nadia grit her teeth.

'She normally wouldn't deign to engage with a mere bus driver,' Sharif whispered in Carmel's ear. 'She must be smitten.'

'Your mother will strangle her if she doesn't go easy with the flirting,' Carmel whispered back with a grin. 'I don't know which is scarier, Zeinab being horrible or Zeinab being nice.'

'So, folks, I thought we'd begin our tour with a trip to Newgrange. Now I took Jen and Luke there as kids, but we haven't gone for ages, and it's all been developed, I believe, so it will be worth a visit. It's older than the pyramids, older than Stonehenge in England. An amazing place. It's a passage tomb, and it is huge. The stones used to build it were pulled from over a hundred miles away as the crow flies, and over five thousand years ago, that was no mean feat.'

'Use the mike, Dad, we can't hear you!' Luke yelled up from the back.

Joe squirmed a bit. 'Ah, I'd be like an eejit, and sure I'm not really a guide, I'm just telling you a few bits that I know...'

'No, Joe, please, use the microphone.' Zeinab leaned forward and tapped Joe on the shoulder almost proprietarily. 'You have a lovely speaking voice, and it is so fascinating – it would be a shame if we couldn't all hear you properly.'

Carmel glanced at Nadia, who looked mortified. Something would have to be done, or poor old Nadia would crack up. Carmel resolved to have a chat with her when they stopped. Zeinab wasn't upsetting Joe in the slightest; he was obviously well aware of her taking a shine to him, and if anything, he thought it was funny. But Nadia was clearly uncomfortable, and Zeinab wasn't exactly subtle.

Reluctantly, Joe pulled the gooseneck mike from its socket on the wall beside his head and put it in front of his mouth, testing it for sound.

'This is the end of the peace and quiet now, lads, Joe has amplification!' Damien joked, and everyone laughed. Everyone except Zeinab, who seemed to be taking umbrage on Joe's behalf.

'We are very lucky to have Joe to show us around, young man,' she said, her imperious tone cutting through the laughter. 'Perhaps you should have more respect for your elders.'

Joe jumped in quickly. 'Ah, he's only messing, Zeinab. I'm well able for him. Now, as I was saying...'

Damien gave a grin and gestured being slapped on the wrist. Luckily, Zeinab didn't see it.

'The lads that built this place were some engineers,' Joe went on. 'It's seventy-six metres wide and over twelve high, and was used to bury people, presumably the kings or whatever in that society. Anyway, it's a passage tomb, and over the entranceway is a thing that looks for all the world like a window, but they call it a roof box. And wait till you hear this! On the winter solstice, twenty-first of December, the passageway into the tomb is perfectly aligned with the rising sun and the light shines in through the roof box, creeps along the passageway – and this passageway is sixty feet long, mind you – and then when the light gets all the way down, it floods the tomb chamber with light. It is absolutely incredible, and they had the technology to do this over five thousand years ago. There's a lottery you can enter to be there on the solstice, but they do a reconstruction when you visit, so we'll get to see that. It's not as good as the real thing, but 'twill give us an idea.'

'It sounds incredible, Joe. How come we've never heard of it?' Sharif asked. 'I mean, in that everyone has heard of the pyramids or Stonehenge?'

'Good question, Sharif. I don't really know, but I suppose it's not pushed as much as other sites, maybe because of the damage being done just by condensation alone from people's breath? They mind it well, and they're strict about not bringing bags in that could brush off the walls and that, but to be honest, I think it's just another hidden Irish gem.'

'Do you remember being here, Luke, with Mam and Dad, and we had a picnic in the car because it was lashing rain?' Jen was reminiscing, but Carmel also got the impression she wanted her mother as part of the conversation. It was harder for Jen than Luke, she noticed. Jen missed her mother badly, and the arrival, albeit posthumously, of Dolly had threatened Mary's memory for a while. Or at least it had changed the narrative of how Mary was remembered. And aside from Dolly's memory and her relationship with Joe all those years ago, Jen was having a very hard time enduring Zeinab's attentions to her father now.

'Yeah, we all got soaked, and she had brought spare clothes for everyone except herself,' Luke said, chuckling at the memory. 'She had to wear Dad's old fishing gear – that was the only dry stuff in the boot of the car. She was complaining that she smelled like a trout.'

'Did she?' Carrie asked, her wide blue eyes innocent.

Luke did a double take. 'Did she what?'

'Smell like a trout? Like, does a trout smell? Maybe if he was dead, but then would he smell different to other fish who were also dead?'

Luke laughed heartily and gave her a hug. Carmel couldn't decide what to make of her, but her ditziness seemed to delight Luke. For such a smart guy, she seemed like an odd choice, but maybe there was more to her than met the eye. They'd find out for sure after a few days on the bus anyway.

'It was a great day,' Jen went on. 'We went to Newgrange and then to the Hill of Tara, and remember, Dad, you used to tell us all the stories about the old kings and queens and warriors long ago, and Mam used to be trying to get you to tone down the violence, but we loved it. The more gruesome, the better. Fellas sliding around on the guts of their enemies, all that kind of thing.'

Carmel turned her head and blinked back tears. It amazed her how emotional she got about her own childhood these days, when for years she'd just accepted it as it was and it really didn't get to her. Sharif said she was thawing from the inside out and finally allowing herself to feel, and maybe he was right. Listening to Jen and Luke reminisce about picnics and day trips with their parents made her so sad. Maybe that was part of her longing to have a baby – so she could finally experience childhood properly.

Sharif placed his hand on hers, and she looked down at his brown skin, his manicured fingernails and his silver wedding ring. Though Sharif wasn't a practising Muslim, the tradition stated that men should not wear gold, so when they married, he chose a silver ring. Wedding rings were not part of Islam, but he said he wanted the world to know he was a married man. To this day, she remembered the feeling she got when he said that. For him, it was a casual remark, but for her, it meant so much that he not only wanted to marry her but that he was proud of her and wanted everyone to know they were together. She leaned her head on his shoulder as they drove along.

CHAPTER 14

*T*im took photographs as they approached the massive tomb. It seemed to glisten in the afternoon sunlight. Luke and Carrie fell into step beside him.

'It's so sparkly, isn't it?' Carrie sighed happily.

'That's the quartzite in the stone,' Luke explained. 'That's how they know how far they brought the stones, because the nearest place to get quartzite is in the Dublin mountains, miles away. They think they rolled them on logs over land. I think that's how they did it anyway, but maybe you know more about it, Tim?'

'I was never here before – sure, what am I saying?' Tim adjusted the lens on his camera. 'I was never anywhere in Ireland but Mayo – and Dublin, the day I got the boat to England.'

'But Carmel was telling me you travelled all over the world with Uncle Brian,' Luke protested.

Tim smiled at the memories. 'We certainly did. We've been all over Asia, Australia, Africa, the States... We even went to Antarctica one time on a boat, three weeks out of Ushuaia, Argentina. I was sick as a parrot the whole time, but it was worth it.'

'I'd love to hear about those trips sometime. We knew he travelled a lot, but to be honest, he was a bit cagey when you asked him about his travels. He was a great guy, but we learned not to pry, y'know?' Luke helped Carrie over some rough ground because the high-heeled wedges she was wearing were totally unsuitable for the terrain.

Tim sighed. 'It makes me sad to hear that, Luke. He wasn't naturally reticent, but he was always trying to protect me, and so he had to hold back from all of you.'

'Protecting you from what?' Carrie asked.

Luke reddened a little; he obviously had not told her the story. 'Er...well...' Luke stumbled. He was absolutely fine with Tim being gay, but it wasn't his story to tell.

'It's OK, Luke,' Tim said kindly. 'Brian, Luke's uncle, was my partner for forty years. But before he and I got together, I was married and had kids. It's complicated.' He shrugged.

'And are your kids here?' Carrie asked.

'No, they live in England, but I don't see them, to be honest. They aren't comfortable around me.'

'Just because you're gay?' Carrie was flabbergasted.

'Yes. I believe that's the reason.' Tim bent down to get a better angle of the tomb.

'That's crazy,' Carrie said. 'You should so say something. I mean, look how the Kardashians took the news about Bruce Jenner becoming Caitlyn! Like, they were totally fine about it, and he actually looks good as a woman. You should just ask them straight out if they're homophobic. Like, it might be totes awks for, like, ten seconds, but then they'd probably have been cool. And if they're not, well, then it's their loss, right? Like, I get that things were different in the olden days. But they don't know what they're missing. I don't really know you yet, but I think you're lovely, and I'd say Brian must have been crazy about you 'cause you are like really fit for an old guy. Like Sean Connery kinda, y'know? Being gay is just so cool right now. My personal trainer, Darryl – he's so ripped, I mean, it's just awesome – but anyway, he's got this Puerto Rican boyfriend who is a dog counsellor. Well, he specialises in poodles, actually – they suffer a lot from anxiety. But anyway, he's like really old, forty or something, and his mum and him go shopping together and everything. Your kids are losing out if they won't have you in their lives. But look at this gang you've got here. Like, all of Lukie's family seem like they totally want you in their crew, so, like, let people go who don't want to know you. As Taylor Swift says, "Haters gonna hate".'

'Well, that is probably the most sensible take I've ever heard on the subject, Carrie,' Tim replied without a trace of sarcasm. 'And you know what? You're dead right.'

Carmel suppressed a smile. A lifetime of staying in the shadows meant she didn't feel the need to join in every conversation and Carrie and Tim were getting along just fine.

Carrie went to examine some 'neat little flowers' and busied herself making a Snapchat story as Tim, Carmel and Luke stood gazing at the ancient edifice.

'She's a bit quirky…' Luke said with a grin.

'There's more to Miss Carrie than meets the eye, Luke. I can see why you like her.' Tim was anxious to put the younger man at ease.

'I really like her. I know she can come across a bit daft, but honestly, she's great, and so loyal and decent and honest. And she might seem a bit…I dunno… But she is really wise about things. She gives me great advice. I trust her, y'know? I'm not seeing her that long, and I'm away during the week so I only see her at the weekends really, and we don't know each other that well, but I really like her. Jen can't stand her, though. I know by the face of her. I just want them to give her a chance.'

'Look, I'm no expert, but I have been around forever, so here's my tuppence worth if you want to hear it?'

Luke smiled. 'Go on.'

'She seems like a really nice woman, certainly no malice in her, and she is beautiful, even I can see that.' He chuckled. 'The others might think she's a bit off the wall, but they'll be kind, and once they know what she's really about, they'll understand why you like her so much. Trust her. I think she'll surprise you.'

'If my sister doesn't choke her first. She's protective of me even if I don't need it.' Luke shrugged.

Jen appeared then at his shoulder. Damian and Ruari were slowly making their way up since the toddler was insisting on walking himself rather than sitting in the stroller, which would have been so much faster.

'I'll probably try to choke who, might I ask?' She held her hand up to her eyes to shield the strong evening sun.

Luke glanced in Carrie's direction and gave a nod of his head.

'Ah, I see.' Jen nodded sagely. 'Well, I don't know what to say to you, little brother. You've picked some beauties in your time, but this one takes the biscuit. Like, is she actually that thick or is it an act or what?'

Carmel saw Luke bristle. Sure, Carrie did come across as a bit of an airhead, but Luke clearly wasn't happy with his sister slagging her off so harshly.

'And you're brain of Ireland, are you? Don't be such a cow, Jen. She's a nice girl, and what did she ever do to you? She's trying to be nice – why can't you do the same?'

Jennifer reeled at the quick turnabout and lashed out at Luke. 'Well, we all know what part of your anatomy has been doing the thinking lately. She's a muppet and you know it, Luke, and I can't believe you're inflicting her on us for the whole trip. You never even asked Dad if she could come along.'

Carmel had heard about Jen's quick temper, and she was well and truly riled now.

'It's none of my business, I know...'

The siblings both turned their gazes to Tim, who looked worried he was sticking his nose in where it wasn't wanted. But he did remember that Irish families were more expressive than British ones. English people valued the stiff upper lip, being stoic and all of that, whereas the Irish tended to say what they felt.

'But I don't think you two want to fall out?' he ventured. 'This is an emotional trip for all of us, in different ways, so maybe we need to try to, I don't know, be a bit more understanding. Look, what do I know? Nothing, except that you two love each other and this is a silly argument. So my advice is to just let it go, and we'll all enjoy ourselves.'

They both stood in silence.

'I will if she will.' Luke gazed at a spot over Jen's head.

'Fine, it's your funeral.' Jen sighed, and Tim shot her a warning glance. 'Fine, fine, I'll play nice. Just watch – we'll be totes, like, besties.' She nudged her brother to show she was just fooling around.

'Thanks.' He gave her a quick hug.

* * *

THE GROUP ASSEMBLED at the entrance to the tomb, and a local guide told them the stories of the people long, long ago who lived and died there. This was the heart of Ireland, very close to the Hill of Tara, where the high kings lived 'in the olden times', as Carrie might have put it.

Carmel watched as Sharif, Nadia and even Zeinab were blown away by the place. Though she'd never been anywhere except Dublin and Ballyshanley, she felt the beginnings of national pride in her country.

And at least Zeinab wasn't complaining. Quite the opposite, actually; everything was splendid as she sycophantically sucked up to Joe.

The rest of the day passed wonderfully. The sun shone on the lush green fields and stone walls. In the evening, Joe took them by Clonmacnoise, a gorgeous monastic settlement from the seventh century on the banks of the River Shannon, the longest in Ireland.

'I knew Ireland was beautiful, everyone says so, but honestly, it is breathtaking,' Nadia remarked as she and Carmel sat on a dry stone wall watching the late evening sun set behind the huge round tower of Clonmacnoise, bathing the entire place in its buttery glow. Tim was taking more photos, and Luke and Carrie were messing around in the old church, laughing. Jen and Damien had gone to the café to get a snack for Ruari, and Zeinab looked like she was holding court with Sharif and Joe.

'It is, and to be honest, I had no idea,' Carmel admitted. 'I can't believe I lived here for forty years and had no inkling it was like this. I mean, I could have come, I suppose, or found out about it on the internet or something, but I just never did. I feel like a very poor ambassador.' She smiled.

'Well, Joe is doing a great job,' Nadia assured her. 'I don't know how he manoeuvres that big bus around those tiny roads, not to mention all he knows about the country. He's better than any professional tour guide, I'm sure. And he's gone to so much trouble.'

'I know, he's amazing, isn't he? And everyone is getting along so well. I was kind of dreading it, to be honest, but so far so good.' Carmel was trying to bring the conversation around to Nadia and Zeinab. She knew Nadia would enjoy the holiday so much more if Zeinab wasn't getting on her nerves so much.

'Well, everyone but my sister,' Nadia grumbled. 'I know. I'm trying not to let her get to me. But the way she's fawning over Joe, I just want to throttle her.'

Carmel wondered just for a moment if there wasn't more to the story. Initially, when Joe and Nadia had met, Carmel thought there might have been a spark between them, but she'd dismissed it. They did get along very well, though, and liked a lot of the same things, but they seemed happy to be friendly. Nadia had no contact with him except when Carmel was there, she was sure of that. But she was starting to think that maybe Nadia's frustration wasn't just embarrassment at the obviousness of her sister's flirting but also maybe a little tinge of jealousy? Joe was lovely to everyone, and he had a way of making whoever he was talking to feel like they were the most important person on earth, including Zeinab.

'But at least it means she's on her best behaviour, right? She doesn't want Joe to think badly of her, so she's being extra nice. That can only be a good thing, can't it?' Carmel's eyes searched her mother-in-law's face.

Nadia sighed. 'I suppose so.' She gazed downwards as she spoke, not looking at Carmel. 'I'm just... I don't know. This is a big thing for you, to come back here, to connect with your family. And for Tim as well. And I just wish she wasn't here. I know it makes me sound so mean and nasty, and as you say, at least she's not being rude, but the way she is with Joe, it's embarrassing.'

Carmel wondered if she should dig a little deeper. She'd lived a whole life of never sticking her nose into anyone else's business, but she felt close to Nadia. Not just as mother- and daughter-in-law, but woman to woman.

'I don't think Zeinab is his type,' Carmel said gently. 'He'll just be nice to her for our sakes and humour her, but it's not like anything is going to happen between them.'

Nadia looked up, her brown eyes searching Carmel's face.

'Do you like him?' The words were out before Carmel even realised it.

Nadia grew flustered and reddened. 'It's not that. She's just so irritating. I just wish she could act normally.' She glanced around. 'We'd better get back. It's getting late and we need to get to the hotel.'

Carmel let it go, but something about the way Nadia had deflected the question made her think. The whole thing would be 'a bit Jeremy Kyle', as her friend Zane was prone to say, referring to the trashy reality TV show where people found out about the paternity of their children or revealed affairs on live television. Her dad and Sharif's mother getting together might look a bit odd, but if life had taught Carmel anything, it was that you needed to seize opportunities for happiness and love wherever and whenever they came along. If Nadia liked Joe and he felt the same, why shouldn't they enjoy a relationship? It would certainly explain Nadia's reaction to Zeinab's flirting.

Joe was single and had been since Mary died. He was a good-looking man, Carmel could see that, fit and well built, and he was a charmer, no doubt about it, but not in a sleazy way. He was just a great laugh, and he saw the bright side of everything. The way he'd immediately embraced her and took her into his life as his daughter was a testament to the kind of man he was.

And Nadia was like a mother to her, as much as she was to Sharif. She and Dolly had been so close. They'd talked about almost everything and shared so much, it was as if Nadia could bring Dolly alive for her daughter – and she did, sometimes in glorious Technicolour. By all accounts, Dolly was larger than life, full of energy and mischief.

Nobody but Nadia, Khalid and Sharif knew the heartache that lay beneath the jovial exterior.

If a relationship between Nadia and Joe was something they both wanted, then Carmel was going to do her best to make sure it came about.

CHAPTER 15

*O*ver coffee and after a delicious dinner in the hotel with the whole group, Sharif whispered in Carmel's ear, 'A nightcap in our room?'

She loved that while he was a sociable man and chatted easily with everyone, his favourite thing to do was spend time alone with her. 'Absolutely,' she whispered back.

They made their excuses and left the gang to it. Zeinab had been monopolising Joe all evening, and Nadia was doing her best to ignore it. She sat beside Jennifer and Damien and heard all about their plans for the extension and the new baby.

Sharif had bought a lovely bottle of gin in duty-free, and he arranged ice, lemon and tonic to be sent to the room. He made them both a drink while Carmel removed her make-up and slipped into her pyjamas.

Handing her the gin and tonic, he tucked a stray hair behind her ear. 'I miss you. It feels like there's always people around. I'm glad to have you all to myself for once.'

She put her drink down, placed his beside it, and wrapped her arms around his waist.

The old version of her would never have taken the initiative, but she was getting bolder with Sharif. The revelations of the reality of his marriage to Jamilla, and the fact that he had made mistakes, that he wasn't the perfect person she thought he was, had brought them closer. He did need her, she was finally coming to accept, as much as she needed him. It evened things out somehow.

Going up on her toes, she drew his lips to hers and kissed him deeply. 'I miss you too,' she whispered, taking his hand and leading him to the bed.

As usual, their lovemaking was passionate and tender, and afterwards, they lay in each other's arms, chatting. They would talk again about the future, but for now they had decided just to enjoy the holiday and deal with it when they got home.

'So Zeinab seems to be behaving better than we hoped,' he remarked.

'Well, she's on her best behaviour for my dad, I think.'

'Really? I knew she was flirting to annoy my mother, but do you really think she likes him that way?'

Carmel smiled. For a smart man, he could be very unobservant sometimes, especially on matters like this. 'Definitely. She's trying to impress him. She fancies the pants off him.'

Sharif laughed. 'Really?' he repeated. 'I suppose that would explain it. Has he any interest, do you think?'

'I doubt it. I can't see her being his type, really. Besides...' Carmel paused. As far as she was aware, Nadia had never had another relationship after Khalid died. She wondered how Sharif would take to the idea of Nadia and Joe. Regardless, she decided to come clean. He loved his mother and would want her to be happy, and anyway, she might need his help.

'Besides what?' he prompted.

'I think Zeinab may not be the only woman with her eye on him.'

'I'm not surprised. He's a great fellow. I'm sure plenty of ladies would be delighted to have Joe on their arm. But I don't think he's seeing anyone, is he?'

'Not now, no. I don't think he has since Mary died, and that was a few years ago now. I asked him before, and he just said he was kept busy with the family and his properties and all of that. But if the right woman came along, I think maybe he would consider it.'

'But you don't think my cantankerous, snobbish aunt is the right woman?' Sharif chuckled.

'No, I don't, but maybe your sweet, kind mother is.' Carmel paused, trying to gauge his reaction.

'What? Really? Joe likes *Ammi*? Are you sure?' Sharif seemed astounded.

'No, I'm not even half sure, but I think she likes him. I think that's why Zeinab flirting her head off is driving Nadia bonkers.'

'Well, they do get on well,' Sharif agreed, 'and they seem to have a laugh together when they meet. But do they see each other outside of us?'

'No, I don't think they ever have. Joe would be afraid we wouldn't approve, and Nadia probably the same. So I was thinking we could test the waters, so to speak, and if there was a bit of something, we could give it a little nudge. What do you think?'

Sharif sighed. 'I don't know. I mean, sure, I really like Joe, but, well, I never really thought of *Ammi* like that. She and my father had such a good marriage, and being an only child, well, after he died, it was just the two of us. I'm not opposed to the idea, I don't think. I just need to try to wrap my head around it, you know? And there may not be anything anyway...'

She knew he was thinking aloud, so she didn't interrupt.

'Has she said anything to you?' Sharif asked.

'No, not directly, but we were talking today, and she was just venting about how crazy-making Zeinab was, and I asked her. She got all flustered and embarrassed and denied it, of course. But there was something, I just know there was.'

'Well, should I ask her?' Sharif wondered.

'No, let's just sound Joe out first. If I can ever prise Zeinab away from him. Maybe you could distract her sometime tomorrow, and I'll get Joe on my own.'

'Sure, I'll take her to a gift shop or something, flash the cash. She'll love that.'

They lay in silence, and Carmel cuddled up to him. Just as she was falling asleep, he spoke again.

'I know we said we'd wait, talk about it later, but I just want you to know that you are the most important person in my life and I want you to have everything you want. I know I didn't sound too enthusiastic about the prospect of having a child. It's nothing to do with you. I just have such sad memories and such guilt about making Jamilla wait and all that turned out to mean. But I want you to know that if you want to try for a baby, then so do I. You'd be such a wonderful mother, I know you would.'

Sometimes, without warning, tears came unbidden to Carmel. She never remembered crying as a child, or even in the years with Bill, but since she'd moved to England, she was prone to tears. It embarrassed her, but Sharif was always telling her that it was just her thawing out – years of frozen emotions finally being given some space to be.

He didn't say anything, just held her until she could reply. She leaned up on one elbow and looked down into his face.

'I don't know if you'll understand this, but I want to have a baby, to have someone to love. I love you so much. And Nadia and Joe, and now Jen and Luke and everything, putting so much love in a life that had absolutely none, but it's not enough. I can't explain it, but the desire to hold a baby of my own in my arms, to hear someone call me Mammy, calling you Daddy, to have a person of our very own, my own flesh and blood, it's...it's so overwhelming sometimes, it scares me. When I heard Jen talking about going on picnics with Joe and Mary, or just things Zane or Ivanka would say about when they were kids, I realised I had no childhood. Not really. I don't have any real happy memories, and maybe I want to relive childhood through my own child, I don't know. I never felt this, not once with Bill, but now it's all I think about. I know the odds are against me – I'm forty-one, and I don't even know if my reproductive system works properly – but I –'

He drew her tightly to his chest. His strong arms around her stopped her disintegrating. 'I know. I understand. Let's go for it, OK? We won't know until we try.'

'You really want to? Not just to keep me happy but for you as well?' she asked, her voice barely audible.

'I really do,' he whispered, and she knew he meant it. She would stop taking the pill immediately.

* * *

SHARIF WAS true to his word, and the following afternoon as they explored the colourful, arty city of Galway, he insisted on taking his aunt to get a souvenir in a very expensive-looking gift store. For once, she wasn't thrilled about spending time with her nephew as she had attached herself like glue to Joe, but Sharif wasn't taking no for an answer.

Carmel had asked Joe quietly at breakfast if they could have some time together during the day, just the two of them, so he gave Luke directions to the cathedral and the Claddagh and the Spanish Arch and made arrangements to meet everyone for fish and chips and a pint in McDonagh's in a few hours' time.

Jen had stayed in the hotel for a rest. While she was feeling good, her energy levels were not what they normally were, so she was happy just to relax there. She promised she'd join them for dinner. Damien was so great with Ruari, and Carmel wondered if Sharif would be as hands-on. She immediately chided herself for the thought. She wasn't even pregnant yet, and it most likely would never happen, so it wasn't doing her any good at all speculating on the non-existent future baby. Time enough for that if she did actually manage to conceive.

Joe put his arm around her shoulders as they strolled down Shop Street licking 99s. She'd protested that she didn't need an ice cream as they'd had scones with jam and cream and coffee before the group broke up, but Joe insisted.

'I never bought you a 99 as a kid, so you'll have to eat forty-odd years of them now.'

As the woman in the shop swirled the thick, soft-serve ice cream onto the cone and stuck a chocolate flake in it, Carmel had been transported back to a time when she was around seven or eight. She'd had a bad tooth and was taken to the dentist to have it pulled.

'No more 99s or chewy toffees for you, young lady,' the dentist had remarked jokingly once he'd pulled the offending tooth.

'What's a 99?' she'd asked.

The dentist and his nurse had looked embarrassed. They'd forgotten she was a child of Trinity House and were talking to her like she was a normal kid.

'It's an ice cream on a cone with a chocolate flake in it,' the nurse had explained.

Then the dentist put his hand in his pocket and pulled out a five-pound note, thrusting it at Carmel. 'Not too many now, but an odd 99 won't do you any harm,' he'd said gruffly.

She'd put the money in her pocket, and when she got back to Trinity House, she hid it in the base of a box each child was given for their personal belongings. She never spent it. It was the only present she'd ever got as a kid.

She considered telling Joe the story now, but she hated to see the sadness in his face when she recounted bits of her life as a child, so she said nothing.

They chatted easily as they walked along, stopping every so often at shop windows to look inside. The streets were busy with locals and tourists alike, and buskers vied for attention. Music was everywhere, and children played and dogs barked and all seemed right with the world.

As they passed one shop, Joe lifted up Carmel's right hand and inspected it.

'Good,' he announced, before leading her into a shop.

'What?' she asked, giggling.

It was a jewellery shop, selling many variations on one product: the Claddagh ring.

Carmel gazed at the array of rings on display. Each had the same basic but intricate design in varying metals and with different stones inset.

'The hands are holding a heart, on top of which is a crown.' The shop assistant began her explanation.

'We know,' Joe said gently. 'We're Irish.' He smiled to take the sting out of his words. 'The hands symbolise friendship, the crown is for loyalty, and the heart is for love.' He spoke directly to Carmel. 'Pick one. I want to buy it for you.'

'You don't need to do that –'

He held a hand out to stop her objections and spoke quietly, out of earshot of the staff and other customers. 'You are my daughter, and I hope we'll always be friends. You will have my loyalty to the day I die. And, well…' He stopped at the love part, suddenly shy. 'Please, let me do this.'

'OK. Thanks.' She kissed him on the cheek, and he gave her a squeeze.

They walked to the counter. 'Can you show us the best ones, please? I want to get my daughter here a really nice ring.'

The assistant didn't need to be told twice. She hastily extracted a tray. 'These are white gold, platinum and yellow gold, set with diamonds, sapphires and emeralds.'

They had no prices, and Carmel began to panic. 'I like the ones over there.' She pointed to the cheaper varieties on open display.

'You're having one of these.' Joe was adamant.

'But they are probably so expensive,' she whispered. 'Honestly, the other ones are just the same and –'

Joe grinned and picked out a gold ring, inset with an emerald, and slipped it on her finger. 'You must wear it with the heart facing in. It tells the world you're spoken for. I think Sharif would rather that.' He winked. 'Though I often thought of getting one for myself, facing it out, to see if there were any bites from gorgeous women!' He laughed. 'Do you like it?'

Carmel looked at it, the emerald sparkling as she moved her hand. She loved not just the ring but everything it symbolised. It was an old wedding ring, traditional to the Claddagh village outside of Galway, and its intricate design was uniquely Irish. Friendship, love and loyalty, absent for so long, and now she had all in abundance. It was a symbol of her new life.

'I love it.' She smiled, trying not to allow her emotions to bubble over again. She took it off, and the lady polished it up and went to put it in a box.

'I'd like to wear it now, if that's all right?' Carmel said.

'Of course.' The woman smiled and handed the ring back to her.

Carmel slipped it on the ring finger of her right hand and smiled. 'Thanks, Dad.'

'You're very welcome, my love. Now outside the door with you till I settle up with this lady.' And he whooshed her out.

CHAPTER 16

*C*armel stood outside, her back to the wall of the shop, and turned her face to the sun, closing her eyes. The street musicians, families and groups of teenagers milled around, and all the chatter settled easily in her ears. She was perfectly content. The talk with Sharif last night had lifted her spirits, and knowing they were both on the same page filled her with happiness. She was wondering if she should raise the subject of Nadia with Joe when she was startled by a voice.

'Carmel? Is it you?'

She snapped her eyes open, and her mouth went instantly dry. She felt as if someone had punched her in the stomach.

'N-Niamh… Oh, hi. H-How are you?' Carmel could hardly speak.

Bill's daughter was standing in front of her, large as life, exuding indignation and righteous fury from every pore. Carmel hadn't seen her in more than a year and a half, but she looked the same. Perfectly highlighted blond bob, Michael Kors handbag, designer clothes head to toe and a bit too much make-up for a day out in the city. She'd gained weight since Carmel last saw her, and she was wearing very tight leather trousers and a low-cut top. It wasn't flattering. Niamh and Sinead were now in their early thirties, but this outfit was for a much younger, slimmer woman.

'How am I? Well, I might ask you the same question. Not to mention, what are you doing here? I thought you'd hightailed it off to London to be with some Indian or something?' The tone was simultaneously accusatory and dismissive. Carmel had forgotten that was how people used to speak to her.

'I'm fine, thanks, fine. Er…yes, I live in London now.' She wished she could be more articulate, but seeing Niamh out of the blue had rattled her.

As she was about to try again, Joe emerged from the shop. 'Are we right?' he asked, not realising she was in conversation with Niamh.

'He's not Indian,' Niamh accused, glancing Joe up and down, her nose wrinkled in distaste.

'Sorry…' Joe stopped, realising this woman was addressing Carmel. 'Who are you?'

'Who am I? Oh, well you might ask, don't mind me. I'm Niamh Sheehan-Condon, just her ex-husband's daughter. You know, the one she abandoned to go off with some Indian, some refugee off the internet or something. Though you're no more an Indian than I am, so he obviously didn't last long.' She snorted, delighted to have caught Carmel out, as she saw it.

Joe seemed to almost get taller and broader, standing slightly in front of Carmel. 'You have the wrong end of the stick there, Niamh Sheehan-Condon,' Joe said, smirking slightly at the affectation of a double-barrelled name. 'I'm Joe McDaid, Carmel's father.'

'What? Oh, I've heard it all now. Her *father*? You are in your eye her father. Sure she's out of a laundry or an orphanage or something. Her mother unmarried, and she was left to the nuns and the taxpayer to rear. You're no more her father than the pope.' She turned to Carmel. 'You might have conned poor Daddy, and now you've this eejit running around after you like a fool, but I'm wise to you, lady, always have been. How dare you come back here, swanning around Ireland with another of your fancy men? Thank God my poor father isn't here. He could do without running into you after everything you put him through.'

Joe put his arm around Carmel, who was trying to formulate a response but failing. His voice when he spoke was one Carmel had never heard before, dark and threatening. 'My daughter has every right to go wherever she likes in her own country. And the day she left that miserable farm was the day her life began. She *is* my daughter, my blood runs in her veins, and I will never allow you, or any member of your pathetic family, to hurt her ever again. And her husband is from Pakistan, not India, you ignorant woman, and he is a wonderful man who loves her as she deserves to be loved, not treated like some kind of unpaid maid for your emotionally stunted father. Now I suggest you take yourself off and leave us alone or I'll have you arrested for harassment. Your *poor daddy*, as you call him, made Carmel's life hell along with that auld wagon of a sister of his, and you seem to have followed in the same path. But no more. You have nothing to do with Carmel, or any other member of our family, so take your obnoxious attitude off now and don't bother us again, do you hear me?'

Carmel smiled involuntarily. Joe sticking up for her, her dad fighting her corner, felt so great. She didn't know where it came from, but the sight of Niamh, so outraged she couldn't actually speak, struck her as so funny.

'How dare you laugh at me, you little tramp?' Niamh hissed, leaning forward, spittle escaping her Botoxed scarlet lips. Just as she was about to continue, a tall, harassed-looking man intervened.

'Niamh, I've been looking everywhere for you!' He noticed Carmel. 'Oh...Carmel? How are you?'

'Hi, I'm fine, thanks.' Carmel smiled weakly at Niamh's long-suffering husband. Theirs was the wedding she had hoped to be involved with in some way. She'd even applied for a passport in case Niamh invited her to go wedding dress shopping abroad, but Niamh had taken Julia instead. Killian was always a nice lad, though. He'd spoken kindly and politely to Carmel on the few occasions they met. What he was doing with the dreadful Niamh was anyone's guess.

'Er, Joe, this is Killian, Niamh's husband.' Carmel introduced the two men awkwardly.

'Killian, if I were you, I'd take your wife out of here before she finds herself up in court for harassment.' Joe was stern. 'Come on, Carmel, the rest of the family will be wondering where we've got to.'

He led Carmel down the street, leaving Niamh seething and snapping at poor Killian.

Joe took her into a bright, sunny pub and, without asking what she wanted, ordered her a brandy. She caught a glimpse of her reflection in the mirror behind the bar; she was snow-white.

She said nothing but took the drink and allowed Joe to bring her to a corner table. He'd got a pint for himself and took a long draught before saying anything.

She sipped the brandy. It was so strong but warming. She realised she was trembling. 'I'm sorry,' she began. 'I should have –'

Joe leaned over and took her hand. 'You have absolutely nothing to apologise for. That woman is a poisonous bitch, and she needed putting in her place. I was glad I got to do it. Who the hell does she think she is? I've never hit anyone in my whole life, least of all a woman, but that was the closest I ever came.' Carmel had never seen him so angry.

'I thought by avoiding Ballyshanley, I'd manage to avoid all the Sheehans, but I forgot Killian is from Galway,' she said. 'They must have been here visiting his family or something. I had my eyes closed, leaning against the shop, the sun on my face. It was lovely. I would never have done that before – I'd have felt foolish. And if Bill heard I was going around Ballyshanley leaning against walls with my eyes closed, he'd have probably had me committed to the county home.'

From nowhere, Carmel felt the urge to giggle, a combination of relief and entertainment at the idea of her sleeping against shops in Ballyshanley – and the image of Bill's perplexed outrage at such mental behaviour. It made her guffaw so hard, the tears flowed down her cheeks and she shook with laughter.

Joe watched in amazement as she chortled at the hilarity of the image, but it was infectious and soon he joined in. Within moments, the two of them were almost in convulsions, wiping their eyes and barely able to catch their breath. Two German tourists looked on in bemusement, and the barman who was wiping glasses nearby grinned.

Eventually, the laughter subsided.

'Oh, Joe, I feel better. I don't think I've ever laughed like that before, but that image just tickled me. Everyone back there in Ballyshanley, full of opinions on everyone else's business, and me just sleeping up against walls… Julia and Bill would need to be sedated to cope with it.' She wiped her eyes once more.

'Well, I'm glad you can see the funny side, pet, even if you have a quirky sense of humour.' He winked and took another drink from his pint of Guinness.

'Look, what can they do to me at this stage? Nothing. And poor old Killian. I always liked him – he's a grand lad.'

'He seemed OK, for the one second I saw him. He's got his work cut out dealing with that one, though. She's a lighting wagon, as my mother used to say.'

'Oh, he does. I remember their wedding. Nothing was good enough, like, the money they spent – well, she spent – it was obscene. And Bill signing cheques away for everything. He never saw any wrong in them, and to be honest, they both grew up very spoiled. Sinead – that's the other girl, Niamh's twin – is a bit nicer, but neither of them really bothered much with me. Julia was in their ear, though, since they were tiny, so they were predisposed to hating me. And then, when I left Bill, well, that was the icing on the cake, as they saw it. I never had a relationship with them, so there was nothing to lose. So I don't actually know why Niamh was so angry…' Carmel was surprised that she could be so reflective and calm about it.

'Well, as you say, small-town gossip. She probably feels that you disgraced her father or something. But there's no excuse for the way she spoke to you. None at all. And I'm glad I got the chance to tell her to her face.'

Carmel looked at Joe, the man she had come to love so much, and said, 'When I was small, I remember this nun in the primary school –

she was horrible. Some of them were nice, but this one, she was really mean. Anyway, at the time, kids got free milk in school, but I hate milk, always have, and it drives my asthma crazy. Sharif says it's often the case with asthmatics – dairy exacerbates breathing problems sometimes, so people who suffer from that tend to shy away naturally from milk and things. Anyway, I asked one of the care workers, not a nun, one of the lay people who worked in Trinity House, to write a note for me to the nun to say I didn't have to drink the milk. So the next day, I was terrified, but I handed her the note, signed by the care worker. Another girl in the class, Julie Murphy, also had a note from her dad saying more or less the same thing. Well, the nun went mad, almost inflated in front of me – and she was huge to begin with. I was only a skinny little eight-year-old. She went mental. Slapped me and Julie with a metre stick and made us stand up for the whole day, no lunch allowed or anything, for having the cheek to ask not to have milk. We were just changing over from feet to metres in those days, so each class had a metre stick, but she used it for slapping the kids.

'Well, Julie went home and told her dad, and the next day he came down and knocked on the classroom door. It was a big timber door with lots of small panes on the top half, solid wood on the bottom. She didn't open the door, just continued on with the lesson, but she held her hand up to the timber bit on the side of the glass to stop him opening it. We were terrified and fascinated at the same time, chanting our eight times tables or whatever, wondering what was going to happen next.

'Well, she's calling out the tables, and next thing, he wraps his fist in his jumper and smashes his hand through the glass pane, grabbing her by the veil and tugging it off her. We never saw a nun's head before – they were always covered – so we were just gazing, horrified and terrified and thrilled all at the same time. He dragged her head close to his and through the door said, "If you ever touch my daughter again, it will be the last thing you ever do, you dried-up auld Mickey Dodger." He left and we all sat there, not knowing what to do. The nun just pulled herself together and carried on as if nothing had happened, but she never so much as looked sideways at Julie Murphy for the whole year after that. I remember that night, lying in bed, wishing I had a dad to stand up for me like that. And today, my wish came true.'

Instantly, just like with Sharif, Carmel regretted telling the story. But she and Nora had discussed it often, and they'd come to the conclusion that Carmel would have to tell remembrances from her childhood, even if it upset Sharif or Joe, because it was the only way of being true to herself. Still, it was hard to see the pain in Joe's face.

'I wish I could have gone down there. I wish I could have protected you, loved you. I wish things had been so different.' Joe's voice was choked with emotion.

'I know you do, and so do I, but I didn't tell you that story to make you sad. I told you because I want you to know it's never too late. Sure, I could have done with parents when I was small. Things would have been so different. But then, it was Dolly who led me to Sharif, and then to you, so who knows? Maybe it was for the best. It seems much worse in hindsight, I know it does, and compared to the childhood Jen and Luke had, well, it's like chalk and cheese. But I'm OK. I'm more than OK – I'm happy. I'm getting stronger every day, and having Sharif and Nadia and all of you, well, like I said, it's a dream come true.'

CHAPTER 17

$\mathcal{W}$ hen everyone met for fish and chips in the big pub on Shop Street, Galway's main thoroughfare, the cacophony of voices was almost deafening. There was a huge group of young people, some of them carrying instrument cases, on one big table and the entire McDaid clan on the other. Jen had strolled in to meet them, and she looked rested. Sharif and Zeinab had yet to appear.

Luke and Carrie were busy telling everyone about how they'd ended up at an African drumming class in the park.

'It was so, like, OMG, like healing or something?' That upward inflection again. 'Lukie and me are going to buy some and go busking on Grafton Street when we go home, aren't we, Lukie?' She was sitting on his lap, her arms around his neck, nuzzling him.

He grinned. 'Er…we'll see…'

'I can just see the Garda Commissioner being over the moon about that, a member of the vice squad drumming away on the street for spare change.' Joe winked and nudged Carmel, who was sitting beside him. 'Just the image the Gardai are looking for.'

'Leave him alone,' Carmel chided. 'I'd love to try drumming. It's supposed to be very good for you.' She wanted to support her brother, who was getting it from everywhere. Jen and Damien were constantly teasing him, and now Joe as well.

'Thanks, Carmel. It's nice to know at least one member of my family isn't picking on me 24/7.' Luke sighed in mock despair.

'Where's Sharif?' Carrie asked.

'Still shopping with Zeinab. He promised to buy her a souvenir.' Carmel grinned and moved to make space between her and Joe as Nadia returned from the ladies'. Carrie and Luke were on the other side of her father, and Tim was across the table, so whenever Zeinab did arrive, she wouldn't be able to monopolise Joe.

With all the business of meeting Niamh, Carmel had never got to raise the issue of Nadia with Joe. Instead, she was just going to observe. She deliberately made chat with Tim, Jen and Damien – Ruari was conked out in the buggy beside them – leaving Joe and Nadia to talk.

Tim told everyone a very funny story about something that happened to him and Brian in Indonesia, and Carrie was very busy nuzzling and kissing Luke, who seemed to have no objections. Every time Carmel glanced over, Joe and Nadia were deep in chat, and they seemed perfectly happy in each other's company.

The food arrived just as Sharif and Zeinab entered the bar laden down with bags. Sharif's face lit up when he saw Carmel, and she pushed over on the bench to make room for him to sit beside her.

He filched one of her chips. 'God, I'm starving. I thought I'd never get her out of the bloody shop.' Then he murmured in her ear, 'I missed you.'

A young waitress with lots of tattoos and piercings and multi-coloured dreadlocks passed Zeinab by, despite her gesticulating wildly to attract the young woman's attention. She instead stopped beside Sharif.

It was something Carmel noticed and often teased him about, how female waitstaff were so attentive. He was gorgeous; of course that was why. Even girls much too young for him could see that. Carmel recognised the admiration in this young woman's eyes as she took the order. He did look particularly sexy today in a burgundy shirt, open at the neck, and petrol-coloured jeans that hugged him in all the right places.

'Carmel, you look like a fox in a chicken coup, gazing at him like that,' Jen whispered to her as Sharif discussed wine with the waitress. 'Not that I blame you, of course.'

Carmel reddened. 'I wasn't... I was just...'

'Just admiring your gorgeous man, I know. As I said, nobody would blame you.' Jen winked and turned her attention back to what Tim was saying, just before they were all distracted by a commotion at the other end of the table.

Zeinab was trying to insert her rather ample bottom into a space between Joe and Luke, despite there being a perfectly good chair on the other side of the table. When it became evident that she simply wouldn't fit, she almost barked, 'Oh, for goodness' sake, Nadia, you know I need to have my back to the wall! I can't sit outside – I've told you that so often, but you never listen. Look, you come out here and sit on this chair, and I'll go in your seat by the wall.'

Nadia was about to leave her seat, despite the fact that her food had already arrived, when Joe piped up. 'Look, my grub hasn't come out yet, so why don't you take my seat, Zeinab, here beside Nadia, and I'll sit out there with Tim?' Before Zeinab could think up any other reason, it was all done, and a very disgruntled Zeinab found herself beside her sister, far away from the object of her desires.

Jen tucked in with gusto. 'I'd love a beer,' she grumbled as Damien ordered another pint. 'Don't ever let me hear you saying the "we're pregnant" remark. If *we* were pregnant, we would both be on the fizzy water.'

'I know,' Damien said. 'I'll make it up to you when the spare arrives.'

'The what?' Sharif asked.

'The spare, that's what we're calling him. Like, y'know, the way the royals have an heir and a spare? Well, we already have the heir, so this one's the spare.' Damien winked surreptitiously, knowing the effect his words would have on Jennifer.

She glared at him. 'That's what *you're* calling him, or her – it might be a girl, you know.'

'Joking! I'm joking, my darling. I know how crap it is, feeling sick and knackered tired all the time. And you're being such a trooper. I mean it, I'm so proud of you.' He gave her a kiss, and her frostiness melted.

The fish was smoked cod, and in the thin beer batter with a tartar dip, it just melted in the mouth. The chips were cut from real potatoes and smothered in salt and vinegar. It was delicious. Sharif finished his huge portion and then started on what was left of Carmel's. She wondered where he put it all. He ate so much but never gained weight.

'So, Joe, what's on the agenda for tomorrow?' Nadia asked.

'Well, tomorrow and tomorrow night and possibly the next day, we'll be in the glorious county of Mayo,' he announced extravagantly.

'Where we're hoping I won't be run out of town,' Tim added wryly.

'Well,' Zeinab said, 'I must say, if we were in Pakistan, a man who lived such a lifestyle...'

Only Carmel and Carrie heard her. All the others were busy laughing at Ruari, who had spread ketchup all over the table surface. But she wasn't done. Carmel was horrified. What was she about to say? She couldn't let the others hear.

'Isn't it so funny how they named a place after a sauce?' Carrie piped up loudly.

Everyone turned to her, bemused.

'What?' Jen was perplexed, and even Luke's brow was furrowed.

'Mayo, like, it's totally random, right? Like there's nowhere called Ketchup or Mustard, is there, Lukie?' She smiled innocently.

Joe stifled a smirk. 'Well, Carrie, pet, I think the name comes more from the Irish word, *Maigh Eo*. When the British changed the place names, they didn't really consider what it meant, just what it sounded like. So that's why we have such funny-sounding place names. In Irish they make perfect sense.' Joe's smile was kind so as not to humiliate her.

'Oh, I see,' Carrie said, and gave her attention to her meal, but not before giving Carmel an almost imperceptible wink.

Carmel exhaled. Carrie had really saved them acute embarrassment. Zeinab was about to launch into her 'gay is a lifestyle' rant. She'd treated Carmel and Nadia to it one afternoon after meeting the outrageously camp Zane, and they had been horrified. Of course, Zane had ramped it up for Zeinab. He'd explained to Carmel once that being gay in his West Indian culture was still very much frowned upon, and he'd endured terrible bullying as a kid, so now he was out and proud and to hell with anyone who objected.

But Zane was only one side of the story. Tim was quite another. He was gentle and quiet, and Carmel would have been mortified if Zeinab had said anything hurtful to him.

Zeinab shifted uncomfortably in her seat, and Carmel shot her what she hoped was a clear warning. She'd known the older woman was still having trouble accepting Tim. One evening before the trip, she'd asked why Tim didn't just take anti-gay drugs or get hypnotised to get him 'back to normal'. She'd then gone on to explain that he'd probably never met the right woman and got nervous so he resorted to his own gender out of fear. And according to her, there were no gay Pakistani men.

Nadia had been beside herself with worry that Zeinab would say something along those lines to Tim, so Sharif had to sit her down before leaving and warn her not to say anything rude. She still looked on him with undisguised suspicion and mistrust, but she'd acted OK up to now – until the potential situation Carrie had so deftly averted. In fact, Carrie had jumped in just in time. Tim was right about her – she might appear ditzy, but she was one smart cookie.

'Ah now, Tim,' Joe said, clearly anxious to get the conversation away from condiments and back to the plan for the next few days. 'I know it must seem strange after all these years, but try not to be too worried about it. You have a fairly formidable posse behind you, so nobody will be running you anywhere, and anyway, I'm sure it will all go grand.' He patted Tim gently on the back and turned to address the rest of the group. 'So Tim will attend to his affairs, and the rest of us will go on a bit of a tour around. There's the most marvellous sea stack out at Downpatrick, then I want to show you the Céide Fields – the first evidence of farming in Ireland that goes back into prehistoric times – and some dolmens and ring forts. And I thought we might walk or even cycle a bit of the greenway. They've turned a lot of the old railway lines into cycle paths, and there's a gorgeous one from Westport, Tim's home town, so I thought we might do that?'

There was general agreement, except for Zeinab, who looked nothing short of appalled at the prospect of cycling anywhere. The chat continued over the meal, and soon the crowd began to disperse. Jen and Damien took little Ruari back to the hotel, and Carrie almost dragged Luke out the door, so anxious was she to get him alone. Zeinab, Nadia and Joe took a taxi, even though it wasn't far and a lovely night, because Zeinab said she simply couldn't walk. They offered to have Tim join them, but he said he'd prefer to walk, so once they'd settled up the bill, Sharif, Carmel and Tim began the stroll back to the hotel.

They could hear the *ting, ting* of sails and rigging as they strolled along the quayside in Galway. Even though it was almost eleven at night, it was only dusk, and when Sharif remarked on it, Tim replied, 'Yes, I'd forgotten that about Ireland. In the summertime, it never really gets dark. It goes kind of dusky around midnight, but by three or four in the morning, it's bright again. The day I left, it was in the middle of June, and I remember walking to Westport town – the farm was about seven miles outside – and even though it was two or three in the morning, it was quite light. I never imagined I'd come back, and yet here I am, a lifetime later, so much done.' It was hard to tell if he was wistful or just sad.

'How do you feel about tomorrow?' Carmel asked. She felt kind of united with Tim by the isolation of their early lives. That's why she'd been the one to break the news to him that Brian was dead. Not to mention that Dolly had confided the whole story of Carmel's conception and birth to Brian and Tim years before. Brian and Tim had been there for Dolly as she told the whole sorry tale, and again, along with Nadia,

Khalid and Sharif, to pick up the pieces every time Dolly returned to London after yet another fruitless search for her daughter in Ireland. When Carmel attended Brian's funeral, the first time she met any of the McDaids, they'd had no idea she was Joe's daughter or that Tim was Brian's life partner. They stood together in the crematorium that day, and afterwards, Tim had cried in her arms at the loss of his one true love.

The family knew the whole story now, of course, about both Carmel and Tim, but for so long they were both outside looking in at life. They were connected in empathy.

'How do I feel?' Tim repeated. 'The truth? Sick to my stomach. I don't know why. It's ridiculous. Everyone I knew is dead and gone. It's just a scrap of land and a few forms. But I don't know... It feels so...so bloody sad, I suppose.'

Carmel linked her arm with his as they walked. He was easily a foot taller, straight as an arrow. As always, his snow-white hair was neatly brushed back off his high forehead. In his herringbone Crombie coat and felt trilby hat, he looked almost like some off-duty duke or lord swanning about. Nothing about his demeanour gave away the inner turmoil Carmel knew he felt. They were both good at hiding what was really going on. She just hoped she hadn't done the wrong thing in convincing him to come here.

'It's bound to be emotional, and you're still raw after Brian,' she said. 'You should just take the day as it comes and accept that you are going to feel something. It's not just any other day, and if you get a bit upset, then that's fine. You don't have to put a brave face on things if you don't feel it.'

Tim chuckled. 'Ah, yes, little miss self-help. How right you are.'

'I mean it,' she insisted. 'I know my life was a train crash for so long, but I didn't go around the bend because of self-help books. Wayne Dyer, Deepak Chopra, Sharon Salzberg – they were my friends, they kept me from tipping over the edge. I know some of it sounds like old claptrap, but most of it makes perfect sense.'

'I know, and you're right,' Tim conceded. 'I'm only joking with you. I want to thank you both, actually. Carmel, you especially, for convincing me to come along, for being with me on this trip. I would have definitely cried off if it wasn't for you.'

Sharif patted the older man's back. 'Sometimes you need your friends, simple as that. We all do. Carmel is right, you know. Just allow yourself to feel whatever you feel tomorrow. Don't try to mask it or bury it. We're all going through things all the time. Everyone has a story – you know that better than most – so live yours. Sure, it was sad, and your parents missed out on so much by not having you in their lives, but you might find that going there tomorrow gives you some peace…some closure, as our American friends say.'

'Maybe.' Tim seemed lost in another world.

'So what's the situation with the farm now, do you know?' Carmel asked.

'It was leased to a local family. When my father died, my mother let the neighbours farm it for a small fee. She wrote to me, just telling me he was dead and the arrangements she had made. I sent a Mass card, and that was that. Then when she died, well, the neighbours wrote to me, asking if the arrangement could continue, so I said it could. I had no interest in the place.

'The house is empty. It was just closed up after my mother died and left there. I don't have a clue what shape it's in, close to derelict, I would imagine, though. The son-in-law of the man we used to rent to wants to buy the land, so I'll sell it to him, and sure if he wants the house as well, he can have it. I don't even need the money, but he seems anxious that it be in his own name, not rented land, so I might as well do the right thing and do the deal. It's something to do with European grants for farmers, don't ask me what. The auctioneer started explaining in a letter, but to be honest, it wasn't long after Brian died, and I couldn't concentrate so I just tuned out.'

'Well, I'm sure it will all go fine,' Carmel assured him. 'Are you going to meet him there?'

'That's the plan. I'm seeing him and his wife at the farm tomorrow at three, with Jim Daly, the local auctioneer. I'm not sure about him, to be honest with you. He seems a bit, I don't know, a bit greedy or something. He suggested a figure, but I think it's too much. They're a young couple with a family. The farm came to her and she married this lad, and they're trying to make a go of it. If they had my land with their own, they stand some kind of chance of making a decent living.

'Daly reckons we can get six thousand an acre, and there's about a hundred acres there. Some of it is bog and a bit under forestry, but mostly it's good grazing land. But I can't see how two young farmers from County Mayo can raise that kind of money. They're terrified it will go on the market and then they're snookered forever, but I won't do that to them. I'll meet them tomorrow and weigh the situation up, and if at all possible, I'll do a deal with them. As I said, I have no need of the money, and my children have made themselves very clear that they want nothing to do with me or my estate, so all that's left is for me to try to do right by these young people at least. Maybe some good can come of the place after all these years.'

'You're a good man, Tim. But be careful.' Carmel felt so protective of him. She would hate to see him taken advantage of. 'I have first-hand experience of Irish farmers and land and all that means. They'll do anything for it. Then most people are nothing like my ex-husband, so maybe they're nice and it would be a good thing to give them a break. Just be careful anyway.'

Sharif grinned. 'Carmel, this man was a banker all his career. I think he's a fairly good judge of character at this stage.'

'Well, it's certainly taught me to look beneath the surface anyway,' Tim said.

As they approached the hotel, Carmel and Sharif went to say goodnight, but Tim looked like he had something else to say.

'Tim?' Carmel prompted.

'Ah, it's nothing. Goodnight, you two, and thanks for another lovely day. See you both in the morning.' He went to his room on the opposite side of the lobby to theirs. Carmel urged Sharif to go on without her and ran after Tim.

'What were you going to say?' she asked as he put his key in the door to his room.

He smiled. 'You're a perceptive woman, Carmel Khan, do you

know that? All those years of just listening and saying nothing. Look, it doesn't matter, I –'

'Do you want me to come with you tomorrow? If you do, I'm happy to.'

'It's stupid, I know. I don't know why I'm being like this. It's just a bloody bit of land. But…'

'It's not stupid. It's hard to go back. I can't imagine trying to set foot in Ballyshanley ever again, or Trinity House. I know our lives took different paths, Tim, but we have a lot in common, not really fitting into the world or something. The others don't get it the way we do. So will I come tomorrow?'

'Are you sure?' Tim asked. 'Joe had such a tempting itinerary planned, I feel bad dragging you away from it. And this is your home-coming trip after all.'

'The places Joe is taking everyone tomorrow have been there for centuries – they'll wait. Tim, I had an empty, lonely life for forty-plus years, and now I have family and friends and people who actually want me around, not just put up with me. Nobody ever needed me before, and it feels so good to be needed. I'm not saying you need me tomorrow, but if it would make it a bit easier on you if I was there, well, that would mean as much to me as to you.'

'Thanks, Carmel. If you're sure, then I'd feel so much better with you beside me.'

'It's a date.' She grinned and went up on her tiptoes to kiss his cheek. 'Goodnight, Tim. I'll be right beside you, and if you ask him to be, so will Brian.'

'I'll certainly ask him. I talk to him every night. Sounds mad, I know, but I do.'

'I talk to Dolly too, and I never even met her, so we can be basket cases together.' She chuckled as she left him and went to join Sharif.

CHAPTER 18

The next day, the group took off in the bus, leaving Carmel and Tim to sort everything out. Sharif was, as usual, wonderfully supportive, delighted Carmel was accompanying Tim and telling her she would be a great help to him. The way he encouraged her in everything never ceased to amaze her. He not only protected her, but he thought there was nothing she couldn't do and urged her to go boldly at life, taking chances and trying new things.

'Will we rent a car?' Carmel asked over a late breakfast. 'That way we can travel on our own and come and go as we like. The hotel reception have a sign saying they will arrange it. I checked earlier, and we can pick it up here and drop it off at the hotel we're staying at tomorrow.'

'Well, I haven't driven since I had my knee replaced last year,' Tim admitted. 'There's no need when we are right on the Tube. So I'd be less than confident, to be honest.'

'Well, I'll drive. I have my licence, so it should be fine. What do you think?'

'I think you are my guardian angel, Mrs Khan, that's what I think. Let's do it. The farm is about seven miles outside of Westport, so having our own transport would be so much better than trying to get taxis or lifts or whatever. But I insist on paying, OK?'

'Fair enough.' She held her hands up in surrender. 'I've never driven in Ireland, but if I can navigate London, then I can surely manage rural Mayo, right?' She smiled. 'Just to be safe, though, let's get good insurance.'

The car was organised in very quick time, and Carmel felt a little surge of pride as she handed over her driving licence and Tim's credit card. She would have loved to travel back in time and show that timid child in Trinity House and then that subjugated woman in a lonely farmhouse just how far she would come.

'If you just take a seat in the lobby there, someone will bring the car over to the front door. They'll come to find you when it's here, Mrs Khan,' the charming young hotel receptionist explained. 'Can I get you some coffee or tea while you wait?'

Carmel looked at Tim. 'We're not long finished our breakfast, but we never say no to a cup of tea, so yes, please, that would be lovely.'

They sat in companionable silence. Carmel sensed Tim was happier not to have to talk, so she read the paper and he just sat, in quiet contemplation, sipping his tea. Within twenty minutes, the car arrived, and Carmel had butterflies as the young man who delivered it handed her the keys. He showed her how everything worked in about five seconds flat and immediately was on his mobile phone, deep in some vital conversation with someone called Macca about a part for a motorbike. It didn't look like he was coming back, so they sat in and Carmel nervously edged the car out of the hotel car park.

'We're about an hour and a half from Westport, according to this,' she said, poking at the satnav. When she figured out how to work it, she followed the directions out of the city of Galway.

Tim seemed to have relaxed a little now that they were actually on their way, and they chatted easily on the trip. After a few minutes, she'd got the hang of the car and was driving confidently. The time flew by as they marvelled at the gorgeous rolling hills, the ruins dotted everywhere and the bustling towns they passed through. As they approached their destination, she saw lots of signs for Westport House.

'What's that?' she asked. 'A hotel or something?'

'Well, no, though I think now there are holiday places to stay in the grounds or a camping site or something. It was the home of the Browne family – they held the title Marquess of Sligo – but it's owned by someone else now. The Brownes made all their money in slave trading between Europe and Jamaica, so it's got a murky past. The house itself was just opening to the public when I left, but my father was often up there, on various matters to do with land. I went with him once or twice as a boy. It's an incredible house, beautiful. It's also got a connection to Granuaile, the pirate queen of Connaught. Her great-granddaughter married in there. There are some wonderful stories about her pirating on the high seas, feared by everyone. Apparently, she met Queen Elizabeth I, and the queen couldn't speak Irish and Grainne couldn't speak English, so they conversed in Latin.'

'Wow! That sounds like a fascinating place. Maybe we'll get time to visit tomorrow. If not, we'll just have to come back sometime.' Carmel indicated to turn down the main street.

'Well, you've changed your tune,' Tim teased. 'I thought this was a one-off trip, never to be repeated?'

'OK, I admit it, I'm having more fun than I anticipated,' Carmel conceded.

'Even crazy ex-step-daughters aside?' Tim asked. She'd told him and Sharif about the encounter with Niamh, and both of them had congratulated Joe on how he handled it.

'Even that,' she agreed.

The main street of Westport was a hive of activity. The shops were all painted different bright colours, and the goods for sale were many and varied, from Asian street food to traditional crafts. There were antique shops, jewellers, sweetshops, cafés, pubs and restaurants to suit every taste. People chatted on street corners, families strolled by licking ice creams, and nobody seemed in a hurry. A traditional band were playing outside a pub, and children were dancing wildly to the music while their parents had a drink in the sun.

Tim was agog.

'A bit different to how you remember it?' Carmel asked gently as they drove slowly down the street, their progress impeded by the nonchalantly jaywalking Irish.

'You could say that.' Tim gazed in amazement at his home town. 'Look at that.' He called out the storefronts as they passed. 'Turkish barbers, Polish shops, a yoga studio... I wouldn't recognise the place, and yet, some parts look the same. Clew Bay, the river, Westport House, even some of the buildings. But it all seems so vibrant now, so colourful and full of life. I remember it being drab, cold, the street covered in horse dung – nothing like this.'

'We're a bit early.' Carmel checked the clock on the dashboard. 'Will we get out, have a wander round?'

'Let's do that.' Tim was still mesmerised by the transformation.

They passed a very enjoyable hour wandering up and down the streets and poking about in the shops, and Carmel bought Sharif a pair of cufflinks in an antique shop run by a very charming young man who seemed to have tattooed every inch of his skin. The cufflinks had a Celtic design on them, and she knew Sharif would love them. He often wore double-cuff shirts, so he had many different pairs of cufflinks already, but he loved getting presents and she loved giving them to him. She enjoyed seeing how his eyes lit up with delight even if it was just one of his favourite cakes from the local bakery or a book from a charity shop.

Soon it was time to make their way to the farm. Tim's sense of dread had dissipated since last night, but now that the return to his home place was imminent, he went quiet again. Carmel could see the anxiety behind his eyes.

She tapped the townland Tim gave her into the satnav and eased the car out into the slow-moving traffic once more.

He didn't speak, so neither did she. He needed to compose himself, and the silence wasn't awkward as Carmel deftly manoeuvred the car around the twisty roads. They turned off the main road and drove up a hill. There was a fine two-storey farmhouse on the left, and the satnav indicated that it was their destination. The hedging all around the house was neatly kept, and the house itself didn't appear derelict – quite the opposite. It looked as if it had been recently painted brilliant white, and the windows gleamed, reflecting the afternoon sun.

'Is that it?' Carmel asked, surprised. She'd been expecting some tumbledown ruin, overgrown and neglected.

'Yes…I think so. Well, I know it is, but it looks much better than it did when I lived here. It's not like I expected.'

They pulled into a neat farmyard, where a newish tractor was parked up in one corner and stables lined one side. Right in the middle of the yard was a cherry-red BMW convertible. *What an impractical car for Irish weather*, Carmel thought. It was such a flashy, showy car, and she wondered who on earth would own such a vehicle.

Tim and Carmel got out, and immediately they were spotted by a middle-aged man who ran over to greet them. He wore a shiny suit and a pink shirt with a really garish tie. Carmel deduced immediately that he was the owner of the convertible. She thought the welcome he gave them, as he pumped Tim's hand, a little too effusive to be genuine, and she didn't like his lecherous gaze and his nudge-nudge remark to Tim along the lines of 'Life in the old dog yet, eh?' His boomy laugh was also very off-putting.

Tim made the introductions. 'Carmel, this is Jim Daly, the auctioneer, and Jim, this is a friend of mine, Carmel Khan.' Carmel didn't imagine the slight emphasis on the word 'friend', but Jim was too thick to grasp it.

'Carmel!' he said, leaning in to kiss her cheek and placing a hand on her waist. He smelled strongly of aftershave. He was paunchy, and his hair had a peculiar plum sheen to it. She'd seen old lads in Ballyshanley dying their hair jet-black when they were in their seventies, fooling no one of course, but this dark-purple colour was a new one on her – and certainly a colour never found in nature. Jim clearly saw himself as a bit of a hit with the ladies, and the double entendres just kept coming.

'So, Tim, as I was saying on the phone, this is good land, and a fertile farm is better than a fertile woman, I always say, and if you've no plans to settle down here yourself, however tempting the company...' He winked at Carmel, and she deliberately remained stony-faced. It put him off his stride. 'Yes, well...eh...if you're not staying around, then I think we should look for 500,000 for the farm, and if they want the house, and I think they will, we'll bring it up to 700,000 for the whole shebang. They're getting a good deal at that, and they can't afford not to take it because they'll be surrounded if they let it go to someone else. You see, this farm almost encircles theirs, so we have them by the short and curlies.' Jim beamed, delighted with himself.

Before Tim could respond, a couple Carmel judged to be in their thirties entered the yard.

'Ah, here we are now, Tim, and Carmel of course, this is Catriona and David Lynch.' Jim was enjoying being the master of ceremonies. 'They have the neighbouring fa –'

'I know exactly who you are,' Tim cut across him. 'We've corresponded, and I knew your mam and dad, Catriona. My condolences on his passing.'

The woman smiled and shook Tim's hand. She was dressed for farming in jeans, boots and a dark-green fleece. She had a pleasant, open face, and her brown hair was tied up in a ponytail. 'Thanks, Mr O'Flaherty. Mam got your Mass card, and she really appreciated it.'

'Call me Tim, please. And how is she, your mother?' Tim asked.

'Ah, Tim, she's OK, but she's in the county home now. She has senile dementia, so she has good days and bad days, you know? Most of the time she's content enough, though.'

'I'm sorry to hear that. Your parents were much younger than me, but I knew the family of course when I was growing up.' Tim turned to her husband. 'And you're a native of Westport as well, I believe, David?'

'I am.' He was tall and balding and very quietly spoken, also dressed for farming. They were an unremarkable couple, but they seemed very genuine and Carmel liked them. They were worried, she could tell. Their whole livelihood depended on what happened here today.

'My family, the Lynches, are farming in this parish for six or seven generations at least. My older brother has the family farm now, out at Scarteen Cross, so myself and Catriona are farming here.'

'And you have children too?' Carmel asked, though Jim seemed anxious to get on with the negotiations, clicking his pen and jingling change in his pocket.

'We have. A boy of eight called Jack and a little girl, Katie, she's three, so we've our hands full. We have a German au pair at the moment helping us to look after them because we're making silage and we need to stay at it for as long as the weather holds.' Carmel loved his soft West-of-Ireland accent.

'It sounds like you're busy so,' she said with a grin.

CHAPTER 19

'So maybe we could have a look inside the house and have a chat in there? You are interested in buying both the farm and the house, I take it?' Jim was practically salivating at the thought of the easy commission he was about to make.

'If you don't mind, Jim, I'd rather stay out here for now,' Tim interrupted. 'I haven't been in there for many decades, so if I go in, I'd like to go alone.' He glanced up at the gable end of the farmhouse.

Carmel was surprised how assertive he was being; he always seemed so mild-mannered. But it was clear he didn't like Jim Daly any more than she did. She had only ever known Tim in retirement, but she could see in the way he was dealing with the obnoxious Jim how he'd risen through the ranks in the bank during his career. There was a quiet confidence and determination to him, and something about his demeanour brooked no argument. It was a side to him she had not seen before.

Jim was chastened, but he was determined to keep his commission on track. He was the kind of guy who had probably been bragging to all and sundry about the killing he was about to make. He wasn't going to have it snatched from him now. 'Right, well, OK so. Well, David, and Catriona as well of course' – he added her in as an afterthought – 'as you know, this is a fine farm of land, excellent road frontage and well drained. As good grazing as you'll get anywhere in the county, and the house is in great shape, from the outside anyway.' There was that boomy laugh again that was really getting on Carmel's nerves.

'It's fine inside too. We go in every week, open the windows in summer and air it out, and in the winter, we keep a heater on.' Catriona was matter-of-fact.

Tim was clearly perplexed. 'You've been doing that since when?'

She looked surprised at his reaction. 'Well, since always. When your father died, Dad used to look in on your mother, check she was OK, do odd jobs around the house, take care of the garden, that kind of thing, and then when she died, he just kind of kept on doing it. So I suppose when we took over the farm, when Daddy died, we took that on as well.'

'So your family have been taking care of this place for years?'

'Yes, well, since before I was born,' Catriona said. 'Your parents were very good to us, and then your mam renting us the land for very cheap for so long, and then you doing the same, it was the least we could do. Our families have been good neighbours for generations.'

'Well, times change, and we must all move on, I suppose.' Jim did not like the direction this conversation was taking. 'Now, Tim here is living the high life over in London, so he's happy to sell this property, but only at the right price, of course –'

Tim silenced him. 'Jim, I'm sorry for dragging you out here, but I think we can manage this ourselves. It seems like my family and Catriona's have had many happy years of peaceful coexistence and cooperation, so we'll continue that. That means, unfortunately, we have no need of your no doubt excellent negotiating skills. Thank you, though, and of course I'll settle up with you for your time to date. If you just send me a bill for hours worked, land registry searches, that sort of thing, if you carried them out?' Tim smiled innocently, and Carmel had to stifle a giggle.

Jim puffed up like a bullfrog. 'Well, this is not advisable at all, Mr O'Flaherty. You could seriously jeopardise your position. If I could just have a quiet word...' Jim clearly felt his commission slipping away.

'There's no need, I assure you. My position is fine, and as I said, we'll take it from here.'

'But...but legally...' Jim was grasping at straws.

'Oh, don't worry on that front,' Tim assured him. 'My solicitor will ensure that whatever we decide today will be all signed, sealed and delivered properly, but I appreciate your concern, Jim. It's so nice to know people care.'

Jim had been given his marching orders in no uncertain terms, and he knew it.

'On your own head,' he muttered as he almost stomped back to his ridiculous red car. It began to spit rain as he drove away, and he had to stop again and struggle to get the roof to close. Realising they were all watching in amusement, he got back in with the top still down and drove off, the rain soaking his purple hair.

'Would you both like to come up to our house, have a cup of tea?' Catriona asked.

Tim smiled. 'That would be lovely.'

As they made their way back to the car, David said, 'We can actually walk. It's only a few minutes through the field, but it's three miles around by car. If you don't mind a bit of drizzle.'

'Not a bit.' Carmel laughed. 'We're Irish and well used to the rain.' They chatted easily as they went through a wooden gate around the back of the farmhouse. But as they turned a corner, Tim stopped, stock-still.

Carmel put her hand on his arm as he stood and stared.

'This...' His voice was hoarse. 'Who did this?'

The garden behind the house was a riot of wild flowers, every imaginable colour and size, and the entire thing was surrounded by a beautiful dry stone wall. Right in the middle of the garden was a stone seat and a sundial. Carmel thought it was like an oasis of paradise in the patchwork quilt of green farmland that stretched down to the Atlantic.

'Oh, the wild flower garden?' Catriona asked. 'That's been there for years and years. We don't do much to it, to be honest – it kind of flowers every year itself. We mow it at the end of the season and let the seeds fall out and then gather up the clippings. That's what my father did anyway. Your mam loved it, but it was your dad that really minded it apparently. 'Twas he built the stone wall around it and added in the seat. I remember my father telling me how he offered to help, but your dad said no, he'd do it himself. Every night, after a full day farming, he'd be out there, fixing the wall or making the sundial. I don't remember him – he died when I was young – but my parents spoke of him often. Your mam loved it too, and right up to the time she died, she'd ask Kathleen – that's the home help, but sure you know that, as 'twas you paid for her to be here – to push her out to the garden in her wheelchair. I remember my uncle visiting once and remarking how it was out of character for the O'Flahertys to have such a thing. They weren't given to that kind of frivolity, I suppose, but they just loved the place.'

Catriona's chatting covered up Tim's shock, and Carmel linked his arm through hers as they walked. He was a deeply private man, and she knew he wouldn't want them to know the origins of the garden. To spare him, Carmel prattled away with Catriona and David about life on the farm and their children until they arrived to a new house.

'Oh, I was expecting another farmhouse!' Carmel remarked as she took in the new brightly painted dormer bungalow.

'Well, we built this when David and I got married. Mam and Dad were still living in the home place. We have their place rented out now, to our au pair and her boyfriend, actually. He's Dutch, and he makes knives. They're happy as Larry there. The place needs modernising, really, but they're kind of alternative, so they like having no central heating and stuff like that.' Catriona grinned.

Their kitchen was warm and bright, the big fridge covered in drawings done by the kids.

'Are Jack and Katie here?' Carmel asked.

Tim was yet to speak. The discovery of the wild flower garden that he'd planted all those years ago had seemingly shaken him to his core.

'No, they're at a camp. It's a community-run thing for the kids of the area. They go to the playground and down to the beach. Kristiana, that's the au pair, is with them. Now can I get you tea or coffee?'

'Tea, please.' Carmel gazed around the sunny room. Toys were stacked in one corner, a pair of tiny shoes under the table, small bright-coloured coats hanging on a hook near the back door. The normal stuff of family life was strewn around – Disney character lunchboxes, colouring pencils. It wasn't chaotic or dirty, just a real working home. To anyone else, it would not have been remarkable, a similar scene represented all over the world in homes where small children were loved and cared for, but Carmel realised she'd never been anywhere like it in her life. Bill didn't encourage friendships with people her own age in Ballyshanley, and as a kid, she wasn't allowed to go to anyone's house to play. Not that she was ever asked, but she often wondered what family houses looked like. And now she knew.

'Tim? What can I get you?' Catriona broke through his reverie.

'Oh, I'm sorry, what a lovely home you have. Tea would be great, thanks.' He seemed distracted, and Carmel wondered if they shouldn't leave the deal for another day.

When David left to answer the phone and Catriona went out to the pantry to get something, Carmel whispered, 'We can do this another day, if you'd prefer?'

Tim patted her hand. 'No...I'm fine. It's just a lot to process, the garden. I just don't know whether to be happy or sad. I'm both, I think.'

Catriona came back with some scones, butter and jam and placed them on the table, moving a stack of colouring books. 'Sorry about the mess. It's like shovelling snow when it's still snowing trying to tidy up after my pair.' She did her best to make space on the table.

'Please, don't apologise. It's lovely. I would have loved to have grown up somewhere like here.' The words were out before Carmel realised she'd said them. She didn't often discuss her past, and never with strangers. She reddened in embarrassment, frantically trying to figure out a way to divert the conversation.

Catriona looked at her for a moment and seemed to understand

her discomfort. 'I know sure. They have so much now.' David came
back in then. 'Everything OK?' Catriona asked him.

He nodded.

'So, Catriona and David, I've been thinking,' Tim began. 'And do
you mind if I ask you a personal question? It's only in relation to what
we're going to do.'

'Of course.' It was Catriona who spoke.

'How are you both, financially speaking?' The words hung in
the air.

Carmel felt she should excuse herself. This was their private business. But to do so now would be rude.

The young couple looked at each other, words unspoken passing
between them.

'We're fine,' David began.

'We're really struggling.' Catriona's voice was louder.

'Cat –'

'No, David, we might as well tell him the truth. Look, Tim, we
came down today, and our plan was to ask you to do us a deal. I know
the place is worth 600,000, more probably, but we just haven't got that
kind of money. Jim Daly has been saying to people that the place
would be up for auction soon, and we'll be almost totally surrounded
if someone buys it. We're doing OK, on the bit that we have. But we're
into organic farming, and producing ethically sound food is much
more expensive than the alternative. Our chickens are free-range, the
cows are grass-fed most of the year, and what we'd love to do is set up
an open farm – you know, for families to visit – and maybe have a
farm shop selling our produce and a café. We run the local farmer's
market in Westport, and we've a great little co-op running, but we are
stuck in that we can only produce so much on the land that we have.
We can't really afford your farm, that's the truth, but we can't afford
to let anyone else have it either. We went to the bank, and they can't –
or won't – lend us that much...certainly nothing like 600,000.'

Tim glanced at Carmel, and she knew he was checking in with her:
Do they seem genuine? She thought they were, and she guessed Tim did
as well.

'So you don't want to buy it?' Tim asked.

'Well, we do, as in we can't let anyone else buy it, but now is not ideal for us. Catriona is right.' David sounded tired. Carmel imagined them night after night sitting at this kitchen table going over the figures, trying to find a way to save their livelihoods, and her heart went out to them.

'But I thought it was something to do with grants from the EU?' Tim was gentle but probing.

'No, we just said that to Daly.' David cut a scone in half and buttered it. 'He's such a blabbermouth, everyone in the place would know our business if you told him. Nobody with any sense tells him anything.'

'I can well imagine that's the case all right.' Tim thought for a minute. 'OK, how about this? I could just say let's keep going with the rent, but I'm not a spring chicken, and when I die, you'll be faced with the same problem. Worse, actually, because I don't have anyone to leave it to, so I was considering leaving whatever I have to charity.'

Carmel knew how hard this was for him, denying the existence of his children, but it was their doing, not his.

'So here is my proposal. I give you the farm, the house, the whole lot. It's either you two or a charity, and the way I see it, you are just as deserving as any other cause. Or, if necessary for legal reasons, I'll sell it to you for a euro or something, and I might come back now and again, for as long as I'm able. I know I didn't want to go into the house today, and maybe I will some other time, but seeing the garden, knowing the place is taken care of... I didn't think it would affect me so much, but it has, and I realise that this place is a part of me, even after all these years. The fact that your family cared for it means more than I can say.'

CHAPTER 20

*C*atriona and David were speechless. The silence hung heavily between them all.

'But...but, Tim, we can't do that.' Catriona was struggling to articulate. 'This is your land, your family's land, and no matter what the situation, we have to pay you for it!'

Tim leaned over and put his hand on hers. 'Please, I'm quite sure this is what I want to do. I'm quite wealthy, I own my own house, and I have everything I need. I've travelled all over the world, and now that I'm getting on in life, my needs are few. You're young, just starting out, and I like the sound of what you're doing – the farmer's market and sustainable farming and all of that. Brian – that was my partner, he died last year – was a great gardener, and he'd love that idea as well. So consider it a donation, whatever you want to call it.'

Carmel saw the confusion on their faces – Brian was his partner?

'It's a long, sad story, but in a nutshell, I'm gay. That's why my father threw me out. I got married and had a family, but for obvious reasons, it didn't work out. And then, luckily, I met Carmel's uncle, Brian, and we were together for many years. I want to do this. My children are grown up and don't want anything to do with me. Your family looked after my parents, and seeing that flower garden today...

I planted that with my friend Kitty Lynch the summer before I was sent away. I thought my father hated me, hated what I was, and my mother never really connected with me either once I left. So I lived all my life thinking they never cared about me. But they did care. They looked after that garden, and that must mean something.' Tears shone in the old man's eyes.

'Hang on a minute,' David said. 'Your friend Kitty Lynch, how old would she be now?'

'Same age as me, I suppose, maybe a bit younger? Early seventies. Why?'

'Because I think your Kitty Lynch is my grand-aunt. She lived here all her life. Her nephew Donal is my dad. She's the only Kitty Lynch in the parish, to my knowledge.'

'And is she still alive?' Tim asked. This day was proving more and more amazing.

'Oh, indeed she is, hale and hearty. She's a bit of a character, never married or anything, but she's been all over the world. She lived in America for years and then in South Africa. I can take you to meet her if you like?'

'If she is the same Kitty, I'd like that very much,' Tim said quietly. 'I owe her an apology, and it's long overdue.'

There was a moment of silence, and then Tim perked up again. 'Now back to the deal! Are we on? I'll instruct the local solicitor here to draw up all the necessary paperwork. You two can take care of the fees for that and any other technical things that need to be done, but as far as I'm concerned, it's all yours.'

Catriona's eyes filled up with tears. 'I can't believe it. Are you certain this is what you want to do? It seems too much, and I don't want you to feel like we pressured you and regret it afterwards. And I mean, what about your family? I know they've said they don't want it, but when they hear you've given it away to strangers, they'll be furious surely?'

'Catriona, David, listen to me,' Tim said seriously. 'My children don't even know this place exists. Their mother made sure that they have no sense of being half Irish, so you need have no worries on that score. Nothing about Ireland, Mayo or me holds even the slightest interest for them. As for me regretting it, I don't do regrets, I just don't. Life is for living, and I'm grateful to be in a position where I might be able to make a real difference to someone. So please just accept it. Will you?' Tim gazed from Catriona's face to David's.

David stood up, walked around to the side of the table where Tim sat and stretched out his hand. 'Thank you very much, Tim. My family will always be in your debt. And if we can ever do anything for you, anything at all, then please just get in touch. And that garden will always be looked after. I promise.'

Tim shook his hand, and Catriona joined them and kissed Tim's cheek. 'Thank you, Tim. You don't know what this means to us.'

Tim put his arms around both of them, and Carmel had to wipe away a tear.

* * *

TIM AND CARMEL drove in the hired car behind the Lynches on the way back into Westport. They were taking Tim to meet Kitty again.

'How do you feel now?' Carmel asked.

'Oh, Carmel, I don't know. Honestly, I don't. Seeing the wild flower garden stirred up so many emotions in me. He tended that so lovingly, for so long – they both did – and that touches me deeply, but then it's such a bloody waste! If they did love me still, why couldn't they say it? They knew how to contact me. I wrote to them, sent Christmas cards and all of that. I gave them an address they could contact me at – a priest, actually, he was very good to me. Mam wrote but never anything but the most superficial of things. And as far as my father was concerned, it was as if I were dead. And now I find out they looked after my garden? I can't help but think they saw it as tending a grave, except I was alive and desperately wanting their love. Those first months in London were the worst of my life. I honestly thought about suicide so often. Nobody wanted me. I felt I was alone in the world.'

'I can imagine what meeting Brian must have felt like,' Carmel said.

'Someone to love, to feel accepted by. Though the circumstances were different, I do understand, Tim, I really do. I felt like you for so long – unloved, unlovable.'

'I know you understand. And even Marjorie... I mean, it wasn't a perfect marriage obviously, but she made me feel wanted. And I was so low, so vulnerable, I suppose, that I grabbed her with both hands – figuratively, if not literally.' He gave a sad little smile. 'She deserved better.'

'Not better, Tim, just different. Try to think of it this way – because of her marriage to you, she has children she dotes on and grandchildren too, so I'm sure she doesn't regret being married to you from that point of view. It's incredibly sad that your kids feel the way they do, but you've tried, often, and nothing is budging, so it's time to let it go. Marjorie deserved to be married to a man who could love her, that's true, but you did not deserve to be frozen out of your children's lives, so she's not without blame here either.'

'You're right, I suppose,' Tim admitted reluctantly.

'I think when it comes to the pain of the past, we just need to take it out, look at it, not bury it or anything, but then relegate it to where it belongs – in the past. All we have is now, this moment, and regrets and recriminations serve nobody. Not Marjorie, not your parents, not Charles and Rosemary, and most definitely not you. You did your best, and you've kept your promise to Marjorie all these years at huge personal cost to you and, in some ways, to Brian, so it's time to stop beating yourself up about it.'

He sighed. 'I'm thinking a lot about Brian today. I wish he were here with me, though he would be saying exactly what you're saying, I'm sure. He was so strong, so good at dealing with people. I left all of that to him. He used to laugh, saying I could be the nice English gentleman while he got to play the rough Paddy.'

'I don't know... You managed to put the run on that creep Jim Daly fairly well.' Carmel grinned.

'He was awful, wasn't he?'

'Dreadful,' she agreed. 'I never saw hair that colour before.'

'And that car. Good lord, what was he thinking?'

'Not much, but men like him really do believe they are God's gift to women, poor deluded eejit.' She giggled, and Tim joined in. It helped to lighten the mood.

'So what will you say to Kitty, if it is the same one?' Carmel asked, carefully following David and Catriona as they drove effortlessly along the winding country roads. The road was only really the width of one vehicle, and the hedgerows grew high on both sides. She hoped they didn't meet a tractor or something. She was getting more confident as a driver, but earlier on, she'd had the trauma of reversing under the gaze of some sixteen-year-old smoking a cigarette and driving a huge combine harvester. She'd managed it, but thinking about it was something that made her come out in a cold sweat. She'd seen it all around the roads of Ballyshanley, when she would sit in the back as Bill and Julia sat in the front seats on the way to and from Mass. Sometimes the farm machinery was only inches from them as they edged past on the narrow country roads.

'I'll apologise first anyway,' Tim decided. 'I just left, and we were such good friends. I never contacted her again. Those early months in London, I wrote to her, oh, maybe fifty times, but every letter ended up in the bin. I was afraid she'd heard about the incident with Noel in the barn and was disgusted. Things were so different then. There was no understanding whatsoever. And I was worried she really thought we were the makings of a match. She was just another name to put on the list of people I'd let down, so I never got the guts to make contact. Then I met Marjorie, and the one time I mentioned Kitty, she went silent on me for a week, so I never brought her name up again.'

'Isn't it odd that she never married, like? In those times, it just was what people did. Love, compatibility, political alignment and all the things people seem to worry about now in relationships didn't feature really. People just got married, usually to someone local, and stayed married and raised their families. I can never decide who had it easier. Their life expectations were so low, but there was a contentment in that. Our life expectations, in our generation, are so high. By reading magazines, you'd be convinced every relationship is doomed nowadays if you're not reading the same newspaper, eating the same paleo, sugar-free diet and swinging from the chandeliers every night of the week.'

Tim laughed out loud. 'Carmel, you're a tonic, honestly. Thanks so much for coming today. I couldn't have managed without you. You're a great friend, just like Dolly was. I remember one time, when Brian was in the hospital and there was a problem with my mobile. I don't know, it's all a bit double Dutch to me, Wi-Fi and hop spots and cellular data. It's like these kids in the phone shop are speaking another language. Anyway, it wasn't working, and I tried dealing with them but got nowhere, so Dolly grabs me and the phone one day and steams into the Vodafone shop, raises all colours of holy hell and makes a total show of us. I was mortified, but in the end, they fixed it. She was a lion, honest to God. She was so loyal. And even though she and Brian didn't agree on her decision to say nothing to Joe about her and about you, we were friends with her. And, oh, did they have some scraps about it, full-on screaming and fighting, but they were cut from the same cloth, well able to stand their ground. They were reared in the same place, where people wore their hearts on their sleeves, and if you had a difference of opinion, it often ended with a punch. But it never changed how she felt about us. She loved us, and we loved her. Sometimes I just can't believe that, now, here is her daughter, being just as good a friend to me.'

Carmel loved these stories about her mother. It was as if with each little tale – from Sharif, Tim, Nadia, people in Aashna – another bit of the huge painting that was her mother's life got coloured in. It was wonderful. She basked in the glow of being needed as well; there was nothing like the feeling that she was really helping someone she cared about.

Ahead, David and Catriona slowed down as they approached the town of Westport. They indicated right up a hill and turned into a lovely development of smallish houses encircling a green area bordered with marigolds. In the centre of the green was a huge rose bed, where a profusion of white roses bloomed.

'It's like the Irish flag,' Carmel remarked as they admired it, 'the green, white and orange.'

They parked and got out. A plaque on the wall of the first house told them this was called St Gerald's Crescent and was an assisted living community for the elderly inhabitants of Westport.

David and Catriona led them up a little path to one of the houses and knocked on the cardinal-red door.

It was opened quickly, and a tiny woman stood there. She couldn't have been more than four-foot-ten, her thinning silver hair tied back in a bun. She gazed past her grand-nephew and his wife, straight to Tim. She just stood for a long moment, taking him in.

'I don't know whether to hug you or murder you,' were her first words.

'I probably deserve the latter, but I would love the former.' Tim grinned.

'Do you hear him and his plumy English accent!' Kitty laughed. 'Come in here to me, Tim O'Flaherty, till I get a good look at you. Come in, let ye…'

David and Catriona exchanged a glance. 'We'll leave you to it, Auntie Kitty,' David said. 'We've to pick the lads up from the summer camp. But enjoy the visit, and sure I'll give you a ring later on.'

'Right so, thanks for finding him.' She patted David on the arm.

'Oh, 'twas he found us, and what's more, he's giving us the farm.' Catriona couldn't contain her excitement. 'He's like a guardian angel.'

'Is he now? Well, isn't that something?' Kitty grinned and bade goodbye to the young couple as she ushered Carmel and Tim into a little sitting room.

CHAPTER 21

'So who have I here, besides my long-lost friend?' Kitty enquired.

'This is Carmel Khan,' Tim said. 'She's a friend of mine from London. Well, actually, she's Irish as well, but we met in London. We're over here on kind of a trip around in a bus with Carmel's family and her husband, so I tagged along.'

'Well, thank God for that,' Kitty said. 'I thought you were like one of those old men who lose the run of themselves and want to have a young one on their arm, fooling nobody of course. So you're giving my nephew and his wife your farm? Sit down, sit down, let ye.'

Carmel settled into an armchair with white lace-trimmed anti-macassars on the back and arms. The huge three-piece suite of furniture seemed to take up most of the floor space in the small room. The fireplace was cleaned out for the summer, the grate filled with pinecones painted silver, and the whole effect was cosy and welcoming. The entire room seemed to be stuffed with ornaments and photos of a variety of children, weddings, first communions. There was a delicious smell.

'I'll make you a cup of tea now in a minute,' Kitty said, 'and I've a cake in the oven. It won't be long.'

'It smells amazing,' Carmel said. 'You have such a lovely home.'

'It's nice all right. The council build these for all the old fogies like myself. They're small, but it does me. I can do a bit of gardening outside, and I potter away. I'm able to get down to the shops and everything, so I'm very lucky, and sure the family are great.'

'We were admiring the display with the marigolds and roses as we came in,' Tim said, never taking his eyes off Kitty.The years had done their work, but she seemed still the same no-nonsense personality.

'Well, I was doing it myself, with an old fella over beyond in number seven, but it got too much for us, the weeding and that. So my other nephew, Paudie – he works for the county council – he organised to send up some fellas every week. They're on community service for blackguarding around the town, drunk and disorderly and the like, and the judge here says a bit of hard work is what they need and they'll have no more energy for acting the clown around the place. So that's who takes care of the donkey work now, and I tell them what to do.'

'I bet you do.' Tim chuckled, and Kitty joined in.

'Ah sure, they're grand lads. I bring them in for tea and a bit of cake after, and sure one fella says to me that he never ate home-baked cake before. Imagine that? But sure the mothers and fathers get everything in the auld supermarket these days, too busy for baking. I won't go there, though, no. I get everything I need in the local shops. Sure 'tis only a few pence dearer, and you're supporting your own. That big German supermarket they have now out the Galway road, sure that's not doing much for Westport, is it?'

'If more people thought like you, Kitty, the towns would be in better shape, no doubt about it,' Tim agreed. 'There is a corner shop at the end of my road. Three generations of a family, the Patels, and he has the same problem. They opened a Tesco Metro on the high street, and the people flocked to it. Poor Sanjay, the grandson of the original owner, doesn't know how long more he can keep going.'

'Things were simpler in our day,' Kitty said. 'People went to the butcher for meat and the greengrocer for the fruit and vegetables, and there was a newspaper shop and a sweetshop everywhere. It's all bundled into one now. The price of progress, I suppose. So where do we start?'

Her question caught Tim unawares, but her blue eyes bored into his. She might've been old, but she was sharp as a tack.

'Well.' He smiled. 'It has certainly been a long time.'

'Well, we haven't either of us much to go to the end, so we better get cracking,' Kitty said matter-of-factly. 'Why did you leave without a word? I went up to your house the next day, and a few days afterwards, but they just said you were gone and you weren't coming back and that was that. I got the impression they hated talking about it. My own family too were just bewildered, and of course I had all the pitying glances for a few months afterwards.'

Tim leaned forward in his chair and took Kitty's hands. 'I'm so sorry. I wrote so many letters to you, but I couldn't post them.' He took a deep breath. 'The reason I left was my father found me in the barn with Noel Togher. Kitty, I'm a homosexual.'

Carmel was kind of shocked to hear him use that word. She was used to him being gay, and Brian and Zane; in fact, she was surprised at how many gay people there were in the world. But that word, *homosexual*, seemed so clinical or something.

'I'll go and make the tea if you like, Kitty?' Carmel suggested. She wanted to give them some space.

'Do, girleen, 'tis all out in the kitchen.'

* * *

KITTY GAZED at Tim and then down to where their hands were intertwined. 'I knew that, even then. But I thought we loved each other. We could have shielded each other, and I suppose I thought it might still work. You should have contacted me, Tim.'

'I know I should have, and I'm sorry. But I'm so glad we didn't marry. You deserved someone who could love you properly. A proper relationship with children and everything.' Tim was trying to make her understand. 'I didn't know much back then, but I knew I could only bring you pain.'

'You're right about one thing – you didn't know much back then. If you did, you would've known that men are not my thing. I suppose that never occurred to you?'

Kitty watched his face as he processed her own bombshell.

'What?' he said, disbelieving. 'Are you telling me –'

'Yes, I'm a lesbian. But at least when we were young, though people in Westport might have been disgusted by you, they knew what you were existed. Girls who were attracted to other girls were unheard of back then. I felt like the only one in the whole world. With you, at least, I felt a bit normal.'

'Oh, Kitty, I can't believe it.' Tim smiled sadly. 'If only I'd known, we could have run away together.'

'Oh, once you left, there was nothing keeping me here, so when I got the chance to go to America, I took it. A local girl, Marie Donnelly – do you remember her? Well, she got work with her brothers in New York, and she came home on holidays and invited me to go back with her, so I did. I spent twenty-four years in New York – Brooklyn. I loved it. I met Georgie Harper there, a beautiful Black girl from Tennessee, and we were together for eighteen glorious years, until she was in a horrible car accident coming home from the shelter. She set up homeless shelters for women and girls. She died of her injuries three weeks after the crash, and I thought I'd die too. I swear, I remember thinking that no human could withstand that much pain. But I did. Every street corner, every bar, every café reminded me of Georgie, and I couldn't bear it in Brooklyn for another second, so I left New York and never went back. An opportunity came up in South Africa, so I went there.' She sighed. 'You're not the only one with secrets, Tim.'

'Kitty…I had no idea. I mean, all these years I was afraid I'd broken your heart too.'

'Ha ha! D'ya hear him?' She clearly found that idea very funny. 'A broken heart by Tim O'Flaherty! No indeed. You never broke my heart, Tim. My heart was broken only once, when I lost my Georgie. You only have that kind of love once in a lifetime.' She shook her head sadly. 'How did life treat you, after you left here?'

Tim told her the whole story – those first awful months, Marjorie, the children, and finally, Brian.

'And how long is he dead now?' Kitty asked.

'Just over a year. People say it gets easier, but I'm not there yet,' Tim admitted sadly.

'Well, would you look at us, two young freaks of nature, and we couldn't even admit it to each other. Do you know what I think, Tim? I think your father did you a great favour by throwing you out. Imagine if he never caught you? Or he did and never said anything? You'd be up there still, a lonely old bachelor farmer, never having known the joy of children or a love like you had with your Brian. Yes, then, 'twas the best thing he ever did for you.'

'I'm not sure that was his motivation, but you're probably right,' Tim agreed. 'We'll never know now, though, will we?'

He told her about the wild flower garden, and she was silent when he finished.

After a moment, she said, 'I met him one Christmas Eve, your father. He was coming out of Hannigan's below, and he had a few drinks on him. He wasn't much of a drinker, I'd say, but he was drunk that evening. 'Twas the first Christmas after you left. Anyway, I was going home after picking up a few things for the Christmas dinner for my mother when he stopped me. I was shocked, first at the state of him, and second because he'd given me very short shrift when I called after you left.

'Anyway, he said something to me. He said, "If you see him, tell him…" And then he stopped. 'Twas as if he just couldn't say the words but what he wanted to say was kind, not harsh. He waited for a second. He was a bit unsteady on his feet. He said, "Tell him I'll mind the garden for him." Sure I never saw you again from that day to this, so I couldn't tell you anything, but he missed you. I'm sure of it, and sure it near killed your poor mother. She'd sit over on St Teresa's side of the church, all alone on a weekday, and she'd cry. She got a Mass said for you every year on your birthday and on the anniversary of the day you left. 'Twas you she was crying for, her only child.'

Tim was hardly aware of the tears that ran down his cheeks as

Kitty described his parents. That part of his head and heart had been locked away for so long, and he'd buried the pain so deeply, that it came as a shock to have it resurface.

'I wish...' Tim managed through his tears. 'I just wish they...'

'Sure, Tim, if wishes were horses, beggars would ride,' Kitty said gently. 'There's no point to wishing now. But you should know they never forgot you, never stopped missing you. That's really why your father got so close to Catriona's family. They were the family he had lost, I suppose. You did a good thing giving herself and David the land. You'll really make a mighty difference to them, and they were very good to your parents. What goes around comes around, as they say. The wheel is always turning.'

On and on they talked about old school friends, about Georgie and Brian, about all the changes to Westport since they were young.

'What made you come back?' Tim asked, curious.

'Well, I had a great few years in Cape Town. I loved it there. I had a little bakery and a café, and I made great friends. Even though the time I was there was difficult – apartheid was still in full force – when Mandela came to power, he changed everything. Really, everything. I was so fortunate to live there in those years. He drew together a nation that was so divided, it was impossible to see how they could ever pull in the same direction. He was a remarkable man. But in the end, I was getting older, the body wasn't what it once was, and I wanted to be near my family. My brothers were always close with me, if they weren't with each other, and I visited home often, so I knew all the kids and everything.'

'And did they know about you? About Georgie?' Tim was gentle.

'Well, I keep a photo of her beside my bed, and I talk to her every night, but they've never asked and I never say who she was. I think they do know, but the idea of an auld wan like me having relations with anyone is enough to put you off your dinner, so acknowledging my being a lesbian would probably finish them off completely. It's not a problem for me or for them, so we just leave it be. Now let's have that tea. I don't know where your friend has got to.'

Tim's mobile phone beeped, and he took it out of the pocket of his coat. *I've gone to meet the others at the hotel. I let myself out the back door. Think you need time alone with K. Talk later C xx*

'Carmel let herself out,' Tim said as he went to join Kitty in the kitchen. 'She probably felt a bit in the way what with us banging on about the Dark Ages.' The cake was out of the oven. Carmel must have taken it out before she left, otherwise it would have burned to a crisp by now.

Kitty stood there in front of him, and suddenly they were not two old people, over seventy years gone, but a boy and a girl, so afraid of the world they'd been born into, where nobody would accept what they were. Tim took a step across the tiny room and wrapped his arms around her, holding her close.

'We did OK, Kit. Despite it all, we did OK. And here we are, together again for the final act.'

CHAPTER 22

*C*armel was delighted to see the bus in the car park of the
hotel. She missed Sharif and longed to tell him about the
day's events.

As she walked into the hotel, she was almost knocked down by a
sea of purple silk that turned out to be Zeinab, and by the looks of
things, she was in high dudgeon.

'Zeinab, is everything OK?' Carmel asked as the woman barrelled
past her.

'Oh, Carmel, no, everything is not OK. Nothing like it, in fact. I
simply cannot stay one more moment, not another second. I'll take a
taxi to the airport this minute and return to Karachi. Have my things
sent on from London.' She seemed to be both upset and furious simultaneously.

'Look, whatever's happened, I'm sure we can sort it out,' Carmel
said placatingly. 'Why don't we just go for a walk, just around the
block, and compose ourselves, and you can tell me what the problem
is?' She knew she sounded like someone dealing with a recalcitrant
five-year-old, but honestly, that was how Zeinab behaved sometimes.

'No, there is nothing anyone can do. Nothing at all.' Zeinab was attracting attention from the people sitting at the tables outside the hotel having a drink.

'Why is that lady in the funny dress screaming and crying, Mammy?' asked a little girl in a high-pitched voice. 'Did she cut her knee?'

A red-faced mother tried to distract the little girl, but the child was not for deviating from this very interesting floor show. The mother mumbled something and tried to get the child to eat some of her sandwich, but the little voice rang out again. 'She looks like Princess Jasmine from *Aladdin*, except way wrinklier and fatter, doesn't she, Mammy? Maybe she's Princess Jasmine's granny?'

The group gathered at the next table were trying to stifle giggles as Zeinab turned on the child. 'Where I come from, children are trained not to be rude to their elders. I see no such efforts are made here.' Her eyes flashed dangerously.

'I'm so sorry,' the mortified mother said, her face burning. 'She's only three, and she doesn't know –'

'She needs a good spanking,' Zeinab cut in. 'That would teach her how to behave. If she were mine, I can tell you –'

'What's going on here?' Just as Zeinab was warming to her theme, a tall man in his thirties emerged with a tray, taking in his embarrassed wife and his daughter, who was now crying behind her mother.

'I was saying,' Zeinab replied in her overbearing way, 'that if that child were mine, she would find herself properly chastised for rudeness.'

The man placed the tray on the table and lifted his little daughter into his arms. 'Well, she's not yours, so you can mind your own business. Now, Lily, did you say something to upset this lady?'

'No, Daddy. I just said she looked like Princess Jasmine's granny,' the girl said quietly through sobs.

'And that's all?'

The little girl nodded, and the man glanced at his wife for confirmation. She nodded too.

'And that's what has you advocating assault on my little girl, is it?' the man demanded of Zeinab. 'Yerra, you'd want to cop on to yourself, going around taking umbrage at nothing. She's only a child! She didn't mean any harm. And anyway, you're not exactly a spring chicken, are you? Go on away now, you mad old bat, and don't be annoying us.'

The exchange seemed to have gathered even more spectators, and Zeinab was the focus of everyone's attentions. Carmel didn't know what to do. She stood by as Zeinab marched back into the hotel without another word.

'I'm so sorry.' Carmel was mortified. 'She's... Well, I'm just really sorry.' There was no way to defend or explain.

'Ah, sure 'twasn't your fault.' The man smiled, and Carmel turned gratefully away.

Carmel got the key to their room and let herself in. Sharif was stretched on the bed reading.

'Hey, you're back, great.' He leapt up and kissed her. He took one look at her face and immediately asked, 'What's up? Has something happened?'

She told him about the business downstairs with Zeinab, and he burst out laughing.

'Dead right too. If someone was telling me to beat my child, they'd get the same response. I can just imagine her face, and her indignant stomp off. Just let her cool down. It was probably nothing. She was driving my mother insane today, fawning over Joe. It was a bit much, to be honest, and I apologised to him when we got back, but you know Joe. He pretended he didn't notice. Maybe *Ammi* had a word with Zeinab – that's probably it – and she didn't like it.'

'Right, well, she was threatening to leave, go to the airport, straight back to Pakistan.' Carmel was still worried.

'She won't, believe me. She won't do anything of the kind. She's just looking for attention and to paint herself as the victim. Ignoring her is the only way to deal with it. Now how did it go on the farm?'

'Fine,' Carmel said, still uneasy. 'Great, actually. We had a lovely day. But, Sharif, can we go for a walk? I feel like I need some air.'

The encounter with Zeinab had really upset her. She wasn't used to dealing with conflict. In Trinity, everything had been calm, because it was such a transactional relationship between the kids and the staff, no emotion involved. And then with Bill, it was years of just nothing, no fights, no arguments, but no conversation, no connection either. But she was learning, listening to her friends in Aashna talking about falling out with sisters or brothers, or having blazing rows with friends, and she was beginning to realise that it was a part of caring about someone. Emotions can run high and spill out as anger just as much as joy and love. This was obvious to most people, but again, she found herself trying to figure out normal interpersonal relationships.

'Of course,' Sharif said.

She smiled and slipped her hand into his.

They walked up to the grounds of Westport House, and it was spectacular. Huge thickets of rhododendron and hydrangea blossomed everywhere, and flower beds provided riots of colour. There was a river running through the grounds, and they walked and talked for two hours. She told him all about Catriona and David, and about Tim meeting Kitty again after all these years. She talked about sitting in the kitchen with the kids' stuff all around and how lovely it all was. He didn't flinch at the mention of children, as he had done up to now – or maybe she'd just always imagined it – and he seemed happy to discuss it. They came back to the incident with Zeinab, and he promised he'd find her once they returned and check she was OK.

'So how was your day?' Carmel asked as he helped her over a huge log.

'Wonderful,' he said, smiling. 'Just amazing scenery. The sea stack is incredible. It's this huge column – I think it's about 170 feet high – just off the coast. It used to be connected, and then there was a storm that broke the land bridge, so they had to get people off with ropes. Joe told us the legend about it, that when St Patrick was converting everyone to Christianity, the local chieftain wouldn't go along with the new religion, so Patrick struck the ground with his crozier and the land split in half, creating the sea stack and leaving the doubting chieftain alone on the rock. I'm not sure how true that is, but the place really is remarkable. You can see all the different colours of the layers of rock; I've never seen anything like it. And the sea beneath, foaming as it crashes, all the colours of turquoise, blue, green, azure. Honestly, I was blown away, literally and figuratively.

'Then we went to the Céide Fields. It's a farm, the first evidence of farming in Ireland, 5,500 years ago. It's hard to get your head around it. And the life there was fairly sophisticated. I'd never seen a bog before – fascinating. Then we went to Killala, a gorgeous little village with loads of ruins and an old monastery, and we had some lunch there. We really had a great time.'

'I'm glad. So what was Zeinab doing that drove Nadia more mental than usual?'

'Oh, she was just being herself really. She sees admiring another culture as somehow disloyal or something, so every time the rest of us were in awe, she'd pipe up with, "Well, there's much better than that in Pakistan" kind of thing. It drove *Ammi* mad, so she openly refuted her by saying she never saw a sea stack or a bog or a pint of Guinness in Pakistan and would she please just give us all a break?

'Well, that went down like a lead balloon, as you can imagine. So Zeinab, knowing how much it drives *Ammi* crazy, turned up the dial on the flirting with Joe. She was making out like she couldn't walk on the rough terrain so had to hold his arm all the time. Then when we were having lunch, she was offering him bites of her food. She even had her hand on his leg at one stage. Anyway, *Ammi* had enough, and when we got back, she told me she was going to have it out with Zeinab, tell her she was embarrassing us by her behaviour and warn her to stop immediately or else.' Sharif grinned; he clearly found the whole thing very amusing.

But it only made Carmel uncomfortable. 'Or else what?'

'Well, I don't exactly know, but she wasn't taking any prisoners. I probably should have gone, but I decided to stay out of it.'

'Well, I think I walked right into the tail end of that particular chat,' Carmel said with a grimace.

'Don't worry. It'll be fine. They get on each other's nerves, that's all.'

Carmel wanted to fight Nadia's corner. It wasn't fair to say they were both to blame. Nadia was lovely and normal and reasonable, and Zeinab was a self-serving lunatic. Carmel said as much to Sharif.

'I know,' he said calmly, 'but she'll be going back to Karachi after this trip, and we won't have to see her for years.'

'Unless she decides to stay and shack up with her favourite nephew.'

'She won't, don't worry,' Sharif assured her. 'And even if she tried, her favourite nephew has a scary Irish wife, so that's not going to fly. It's all going to be fine. Now we better start heading back. We're eating in the hotel tonight. The table is booked for eight, and it's seven now.'

* * *

DINNER WAS ANOTHER LOUD AFFAIR, with Carrie entertaining everyone with a story about her and her sister in a Botox clinic. Even though she came across as a bit vacuous, there was something wise and endearing about her, Carmel thought. And she was crazy about Luke, so that was good enough for Carmel. Jen was even warming to her a little bit, especially as it turned out she was like a toddler whisperer with Ruari. He, like his uncle, was mesmerised by her, and she seemed happy to play with him for hours.

'She took him to the pool this evening, let me have a spa treatment,' Jen whispered to Carmel. 'I was terrified she'd let him drown and insisted Luke went too, but apparently, she spent the whole time with him, playing away. I think my son is as besotted as my brother.'

'It certainly looks that way,' Carmel whispered back as both Ruari and Luke gazed adoringly at Carrie as she explained just how badly wrong Botox can go if the therapist is in the middle of a text fight with her boyfriend. Apparently, the boyfriend had been at a stag party the night before, and the girl hadn't heard from him all day, and all his friends were being very cagey.

The upshot of the whole thing was the boyfriend was supposed to be doing a couples' photo shoot with their cats that day, and he'd accidentally found himself on a lorry heading out of Dublin Port for

Poland. The therapist's frustration resulted in the client, who happened to be Carrie's sister, leaving the salon with a permanent expression of panicked disbelief. Carrie did a wicked impression of her sister at every social gathering for the next three months, with her eyebrows practically in her hairline and her eyes unnaturally wide.

Nadia and Joe wiped their eyes as the story was further embellished by Carrie, clearly a *raconteur extraordinaire*. She recounted the conversation in a flat Dublin accent, nothing like the mid-Atlantic drawl with the upward inflection she normally used. It turned out she was a brilliant mimic. She had the whole table in stitches by the end.

'I suppose, like, being in the whole medical thing, you totally, like, hate the idea of cosmetic surgery, Sharif?' she asked, her blue eyes innocent. Carmel suspected they may have misjudged Carrie; she wasn't as dumb as she let on.

'I suppose you might believe that, Carrie, but in fact, I don't think like that. I think we get one body, and it is an amazing piece of engineering, and if you take care of it, it may last you for a long time and stay in good working order. But equally, if you don't, then that's your choice. Some people like to be vegan, don't drink or smoke, take lots of exercise, and they might live to a hundred, or they might get cancer at twenty-five. Equally, you can abuse some bodies and they keep on going regardless. Look at Keith Richards.'

The whole table laughed.

'I'm in the "whole medical thing", as you put it' – he grinned – 'at the end of life, when people are dying. And I'm not sure that being very good, no meat, no booze, no Botox, is actually the way to go. In Aashna, we let people do whatever they want. We all have choices, and as Dolly was fond of saying, none of us is getting out of here alive.'

'Well, I think that calls for another bottle of red.' Joe motioned to the waiter. 'We're all going to die anyway, so we might as well live while we can.'

'I totally agree, Joe,' Zeinab said, the first thing she'd said all evening. She'd barely acknowledged Carmel and totally ignored Nadia.

Joe, clearly relieved that her dark mood was lifting at long last, was happy to jolly her along. 'Sure I know you don't usually, but could I tempt you to a small glass of Malbec from sunny Argentina? It's lovely, so it is, no more than yourself.' He was determined to charm her.

'Well, Joe, if you think I should, then maybe I will. I'm not used to drinking, mind you, so you'll have to catch me if I fall.' She gave one of her tinkly laughs, the one that drove Nadia insane.

'Oh, there's plenty of strong men to lift you if you need it, Zeinab, but I promise it won't come to that. One glass, and we'll have you tucked up in bed.'

'Joe McDaid, I hope you mean alone,' Zeinab tittered. 'I'm a respectable lady.'

Carmel saw that Nadia was gritting her teeth and focusing on her dinner. Nobody else noticed the flirting, really, or they were so used to it now, they just ignored her.

Apparently, Joe decided the safest course was to turn to speak to Carmel. 'So, pet, how did it all go today with Tim?'

Just as she was about to reply, Zeinab nearly climbed into Carmel's lap to involve herself in the conversation. It was too much for Nadia.

'Please, Zeinab,' she interrupted, 'perhaps we'll let Joe and Carmel have some time?' Her brown eyes pleaded with her sister to just be normal, but Zeinab was having none of it.

'I'm quite sure Joe is perfectly capable of deciding who he would like to spend time with, Nadia. He does not need you like some kind of human Rottweiler.' Zeinab's voice carried over the hubbub of conversation, and the chat at the table stopped as everyone watched the exchange between the sisters.

Joe, mortified, tried to smooth things over. 'Ah now, ladies, I'm sure we can –'

'No, Joe, please,' Zeinab interrupted. 'I'm sorry if my friendship embarrasses you. I was merely trying to blend in with the lovely friendly Irish ways. Clearly my sister here thinks otherwise. She denies me a little comfort even in the aftermath of losing my darling Tariq. But some sisters are like that. It is hard to accept, but it is how it is.'

'Zeinab, please,' Sharif tried to intervene. '*Ammi* didn't mean anything like that. Let's just all enjoy our dinner –'

'No, Sharif, it must be said. When Khalid died, oh, how she mourned. Going about like a wet week for ages. But yours and Khalid's marriage was so good, so perfect, wasn't it, Nadia?'

Nadia sighed wearily. 'Zeinab, I don't see what that has to do with anything.'

'Zeinab.' Sharif tried again as everyone else looked down at their plates. 'Let's not do this –'

'Sharif, let your mother speak,' Zeinab went on. 'Let her tell us how heartbroken she was, how much sympathy she got from everyone. But when the same thing happens to me, no such consideration. There you are, looking so innocent and reasonable, poor Nadia, putting up with her sister – isn't she a saint? Don't think I haven't seen the looks, the eye-rolling, the martyred expressions you have given to Carmel and Sharif behind my back. I'm not blind, you know.'

'Tariq and Khalid were nothing alike,' Nadia said gently. 'Our marriages were totally different. And of course I feel for you, I just… Look, let's discuss this another time.'

Carmel had never seen Nadia so upset. She was shaking, so embarrassed in front of all the McDaids.

'Another time?' Zeinab snapped. 'Why not now? You can give us all some tips on how to have the perfect marriage.' She laughed bitterly. 'Oh, yes, the perfect Khalid, the wonderful Khalid, not the same Khalid Khan who had an affair with Shanti Chutani, is it? The girl who was told by your precious Khalid to pack her bags and was sent back to Karachi in disgrace after he used her and then rejected her, making sure his silly wife never found out? She never got to tell her story in London, but you know Karachi, Nadia – gossip spreads like wildfire. I had the whole story within days of Shanti's return. So to protect my little sister, I confronted him the next time I met him, and you know what he says? It was nothing, a brief affair that meant nothing, and then he begged me not to tell you. So I didn't, out of kindness to you and to his memory. But I see now you are not worthy of such kindness.'

Carmel wanted to run to Nadia and wrap her arms around her. Darling, kind Nadia, who'd loved one man her whole life.

'I don't believe you,' Nadia said quietly, and stood up, pushing her chair back. Sharif was there, right beside her, and he put his arm around his mother.

'It's not true, Sharif.' She was trying to reassure him, like he was a little boy again, but something on his face stopped her in her tracks. 'It's not...is it?'

'Come on, *Ammi*, let's go.' He led her away from the table.

Carmel wanted to follow, but Joe put his hand on her knee. 'Maybe give them a second, love,' he whispered.

He was right. She loved them both so much, but this was a conversation they needed to have alone.

'So are we having desserts?' Zeinab asked cheerfully, as if nothing had happened.

CHAPTER 23

The rest of the group finished dinner quickly and made their excuses. Carmel sat with Joe and Zeinab once the others were gone. Tim had yet to appear, but she figured he was probably still reminiscing with Kitty.

'Should we go to the bar? I think there's music tonight,' Zeinab said brightly, still pretending it was all perfectly normal.

'No, Zeinab,' Joe said. 'I won't anyway, not tonight. And I think Carmel here is in need of a rest too. It's been a long day.'

Though Carmel had known Joe for only a short time in the great scheme of life, she felt connected to him and was getting good at reading his signals. He was clearly disappointed that the future of the trip was now in jeopardy, given what had gone on between Nadia and Zeinab. And that she showed no remorse or even awareness of the hurt her words had caused was not helping.

'Let me buy you one drink, please, as a thank you for organising this lovely holiday.' Zeinab was wheedling now, and it made Carmel cringe.

'I won't,' Joe said, firm. 'And to be entirely honest with you, Zeinab, I think you should find your sister and try to put right some of the damage done here tonight. I'm not claiming to know anything about it, and I don't really know you or your family, but Nadia seems to me to be a very kind person who never has anything but good to say about people. And she was badly hurt this evening.' He stopped short of blaming Zeinab for the hurt caused, but the implication was clear.

'But, Joe, you don't understand,' Zeinab insisted. 'She comes across like that, all sweetness, but she isn't really like that. She –'

'I don't want to get involved,' he interrupted her. 'It's between the two of you to sort it out, but I do know this – we never know when the people we love will be taken from us, anyone, any time, anyplace. So we shouldn't squander those relationships. Nadia is a good person, as are you, I'm sure, and though we all have our hang-ups and faults, every single one of us, if you don't make things right with her, you'll regret it. That is a fact. Now, Carmel, will we go for a short walk? I feel like I haven't seen you all day.'

'That would be lovely,' Carmel responded. She almost felt sorry for Zeinab sitting alone at the dinner table, but she couldn't think of anything kind to say, so she said nothing.

Joe exhaled heavily as they left the hotel grounds. 'Well, that was unexpected.'

Carmel linked her arm through his as they walked down the main street of Westport, still a hive of activity.

'Is it true, would you say?' he asked.

Carmel thought for a moment. Sharif had revealed the affair to her in confidence ages ago. His father made a confession to him before he died, and Sharif had been so angry, but it was Dolly who talked him down. She told him how sometimes the truth was overrated, and if Khalid had come clean to Nadia all those years ago, she would have left him and Sharif would have come from a broken home. Nadia and Khalid genuinely had a great marriage, but he'd made one stupid mistake and decided to bear the guilt alone in order to not destroy his family. Eventually, Sharif calmed down and saw it the way Dolly did. But he'd had no idea that Zeinab knew.

Still, there wasn't much point in keeping the secret now, not after Zeinab had blabbed the whole thing out over dinner. And Joe was very discreet anyway. So Carmel decided to tell him the truth.

'Yes. It is.' She explained what Sharif had told her, and Joe listened without interrupting.

'Poor Nadia,' he said, when Carmel was finished. 'That's awful for her. The man is dead, so she can't have it out with him, but now the memories are gone too. She'll see everything they had through this lens now. It's not fair.'

'No, it isn't,' Carmel agreed. 'I love Nadia. I feel like we should have stopped Zeinab, but Sharif had no idea she even knew the story. And when she's on a roll, there's no stopping her anyway. It was horrible for Nadia to find out, but to find out like that, in front of everyone... I don't know. What makes someone be so cruel? To their own sister? I would have loved a sister growing up, and now that I have one, I can't imagine ever hurting Jen like that, or her me.'

Joe put his arm around her shoulders and hugged her close to him. 'I love that you and Jennifer really feel like sisters. And thanks for smoothing the Carrie situation too. I know Jen was savage when she met her, and I know Carrie comes across a bit ditzy, but Luke is stone mad about her and she makes him happy, so what's the harm? Jen is overprotective of him, always has been, but seeing you be nice to her and keeping the whole thing going changed her. The old Jen would have been farting fire, as my mam would have said, God rest her.'

Carmel pealed with laughter. 'Farting fire, I love that.'

'Seriously, though, having you in the family, it's just brilliant. I'm so delighted. You hear how, often, when people find their birth families, it doesn't work out. But with us it really has, don't you think?'

Carmel smiled at his need for reassurance. 'It's worked out better than anyone could ever have imagined.' She squeezed his arm.

He was so strong, but there was a vulnerability to him that she loved. She thought about it as they walked along in companionable silence.

He came to visit them in London every two months or so, stayed with them, and they all enjoyed it. She called him Dad now more than Joe, but she never actually said the words 'I love you' to him. But she did love him. He'd never said it either; the closest he'd come was the day he bought her the Claddagh ring. Though she was in no doubt about how happy he was to have her in his life.

She wondered now, should she say it? Sharif had been the first person to ever say those words to her, ever in her whole life. And while her friends bandied the words around in a jokey way – like 'Much as I love you, we're not seeing that film again' type of way – she'd never said it first to anyone.

The old familiar feelings of insecurity and worry bubbled to the surface. What if she made a fool of herself? What if he was embarrassed and didn't know what to say? Should she wait for him to say it first?

She took a deep breath. She was going to have to take responsibility for herself and her emotions. Own them, as Nora was fond of saying. Instead of dismissing them and all her thoughts, she was supposed to try to give them airtime. *You're allowed to have feelings*, she told herself.

'Dad?' she began.

'Yes, pet?' he asked, turning his head.

'I love you.'

He let her go and turned towards her, saying nothing. She wondered why he didn't respond until she saw the tears. Joe was a big, tough Irish man of a certain age, not given to crying fits, so she got a bit of a fright until she realised they were tears of joy.

He said nothing but drew her into a hug.

Eventually, his lips in her hair, he managed to croak, 'I love you too, sweetheart, more than you'll ever know. I wanted to tell you, so often, but I knew you had to come to me, not the other way round. I'd have waited forever, but I'm so glad I don't have to.'

She realised then that she was crying too. 'What are we like?' she managed, when Joe gave her his handkerchief to blow her nose. 'Everyone passing will think we're mental.'

People were milling about, all caught up in their own lives.

'Sure in my case they'd probably be right.' He grinned.

They strolled back as the clock on the top of the main street rang eleven. She texted Sharif. *Is Nadia OK? Will I come back to the room? Can stay in another room if needs be? Xxx*

He texted back a few moments later. *She's asleep. I had some mild sedatives in my bag so I gave her two. I'll meet you in the bar in twenty minutes, OK? xxx*

As they entered the lobby, they spotted Zeinab sitting on one of the huge overstuffed sofas dotted around the reception area. Joe glanced over, and Carmel put her hand on his arm. 'I'll talk to her,' she whispered, and Joe nodded.

'I'll be in my room if you need me.' He kissed her cheek and left.

Carmel felt the familiar butterflies as she approached Zeinab. Anything could happen. 'Hi, Zeinab,' she said quietly. 'Can I join you?'

The older woman looked up and locked eyes with Carmel. 'I can't imagine why you'd want to, but yes, sit down.' She sounded exhausted.

'How are you?' Carmel asked.

Zeinab stared straight ahead and eventually sighed. 'I don't know, Carmel. I honestly don't know. I feel…empty inside. I should probably feel something, some remorse for telling Nadia about Khalid's affair, and for…well, for everything really, but I just feel hollow.' Her voice was a monotone; she was not her usual animated self.

Carmel said nothing but just sat beside her.

'I suppose you and Sharif and everyone hates me now?' She shrugged. 'Of course you do. I'm a terrible, wicked woman. Hurting my sister like that, humiliating her. I deserve your contempt.'

Carmel wasn't sure if this was another of her attempts to garner pity, if she was waiting for everyone to rush over and say, 'No, don't be ridiculous – it was nothing.' But she didn't think so. There was a resignation in Zeinab's voice that Carmel had never heard before.

'I don't think contempt is what we feel, but we are confused. Nadia didn't deserve that. Why did you do it?'

Zeinab turned and looked at Carmel. 'You have lived a long time. It was a long life before you met my nephew, observing, watching, listening. It gives you a certain, I don't know, a sort of stillness, a serenity.'

Carmel didn't know how to take that; it sounded like a compliment, but she couldn't be sure.

Zeinab went on. 'Why did I do it?' She paused and gave a sad little smile. 'Because I hate her. There. I hate my only sister.'

'Why?' Carmel asked, trying to keep the shock from her voice.

Zeinab waved her jewelled hand dismissively. 'Oh, for so many reasons. Our parents loved her more – she was prettier, better at school. She married for love, to someone who loved and respected her, despite what I revealed. He loved her to the day he died, and he was eaten up by guilt but didn't want her or Sharif to suffer for his mistake. Khalid was such a good man.' She sighed again, her thoughts straying to the past.

'But you loved Tariq. You're always telling us how good he was.'

Zeinab's harsh laugh rent the air in the quiet lobby. 'Good? Oh, he was good all right. Good at making money, good at having affairs, good at never coming home. Yes, he was excellent at all of those things.'

Carmel had heard as much from Nadia, but it was a shock to hear Zeinab be so candid. 'So because your marriage was a bad one, you wanted to hurt Nadia?'

One part of Carmel felt she had no right to pry, but they were here now, and maybe she could get Zeinab to see how hurtful she had been and set about fixing the relationship.

Zeinab leaned her head back against the cushions and closed her eyes. As she did, Sharif came out of the lift. Carmel spotted him but shooed him away with her hand. He looked perplexed for a moment but took in the scene and nodded, indicating he was going to the bar.

Zeinab sighed once more, a sigh of pure weariness that seemed to come from her toes. 'I suppose so. She had everything – the nice life in London, a husband and son who adored the ground she walked on, even a meaningful career. And Dolly, your mother, she and Nadia were so close, and I knew your mother couldn't stand me. Whenever we would visit, I'd see them, the knowing glances, the sympathetic smiles. "Poor you, stuck with your stupid sister again." She chose Dolly over me every time. And of course, she couldn't stand Tariq. She should have been respectful to him because he was my husband, but she wasn't.'

'Where Tariq was concerned, she had her reasons, Zeinab,' Carmel said. 'It wasn't based on nothing.' She was anxious the conversation stayed in the realm of reality, not some sad narrative of Zeinab's where everyone was mean to her and she didn't deserve any of it.

'She said that to you?' Zeinab snapped her head around to face Carmel once more.

'Yes, she did,' Carmel said honestly. 'She didn't like him because she thought you were worth so much more. She disliked him because he wasn't a good husband to you. Her aversion to him was because she loved you. She knew you married him because it was what your family wanted, and that she was the lucky one who got to defy their wishes because they already had one daughter in a good match, as they saw it. You marrying Tariq set her free. That's how she saw it. And then to see him treat you badly – it upset her. She wanted to be close to you. My mother and Nadia were friends, sure, but there is room for more love in a person's heart. There's always room for more.'

Zeinab smiled. 'For one who hasn't known much love, you seem to believe in it.' The words weren't harsh, just bemused.

'Maybe it's because of that. It's true I never had anyone love me, not for the first forty years of my life – except my mother, and I never got to meet her. But now that I do, I can see how precious it is. It's why I can't understand how someone who has a sister could choose to reject them. I know Nadia wasn't without fault in this. And if you felt left out or whatever when you visited before, then that was wrong too. But what you did tonight was so cruel. And I think you know it too. I don't know if there's any way back for you two, but I really hope there is. And if there is a way you can make it up to her, I think you should try.'

Zeinab rested her body back against the couch again and nodded slowly. 'I'm not a nice person, Carmel. I used to be. I was a kind child. But I don't know, something along the way, I…I just changed, and I don't like who I've become.' There was a cheerless acceptance in her voice.

'Zeinab, people change,' Carmel assured her. 'I'm not the same person I was a year ago. I was afraid of everyone and everything, and I was living out a life of drudgery because I thought that was all I deserved. Then I met Sharif and everything changed. You've a perception of your life, and maybe some of it is right. Maybe your parents did love Nadia more, she *did* have a great marriage with Khalid, and Tariq treated you badly. Believe me, Zeinab, I know how undermining a toxic relationship can be. But the point is, Tariq is gone and you are your own person with your own path to follow. Did you meet Oscar, the yoga teacher at Aashna?'

Zeinab shook her head.

'Well, he used to be an investment banker, making tons of money,' Carmel explained, 'but so miserable – drinking, being a crap husband and father. He had a breakdown and trashed the house, terrified his wife and kids. But look at him now. He's calm and happy. He has a great relationship with his kids and even with his ex. It was hard work earning their trust again, but he stuck at it, and now they love him. People can change, but you have to want to change.

'Maybe get some sleep and see if you can talk to Nadia tomorrow. She's sleeping in our room now, and we'll leave her there. Sharif and I will sleep in Nadia's room. But in the morning, I'll go up to her and see if she'll see you.' Carmel wanted to pin down a plan rather than leave it up in the air. Zeinab could well return to her awful self once the guilt wore off, but if there was a plan, maybe she would follow through with it.

'Very well.' Zeinab dragged herself up and gathered her things. 'Goodnight, Carmel.'

'Goodnight, Zeinab.'

Zeinab started to leave but then turned back, suddenly looking very old. 'And thank you.'

'You're welcome.' Carmel gave the older woman a smile as she stood and watched her walk slowly towards the lift.

CHAPTER 24

*C*armel entered the bar, which was still buzzing with people. Sharif was sitting with two gin and tonics, reading a medical journal. She sat beside him.

'I got you one. I imagine you'll need it after that.' He gave her the drink, which she sipped gratefully.

'Thanks.' She exhaled fully. 'What a day.'

'What happened with Zeinab? That conversation looked pretty intense.'

'Well, I think she regrets what she did to your mum, but she's just so…I don't know…like her life has been kind of empty and she feels like it's OK to be mean or something. But she's full of guilt and shame and self-loathing. She feels like Nadia got everything and she got nothing out of life. It's just hard to connect with her.'

Sharif sighed. 'I just can't believe she would do that to *Ammi*, you know? She is devastated, really heartbroken. It's so hard to watch.'

Carmel put the glass down and tried to process the last fifteen minutes. 'Well, as I said, she knows that what she did was horribly cruel. And she admits she was jealous of your mother and that her marriage to Tariq was terrible. She was more open and honest than I've ever seen her. She seems to think she's an awful person, and I think she wants to apologise to Nadia but is not expecting her forgiveness. I told her to leave it until the morning, that Nadia's sleeping now, so we'll see. How is she?'

'If she does forgive her, it's going to take time,' Sharif said. 'I've never seen her so crushed, even when he died. It's like every memory is tainted or something, and she's angry with me too, for knowing and not saying it. I tried telling her – I explained all about going to Dolly when I wanted to hit him, I was so angry, and how she talked about the truth being overrated. I tried to say what Dolly would say if she were here. That my father loved her – and only her – his entire life and that he made one stupid mistake and regretted it instantly. He was torn apart with guilt and shame.'

Carmel sighed and took his hand. 'Let's just see how things go in the morning. Honestly, this feels like the longest day in history. It's been a roller coaster.' She leaned against him, and he put his arm around her while she told him about the exchange between herself and Joe.

'Well, the situation with *Ammi* and Zeinab might be broken permanently,' Sharif said, 'but for Tim and that young couple and his friend Kitty, it's a happy ever after, so the day wasn't a total washout. I'm so glad you and Joe are getting even closer. We don't stop needing our parents just because we grow up. I have that with my mother, as you know... Or at least I did.'

'She'll forgive you, Sharif, of course she will. But she's hurting, and we have to give her time.'

He sighed. 'When I was starting out in Aashna – actually, even before that – it was *Ammi* who always backed me. She was there beside me and Jamilla. When Jamilla got sick, and when we had to end our baby's life, she was there. When Jamilla died, it was *Ammi* I called. And then, setting up Aashna, she has always been there, right by my side. Such loyalty is rare in life, even from blood relatives. And now she thinks I betrayed her. My father did – that is a fact. But she believes I should have told her. Maybe she's right. She's been so steadfast, so dedicated to my happiness and success, and now... Well, now everything is different.'

186

Carmel heard the desolation in his voice and longed to help, but there was nothing she could do.

'I think I'll take her back home tomorrow. Is that OK? I don't think she can keep going with the trip now, after everything. Can you understand that?'

Carmel felt panic. Was he leaving her? She forced herself to be calm. 'Well, I'll go with you. I don't want to leave you to do that on your own, and I –'

He turned and faced her, holding both her hands in his. 'My darling girl, please don't do that. I know how much you were looking forward to this wedding and how Joe can't wait to show you off to everyone. This is a really big thing for you, and I do wish I could be in two places at once, but *Ammi* needs me now. And you'll have Joe and Luke and Jen and everyone, while she only has me. I was so low after Jamilla died, and she didn't leave my side for weeks, making me eat, talking, not talking, just being this constant strong presence. And having that helped me get through those first horrific months. I can't let her down now, even if she's angry with me. She needs me. I know you might feel a bit intimidated facing that gang on your own, but you won't be on your own, my love. You'll have your family, the ones who will love you as much as I do. I've been thinking about it, and this is the only thing that makes sense, so I'll take *Ammi* home tomorrow.'

He glanced at his watch. 'Actually, we should probably go in a couple of hours and try to get to Shannon in time for the first flight back to London. Zeinab can stay here, or go back to Pakistan, or... Well, to be honest, I don't care what she does. But you go on to the wedding as planned, and then you can fly home to me when it's all over and you've met your family.'

His chocolate-brown eyes were pleading with her to understand and give in, but she dreaded the thought of him leaving her. She knew she was being pathetic, and of course she had Joe and everyone, but Sharif was her rock. Still, she would have to do it, let him be with Nadia. His mother needed him more right now.

'Of course, come back with me if you really want to,' he said, trying again. 'I'm not laying down the law here – I know better than that.' He grinned. 'But I believe it would be best for you, and I really think you'd regret it if you missed out on the chance to meet your whole family.'

'It's fine, Sharif, and you're right. I should stay. Joe would be so disappointed if I left, and Nadia really does need you. OK, I'm a big girl.' She smiled weakly. 'I can do this.'

They went to bed in Nadia's room, and Sharif booked himself and his mother on the first flight back to London. Eventually, they fell asleep, entwined in each other's arms. She woke when his alarm went off, though the room was still in darkness.

'Go back to sleep, my love,' he whispered. 'I'll call you later, when we're back at Aashna. I'm just going to get *Ammi.*'

He kissed her gently and tucked her in. He dressed quickly, and as all his things were in the other room, he was ready to leave in a matter of moments. They'd packed for Nadia the night before, so he just needed to bring her suitcase with him. He rubbed Carmel's head and bent over to kiss her goodbye.

'I love you,' she murmured.

'I love you too.'

She must have drifted back to sleep, because when she woke an hour later, it took her a moment to remember where she was.

She lay there, in the dark. The distant sounds of occasional traffic and the odd muffled conversation from the car park behind the hotel was all she could hear. She pulled the blanket up to her chin, and soon she wasn't forty-one, she was seven or eight again, in her small iron bed in Trinity House. A memory returned, of a nun, Sister Bridget, who had been very kind. She played with the children and showed exceptional warmth; all the kids loved her. One day, Carmel had made her a card at school. It was coming up to Mother's Day, and all the other children were making Mother's Day cards so she decided to make one for Sister Bridget. She was so proud of it – it had a blue butterfly on the front, and inside she had written in her best writing, *To Sister Bridget, Happy Mother's Day, love, Carmel.*

She didn't let any of the girls in her class see it because she didn't want to have to explain. But it felt so good to have someone to make a card for.

When she'd got back to Trinity, there'd been no sign of Sister Bridget, and when she asked Mother Patrick, the Reverend Mother who ran Trinity, where she was, she got a curt, 'Sister Bridget has gone to another convent. She won't be coming back.'

Carmel couldn't believe Sister Bridget would go without saying a word. Just leave. She was heartbroken, and she scrunched up the card she had taken such care to make and cried tears silently into her pillow.

As an adult, she'd once asked what had ever become of Sister Bridget, and one of the care workers who had been there the longest said that poor old Sister Bridget suffered from her nerves. She'd apparently imagined some kind of relationship between her and Father Delaney, who said Mass in Trinity once a week, so she had to be moved for her own sake, before she disgraced herself and the entire congregation.

That was the last time Carmel had experienced such an acute sense of loss. She had loved and been let down, and she'd vowed at age eight never to get that close to anyone again. It was a promise easy to keep all those years – nobody ever tried to get close to her either. But Sharif, he'd changed all that.

She knew she was being ridiculous – it was only a short time, and she'd survived for over forty years on her own before she met him – but she could not shake the bereft feeling she felt in his absence. She got up and dressed and went back to their room. It was still early, and the others probably weren't up yet.

All of her things were where she'd left them, but all of Sharif's stuff was gone. She sat on the bed, took the pillow from his side and held it to her face. It still smelled faintly of him, the woody, spicy scent he always wore. She held it close and allowed the tears to come.

CHAPTER 25

*C*armel was trying and failing to read a book when the sound of gentle tapping came on her bedroom door.

'Who is it?' she asked through the door, suddenly nervous.

'It's Zeinab.' Her voice was uncertain.

The very last person on earth Carmel wanted to see was Zeinab. But she'd have to open the door.

Zeinab stood there, looking positively dowdy compared to usual. Gone were all the jewels and the heavy make-up, and her hair didn't even have its usual sparkly clips. She wore a plain, dark plum-coloured *shalwar kameez*.

'Carmel, I'm sorry to come so early, but I just wanted to –'

'Zeinab.' Carmel stopped her. 'I'm sorry, but they're gone. Both Sharif and Nadia, back to London. They left early this morning.'

Zeinab must have heard the despair in her voice. 'I'm sorry.'

'Yeah, me too.' Carmel couldn't summon up the strength to be anything but blunt.

'Is everything OK between you and them, you and Sharif?' Zeinab took in the empty room, Carmel's bloodshot eyes.

'Yes, fine, but I decided I wanted to stay and go to my cousin's wedding. My dad has gone to lots of trouble for us to be here, so it wouldn't have been fair on him if I just took off. But Nadia couldn't face it, not after everything.'

'This is all my fault, isn't it?' Zeinab spoke quietly.

Carmel didn't answer.

'So what should I do now?' the other woman asked.

'I have no idea, not one,' Carmel responded wearily. Last night, Zeinab had seemed so despondent, and she still was, but not to the same extent. And anyway, the more Carmel thought about it, the more appalled she was at what Zeinab had done.

'Does Joe know they are gone? Should we tell him?'

Carmel thought she detected a bit of enthusiasm in Zeinab's voice. Surely the woman wasn't still trying to have a crack at her father, after everything? She was incorrigible.

'*We* won't tell him anything, Zeinab. If *anyone* is going to speak to *my* father about this situation, it is me.'

'But what should I do? I'm at a loss...' Zeinab clearly wanted Carmel to solve her problems and salve her conscience, and Carmel was in no position to do either of those things.

'That's up to you, Zeinab. I don't know what you should do, to be honest, but I do know that Nadia doesn't want to see you. So if you do go back to London, perhaps make arrangements to collect your things from her house through Sharif or something. Maybe going back to Pakistan is the best option, for now anyway?'

'Well, I don't want to miss the wedding. I mean, Joe did invite me, and it would be so rude –'

Thankfully they were interrupted by Carmel's phone ringing. 'Sorry, Zeinab, I've to take this.'

She managed to hustle the old woman out the door and gratefully shut it after her.

'Hi, Jen,' she said as she answered the phone.

'Hi, Carmel. Are you all OK?' Jen sounded hesitant. 'I wanted to call last night, just to check, but I didn't know...'

'I'm fine, Jen. Well, fine is probably a bit strong, but I'm all right. Sharif and Nadia are gone back to London.' She filled Jen in on the rest of the night's events, and her sister was supportive and sympathetic.

'I'm so glad you're staying for the wedding, though, I really am. Don't worry, you won't be on your own for a second. We move as a pack, us McDaids.' Jen was joking, but she seemed to sense Carmel's anxiety at facing the whole family without Sharif by her side.

Carmel ended the call after arranging to meet Jen for breakfast in an hour. Jen was going to get Joe and Luke to come too, but the meal would be just the four of them, so they could have breakfast together as a family.

Carmel texted Sharif, knowing he wouldn't even have landed yet. *Have a safe flight. I love you and Nadia.*

She pressed send and threw the phone on the bed. As it landed, it pinged. A text.

She grabbed the phone but saw it was only from Zane. *Alrite luvburdz? Out clubbin' till stupid-o-clock Ivanka is to blame.#deadbodytomo #workinhospicejoke Miss yo sweet li'l Irish face. Z xxx*

Normally, she loved to get his messages – he always cheered her up – but not now. He always called her and Sharif *luvburdz*. It was kind of an in-joke after he planned their engagement party last year, threatening to have a hundred white doves delivered.

Suddenly, the room seemed to be closing in on her. She needed some air. She pulled on some tracksuit bottoms, a t-shirt and a hoodie, slipped into her trainers, and let herself out. The streets of Westport were almost deserted. There was the odd milk truck or delivery van, but the tourists had not yet surfaced after the revelry the night before.

She walked fast, almost trying to run away from the thoughts swirling frantically round her head. She attempted to rationalise the sense of abandonment and the frustration with herself at feeling so frightened and alone. She had her family here, she'd lived without Sharif for forty years, and now she was distraught at spending a few days away from him. It was stupid; she knew it. But Nora was teaching her that her reactions were informed by her experiences. Her fear of abandonment, of being alone, stemmed from her childhood.

Round and round the thoughts went, and she was getting more and more frustrated with herself. In the pocket of her hoodie, she found her earphones. She liked to listen to podcasts when she walked at home, so she stuck them in her ears. She scrolled to her podcasts and selected one from Wayne Dyer. His lovely voice always soothed her, and he seemed to always know the right thing to say.

She was engrossed in her phone so she never saw the broken pavement, or the van that was going too fast, too close to the kerb.

* * *

SHARIF'S PHONE FLASHED 'INCOMING CALL' as he waited at the carousel at Heathrow. His mother had hardly said a word since they left Ireland, except to ask why Carmel wasn't coming back with them. He explained that she'd be back next week, that she was going to go to the wedding – he never mentioned her speaking to Zeinab – and that everything was going to be OK. Nadia was still a little sedated, and for that, he was grateful.

He answered his phone. 'Hello.'

'Sharif? It's Tim.'

'Oh, hi, Tim. Em…my mother and I are actually back in Lon –'

'I know,' Tim interrupted. 'Zeinab said. I'm sorry to have to tell you this, but there's been an accident.'

'What happened?'

'It's Carmel. She's been knocked down by a van. The young fool driving it was out late and drove to work early this morning – he was over the limit. Carmel is in University Hospital Galway. She was taken from the scene by ambulance.'

Sharif felt sick; blood pounded in his ears. 'How is she? Is she badly hurt?'

'I don't know, Sharif. Joe and Luke are following the ambulance in the hire car. I actually came on the accident. I stayed at my friend's house last night and was walking back to the hotel early this morning. She must have gone out for a walk or a run or something. She was wearing sports clothes anyway. The paramedics wouldn't let me go with her, and the Guards wanted to talk to me as well, get her details and all of that. That's how I know the driver was drunk.'

Sharif swallowed. 'Was she conscious?'

'I don't think so, Sharif.' Tim sounded so upset. 'I'm sorry.'

'And was she injured – I mean – could you see any external injuries?'

There was a pause.

'There seemed to be a lot of blood. I'm sorry, Sharif. I'll go to the hospital now. Jen and Damien are coming too. I'll ring again when I know more.'

'I'm on my way back, Tim. I'll get the next flight hopefully.'

Shaking, Sharif went over to where his mother was standing. '*Ammi*, Carmel's had an accident. She's been knocked down. Tim just called. She's in an ambulance on the way to hospital, and he said she wasn't conscious and there was a lot of blood.' He was trying to stop the panic rising up in him.

'Come on, get to the desk and get a flight back.' The news seemed to have jolted Nadia out of her trance-like state. 'Move, Sharif, come on.' She grabbed him by the arm and pulled him to the Aer Lingus desk.

They explained the situation, and the woman on the desk was very understanding but told them the flight was fully booked and the next available wasn't until seven that evening.

'But you can go on standby, and if someone cancels –'

'Not good enough,' Nadia muttered. She left the desk and headed to the security queue.

'Is anyone flying to Shannon?' she yelled at the top of her voice. People stopped and stared at this tiny Asian woman asking over and over for people flying to Shannon. Eventually, a young couple said they were.

Nadia stood before them. 'If you let me and my son take your seats, I will give you a thousand pounds in cash right this minute. I will go to the cashpoint over there and draw it out and hand it over. All you need to do is come with me to the Aer Lingus desk and tell them we are taking your seats. It's an absolute emergency – my daughter-in-law is critically ill in hospital, and we need to get to her.'

The couple looked at each other. The man wasn't keen, but the young woman said, 'It's fine. We can stay another night.'

'Marvellous.' Nadia led them to the Aer Lingus desk, and Sharif went to the cashpoint. They handed over the money, and the change of name was done. Sharif and Nadia had to run to make the flight, their luggage presumably still circling the belt in the arrivals hall.

Nadia took total charge as Sharif tried over and over to contact the hospital. Carmel was in accident and emergency so was not yet on the hospital system, he was told. Eventually, he managed to get through to the emergency department.

'A & E, Moira speaking.'

'Hello, my name is Dr Sharif Khan. My wife, Carmel Khan, was admitted in the past hour, a road accident?' He tried to keep the panic and frustration out of his voice. He knew first-hand the level of pressure staff in emergency medicine were under, and he also knew adding to it wasn't going to get him very far.

'OK, let me check. Please hold.'

Some horrible tinny music played while he waited. He began to think she'd forgotten about him, but he continued to hold as his mother showed both passports and they boarded the plane. She found their seats, and he still waited. The music was on a loop, and he felt the ridiculous tune drilling into his brain.

'Sir, you'll need to end your call.' The stewardess tapped his shoulder. 'We are about to take off.' She was about fifty, and despite a lot of make-up, she still looked like a bulldog chewing a wasp, so Sharif didn't defy her. He had seen people removed from flights for security infractions in the opinion of the cabin crew, so he couldn't take a chance.

'Now, sir,' she added with a steely glare.

Reluctantly, he pressed end. It was an hour and ten minutes to Shannon, and the cabin crew were just going through the security demonstration. He glanced at his watch. 9:15. They'd be there by

10:30, rent a car, and he could be in Galway an hour later if he put the boot down. But what if he was too late?

He couldn't allow himself to think like that. She was going to be OK. She had to be OK.

Nadia leaned over and put her hand on his as they took off, back to Ireland.

He looked at her. 'I should never have left her. If I –'

'Sharif, stop this now. We must pray that our darling girl is all right. Nothing else matters.'

'But if I hadn't left her – she didn't want to stay alone...'

'Why?'

Sharif ran his hands through his silver hair. 'I talked her into staying for the wedding. She wanted to come with us. What will I do, *Ammi*, if she dies? I can't go through it again. She might die – she might be dead already...'

'Stop that now. Sharif Khan, you need to pull yourself together. Your wife needs you, and we'll find out how she is the moment the plane touches down. But for now, we will just pray to Allah to keep her safe.'

For the first time in his adult life, Sharif prayed. He asked Allah to protect Carmel. He didn't know who or what, if anything, he was speaking to – Allah, God, Buddha, the Universe, something, nothing, some power other than himself, something stronger than him, some force to keep her alive.

He shook his head when the same stewardess offered him tea or coffee; he couldn't swallow anything. After what felt like an interminable hour, the captain announced to the cabin crew that they should take their seats for landing, and the lights to indicate no more walking in the cabin came on. Sharif wondered if he could get a signal on his phone as they came in to land. He decided to risk it, despite the clear instruction not to switch it on until the plane had touched ground. He didn't care what the Aer Lingus woman thought – he took out his phone and switched it on. 'Searching for network' flashed up on the screen.

He pressed several buttons in frustration. Still searching for network. They disembarked, and as they hustled their way through the crowd to get to the immigration desk, he was so glad of his British passport. His mother had one too, which spared them the added wait of travelling through the much longer non-EU queue they would have had to endure with their Pakistani passports.

Ping. A text. *Welcome to Ireland...*

Sharif rejected the text, and two more, both offering competitive rates for roaming. Then one from Joe. *At hospital now. No news.*

And one from Tim. *Carmel in ER. Team with her. She's alive but no other update.*

Sharif showed it to Nadia, too relieved to speak. Then he found Joe's number in his phone and rang it.

It was answered on the first ring. 'Sharif, it's Jen.'

'How is she?'

'Dad is just gone off with someone now. We're waiting for him to come back. I'm not supposed to have the phone on here. One sec – I'll go outside and ring you back. Where are you?'

'At the airport. I'm just renting a car now. Call me as soon as you can.' He hung up and relayed what she'd said to Nadia.

Nadia dealt with the car hire, shoving things to sign at him, taking his driving licence and credit card out of his wallet, nudging him to enter the pin. Eventually, it was all done. Sharif just stared at the phone, waiting for Jen to call back.

He knew the protocol well. If a doctor had good news to deliver, they were usually happy to do it in front of the gathered family or friends. If it was bad news, they took the next of kin aside.

He couldn't bear to go further down that line of thought. Why wasn't Jen ringing back? He tried Tim. It rang out. He hung up, frustrated.

Then the phone rang. Joe.

'Sharif, it's Joe.' His tone was terse.

'Tell me.'

'She's going to be OK.'

Relief flooded his body. He felt tears well up. 'I...I'm just so relieved. I'm on the way. How bad are her injuries? Tim said there was a lot of blood. What happened?'

There was a long pause, and then he heard Joe's voice. 'She was out walking or running or something when she was knocked down by a van. She did lose a lot of blood, but the ambulance arrived quickly. They're taking her to theatre now to set the broken bones in her arm and leg. She had a fracture to her skull as well, but they think it's not too serious. No internal bleeding as far as they can see, but she'll have a scan when she goes down to theatre.' Joe's voice had softened.

'OK. Is she even a little aware?' Sharif asked.

'I haven't seen her, just spoke to the head of the assessment team, and that's all he told me. They're fairly sure there's nothing internally, and her vital signs are strong.'

'Well, if you get the chance to see her, can you ring me? I want to speak to her, even just for a second.'

'OK, I will. Drive safely. Oh, Sharif, is Nadia with you?'

'Yes. Do you want to speak to her?'

Joe hesitated. 'Ah no, I'll see you both in a bit.'

CHAPTER 26

*J*en, Damien, Zeinab, Tim and Joe all sat in the hospital canteen, sipping drinks they didn't want. Luke and Carrie were gone back to the hotel to get some of Carmel's things. She'd been in surgery for two hours now, and there was no word. The nurse had told them to go off and get a coffee and she'd call them when Carmel was back from theatre.

Luckily an old college friend of Jen's was married to a Galway man and lived there now, so she offered to mind Ruari. She had a little girl of more or less the same age, so he went off happily.

When Sharif and Nadia arrived to the emergency department, they went in search of the rest of the family and guessed they'd be at the café.

As they entered, the others stood up. Seeing the whole family there made Sharif even more worried. If it was just a broken arm, surely they would have gone home.

Zeinab kept her distance, and neither Sharif nor Nadia acknowledged her.

Nadia went straight to Joe, who drew her into his arms for a hug. Seeing her seemed to melt his stoic exterior. 'My poor girl. Hasn't she had enough crap to deal with already? I'm glad you're here,' he mumbled so only Nadia could hear.

'Yes, well, Sharif had to come back. We should never have –'

'I'm glad he's back too, obviously,' Joe interrupted her, glancing to see Sharif in chat with Jen, Tim and Damien. 'He is of course who she'll want to see, but…' He looked around to verify that Zeinab had gone to the ladies'. 'But I'm glad you're back,' he said.

She looked up at him. He wasn't letting her go.

'I'm glad to be back too. What's the latest?' Nadia asked.

Just as he was about to tell her what he knew, his phone rang. 'Hello, Joe McDaid.'

The others all turned to watch him.

'Right, great,' he said into the phone. Then there was a pause. 'Yes, he just arrived… Sure… Right. Thanks.'

They all stared at him, faces expectant, as he hung up.

'She's back and seems OK,' he said. 'The doctors want to see you, Sharif. The rest of us are to wait here, and they'll let us know when we can see her. She's in recovery. Follow along the green tile. It's sign-posted, the nurse said.'

Sharif didn't need to be told twice and virtually bolted out of the canteen. He passed medical staff of all varieties but saw nothing. Normally, he was very interested in hospitals and how different places did things, but now all he wanted was to see Carmel. He found recovery easily and gave his name at the reception desk.

'She's in cubicle four, second on the left. The curtains are pulled, but you can just go in.'

He found her spot and heard voices coming from the other side of the curtains. So often in his life he'd been the one the family were quizzing, needing information, some good news. It felt strange to be on this side of it again.

He parted the curtains, and there she was. Her blonde hair was matted with blood, her face bruised. Her arm was in a plaster cast from wrist to shoulder, and her leg was covered by a metal cage to keep the blankets off it. All the injuries seemed to be on her right side.

'I'm Sharif Khan, Carmel's husband.' He introduced himself to the very young-looking African doctors consulting at Carmel's bedside.

'Hello, Dr Khan, oncology?' the shorter of the two said with a smile. 'Carmel's aunt mentioned it.'

'Yes, that's right. How is she?' The last thing on his mind was Zeinab. He could just picture it: *My nephew is an oncologist, you know!* Guaranteed to annoy the medical staff treating their patient. They would do their best if her husband was a binman or a plasterer either.

'She's OK. Mild linear open fracture to the skull, but neurosurgery had a look at the X-ray and are confident painkillers will do, no need for their involvement. There's no evidence of cognitive impairment. There's a fracture to the ulna, distal, and a tibia fracture as well.'

'Is that it?' Sharif asked.

'Yes, she's been fully scanned,' the doctor told him, 'though it would have been better to know about the pregnancy before the MRI. But your wife was unresponsive in the ambulance. She woke up briefly in the A & E pre-theatre, but we sedated her. Thankfully, baby seems to have survived the jolt, and the heartbeat is good and strong.'

Sharif sat down on the seat beside Carmel's head. 'I didn't know... We... I don't think Carmel knew either.' He was trying to sound coherent. 'We were trying, but...'

'Well, it's a dramatic way to find out, all right, I suppose.' The taller doctor chuckled. 'Yes, she's about six weeks, so it's early days, but everything looks fine. Congratulations.'

When they left, Sharif just sat watching Carmel. She was pregnant. He was going to be a father.

An hour ago, he was afraid he might lose her, and now here she was, growing their child inside her poor broken body. Six weeks. He knew she was on the pill, but he was trying to think back. Then he remembered the bout of food poisoning – vomiting and diarrhoea could render the contraceptive pill ineffective. That must have been it. He was sure she had no idea. She would have said.

He rubbed the uninjured side of her head, brushing her hair back off her forehead. The injury to her skull meant the skin was broken, dark blood congealing around her ear. The bruising was extensive;

she was going to be very sore for a few weeks, and there would have to be physio to get the range of movement back in her wrist and ankle. But she was alive.

He kissed her head and held her hand. With his free hand, he texted Joe. *She's still sedated. Set her wrist and leg and stitched up her head. The bruising is extensive but she's OK. Only one visitor today but come on your own and I'll sneak you in for a second?*

Almost immediately, the response came. *On my way.*

Joe appeared at her bedside ten minutes later, and he held one of her hands while Sharif held the other.

'She'll probably be out of it for another hour or so.' Sharif spoke quietly.

'Maybe I'll let the others get back. We were to check out and move on today, but now we're probably best off staying put till we know what the situation is.'

'You should all continue, of course,' Sharif insisted. 'Carmel is going to be fine. I'll be with her. You should all go.'

'I don't know. We'll see, Sharif. The way things are with your mother and Zeinab is another thing. Nadia has had enough upset. I don't want any more. But Zeinab has been very nice, trying to be helpful and all of that. I think she is really sorry.'

Sharif sighed. 'Nearly losing my wife this morning puts everything into perspective. What Zeinab did was cruel and hurtful, but – and I should know this better than most – we never get enough time, we all leave too soon, and there's not a moment to waste on anger or bitterness. If my mother accepts her apology, we'll leave it at that. But it's up to *Ammi.*'

They sat in companionable silence as Carmel rested. She'd get a fright when she woke up, but the injury was all superficial, Sharif could tell. *It will take a few months, but she'll be fine.* He watched her. How would she take the pregnancy news? He imagined she would be thrilled. He hadn't really allowed himself to think about it much, his overriding emotion being relief that she was OK.

'If I hadn't gone off like that...' If he'd stayed, she would have been in bed with him, not running around Westport.

Joe sighed. 'Did you ever hear the phrase, if wishes were horses, beggars would ride? You were looking out for your mam. Nobody could have predicted this.'

Sharif nodded.

'Now, I'd better get back to the others, though to be honest, I'd rather stay here, just to be one hundred percent sure. But you'll look after her, I suppose, and poor old Nadia will need a bit of backup.' Joe rose from his seat and bent to kiss Carmel's head gently. 'I'll be back later on, pet, and Sharif is staying here. You'll be fine, darling, don't you worry. We're all looking after you.'

Sharif stood.

'Let me know when she wakes, OK?'

'I will. And thanks for taking care of my mother. She's very fragile right now.'

Joe smiled. 'I know. She got an awful blow, but she's a tough old bird, your mam. She'll be fine.'

Sharif chuckled. 'I'm not sure she'd be happy to be described as a tough old bird.'

'Ah, Nadia knows I'm only joking. Sure I'm fierce fond of her.' Joe felt in his pockets for his keys.

As Joe turned to go, Sharif heard himself say, 'Are you?'

'Am I what?' Joe replied.

'Fond of *Ammi?*' Sharif looked directly at his father-in-law.

Joe coloured slightly, uncomfortable with the turn the conversation had taken. 'Well, I –'

'All I'm saying,' Sharif interrupted, 'is if you do like her as more than a friend, Carmel and I are happy for you.' Suddenly life was so precious, every single minute, because one never knew what was around the corner. 'And I think *Ammi* might feel the same way,' he added. 'If you don't, no harm done, and we won't talk about this again. But I just wanted to give you a bit of an edge. We men so rarely have that when dealing with the fairer sex, do we?'

Joe blustered. 'Well, I don't know about that. Sure, we're a bit old for all of that stuff now and… Well, sure… Anyway, I better get going, and you'll give me a shout when Carmel wakes, right?'

203

'Of course.' Sharif smiled and went back to his wife. After an hour of just sitting there, his thoughts racing, trying to rationalise the last few days, Carmel's consultant appeared on his rounds.

'Good afternoon. I'm Donnacha O'Halloran. Your wife is under my care.'

Sharif stood and shook his hand. 'Sharif Khan. Thanks for all you have done for her. If you hadn't worked so quickly to stem the bleeding...'

'Well, it was the paramedic really. She was in bad shape coming in to us, but if it weren't for them, she'd be a lot worse. The nurse on duty tells me you're an oncologist?' He checked the chart hanging on the end of Carmel's bed as they spoke.

'Yes, I – well, we, actually, Carmel and I and my mother – run a hospice in London.'

The doctor checked Carmel's vital signs and her IV line. He briefly gave Sharif the update of her progress, and as he did, Carmel's eyelids fluttered. They both turned, and Sharif went straight to her.

'Sha...Sharif,' she managed, her voice raspy.

He held a Styrofoam cup of water to her dry lips, and she sipped and swallowed. Her eyes closed again.

'It's fine, Carmel, I'm here. Just go back to sleep. I'll be here when you wake up.'

CHAPTER 27

*T*he other doctor left, and Sharif held Carmel's hand. Over the next twenty minutes, she regained consciousness.

Eventually, she made another attempt to speak. 'My head hurts. What happened to me?'

'You were knocked down, my love, but the ambulance came quickly and you're going to be fine,' he soothed. 'A bit sore, but apart from a broken arm and a broken leg, you're OK.'

'Everything hurts,' she croaked.

'I know, my love. You got a few nasty cuts and bruises, so that's why you feel so sore, but now that you're awake, we can get your meds regulated to manage the pain.'

'OK.' She sighed and seemed content to drift back to sleep.

As she dozed, half in and half out of consciousness, Sharif texted Joe. *She's awake and talking but very tired. If you're coming back, I'd say give her another hour at least.*

Joe messaged back instantly. *What a relief. See you later.*

The next time Carmel woke, Sharif called the nurse, who administered some painkillers, and within twenty minutes, Carmel was much more alert and seemed comfortable enough.

'Carmel, I'm so sorry,' Sharif said. 'I should not have gone off like that. I feel so guilty. This is my fault.' He knew he shouldn't be laying this heavy stuff on her so soon after her surgery, but he needed her to know how sorry he was.

'It's OK,' she whispered, and swallowed. He offered her some more water, and she smiled weakly.

'I love you. So much. When I thought it was worse, Carmel, I...' His voice cracked.

'You won't get rid of me that easy.' She smiled again and added, 'Can you help me sit up a bit? My back is sore.'

'Of course.' He lifted her gently, making sure her leg wasn't dragged, and though she winced in pain, she relaxed back against the cushions. She put her hand to her face. 'My face feels all...I don't know...puffy or something.'

He gently removed her hand from the worst of the bruising. 'I know, and you have a bit of bruising and swelling to your face, but it will go down in a few weeks. You'll look a bit colourful for a while, though.' He smiled and kissed her palm as he placed her hand back beside her hip.

'Oh God, do I look desperate?' she groaned.

'You look gorgeous, and what's more, you look alive. At this moment in time, that is all that matters to me.'

She grimaced. 'I don't feel very gorgeous, I can tell you.'

He was sure she didn't know about the baby. She would have asked about it first if she did. 'Carmel.' He paused, and she turned her head slowly, the pain registering on her face.

'What?'

'When they brought you in, they did a scan to check for internal injuries, and in the course of that, they discovered something.'

What bit of colour she had drained from her face. She swallowed and winced. 'Tell me. Don't drag it out, just say it. Is it bad?'

'No.' He smiled. 'It's very good. You're pregnant, six weeks roughly, and the baby is fine. Heartbeat is strong, and the accident didn't do any damage to him or her.'

Carmel said nothing. She just stared at him.

'Are you OK? This is great, isn't it?'

She nodded. Her good hand went to her abdomen and rested there. 'Are they sure? That everything is OK?' Tears slid down her cheeks.

'Yes, everything is fine. Our little prince or princess is cosy and happy in there.' He placed his hand on top of hers.

'And you're happy? Like really, not just saying it because you think it's what I want?'

Sharif held her good hand in both of his and leaned close to her, his face only inches from hers. 'I'm going to be honest. I wasn't sure, even when I said we'd try. I was partly doing it to please you. If you'd said you never wanted kids, then that would have suited me fine. But now, knowing our son or daughter exists, Carmel...' He swallowed, trying to get the words out. 'All the time you were sedated, I just sat here, knowing, imagining what he or she will be like, what they'll look like, sound like. What it will feel like to have someone call me *Abba*...'

'Like the Swedish pop group?' She chuckled but stopped instantly – it hurt to laugh.

He grinned. 'No, it's Urdu for Da –'

'I know, you eejit, I'm only messing.' She smiled on her good side then sighed. 'I can't believe it. We're going to have a baby. I'm going to be a mammy, like some person is going to call me that. Mammy and *Abba*. The poor kid will be culturally confused.'

'We can send them to an Islamic school taught through Irish maybe?'

She laughed. 'Stop. You can't make me laugh!' She groaned again. 'I feel like I've gone ten rounds with Mike Tyson. Every bit of me hurts.'

'OK. Misery and tragedy from now on, I promise.'

'Stop it, I said!' She tried not to laugh.

'OK...OK. I don't want Dr O'Halloran throwing me out for distressing his patient. Are you sleepy? Will I let you rest? I can just sit here, and you sleep if you want to.'

'No, I don't feel sleepy. Sore and a bit groggy still, but I've slept enough. Can we talk about the baby? I just can't believe it. I never thought for a second that it could really happen for me. Having someone of my own... Like, I know I have you and Joe and all the family, but a baby, my own child...' She was still trying to make it a reality in her head.

'Do you think it's a boy or a girl?' Sharif asked.

'A girl.' Her answer was instant and definite.

'You sound sure.'

'I don't know why, but I am. I think it's a girl. What will we call her?'

'Isn't it obvious? There's only one name our daughter could have.'

'Dolly Khan. I like it.'

Sharif leaned over and gently kissed her abdomen. 'Hello in there, little Dolly. This is your *abba*, and I love you already, so very much. So be a good little girl and grow healthy and strong, and your mammy and I will be waiting to meet you next spring.'

Carmel rubbed his head with her good hand as he spoke to their baby. 'How... I'm amazed. I was taking the pill until recently.'

'I think that dodgy sushi is what we have to thank. You were throwing up for days, and that interrupts the effectiveness of any drugs in the system.'

Moments later, the porter arrived with a senior staff nurse. 'We're going to take you to the ward now, Carmel. You'll be with us for a few days, just till we can be sure everything is healing properly, OK?' The nurse was already preparing the bed for transport.

'I don't think I can get up...' Carmel started to panic.

'No, we won't be getting you up at all,' the nurse explained. 'We'll wheel the bed up and leave you in it. Now if your husband could just move out of my way?' she remarked pointedly.

Sharif stepped into the corner of the small room and made a face behind her back, which made Carmel giggle.

Thankfully, a private room was available, and she was soon settled in.

'Is my phone dead?' Carmel asked.

'I'm afraid so, but I'll get you a new one just as soon as I can.'

'No, it's OK, I just wanted to text Jen to maybe get some of my things, pyjamas, toothbrush, stuff like that.' She leaned back on the pillows again. The effort of moving exhausted her.

'Don't worry, Luke's already on it,' Sharif told her. 'I'm sure they're on the way back here now.' He could see her eyelids drooping once more. 'Go to sleep now, and I'll just wait here, OK?'

'OK...' And within a moment, she was asleep again.

He dozed in the hard chair and only woke when he felt a hand on his shoulder.

'*Ammi.*' He woke to find Nadia and Joe in the room. Nadia was carrying Carmel's smaller suitcase.

'How is she?' Nadia asked, her face registering shock at how battered Carmel looked.

'It looks worse than it is,' Sharif assured her. 'She's going to be fine. A fractured skull, ulna and tibia, a deep gash on her head... She has some dissolving stitches there, and some soft tissue damage to her face and chest. But nothing she won't recover from with love and care.'

'Oh, Sharif, thank goodness she is alive. I...' Tears came to Nadia's eyes for the first time since they'd heard the news.

Carmel's eyes opened. 'Hi, guys,' she said weakly.

'Hello, my darling girl. It's so good to see you awake.' Joe held her hand and kissed her forehead.

Nadia was crying. 'Ah, Nadia, I'm grand...honestly. I'll be fine.'

Sharif was about to put his arm around his mother to comfort her, but Joe got there first. He also noticed how his mother relaxed into the man's embrace. Surely Joe hadn't taken him at his word that quickly.

His face must have registered some confusion.

'Are we missing something here?' Carmel asked straight out, trying not to smile.

Joe looked from Sharif to Carmel and then down at Nadia. 'Well, I suppose we have to come clean sometime.'

CHAPTER 28

*N*adia looked sheepish, but she explained. 'Darling Sharif, Joe told me what you said this morning, and I'm sorry for not being honest earlier, but we were worried how you and Carmel would take it. Jennifer and Luke too, but... Joe and I, well, we have been seeing each other a bit...'

Joe helped her out, his arm still firmly around her. 'We liked each other for ages, since the very start, if I'm honest, and we've gone out to dinner a few times. We talk on the phone most days, but as Nadia said, it was a bit weird. Not the dates, they were lovely, but just the whole setup. And so we thought maybe it would be better to be friends and that. But, eh...well, we didn't manage that so well. So when you said what you said this morning, Sharif, that you and Carmel had discussed it and that you were OK with it...'

'Joe came back and told me,' Nadia continued for him. 'And, well, I hope you meant it and that you spoke for Carmel too?'

'So you two have been together for ages? Is that what you're telling us?' Carmel was stunned. They were a pair of dark horses.

'But how could we not know?' Sharif asked, equally perplexed. 'Whenever you come over, Joe, you stay with us, and *Ammi*, you've only been away for those weekends on the yoga retreats... *Ammi*,

210

those *were* yoga retreats, weren't they?' Sharif seemed genuinely shocked.

This time, Joe and Nadia really did look like teenagers caught getting amorous on the couch by early returning parents.

'I don't know, Sharif. The elderly of today, there's no dealing with them,' Carmel teased. 'Sex mad. I blame the kids, myself, or maybe it's the vitamins they all take now. Has them like goats in spring.'

'Stop that talk, you! Respect your elders!' Joe chuckled but then grew serious, worried. 'Are you sure you are OK, though, seriously?'

'Of course we are, you silly man!' Carmel said. 'We're thrilled for both of you. And now we can all go on one of those trashy shows on daytime telly – "Long-Lost Irish Dad in Romp with Paki Mother-in-Law". I can just see the headlines.' She giggled again and immediately winced with pain.

'Hey, less of the romping images if you don't mind, please.' Sharif shuddered with mock horror. 'That's my mother we're talking about, and she does not romp.'

'Indeed,' Joe said sincerely. 'She's a perfect lady, and she means a lot to me.'

'Does anyone else know?' Carmel was fascinated at how they'd kept it secret for so long. Nadia had been going to so-called yoga retreats for months.

'Zeinab,' Nadia revealed.

It was the first time her name had come up since the accident.

Carmel and Sharif waited for an explanation, and Nadia began. 'When we went back to the hotel, I decided she and I needed to talk. So we went for a long walk, and she apologised for the way she'd blurted out about Khalid's affair. I was so hurt, but I realised my hurt was at him, not her. I could have found out anywhere in Karachi on any of the occasions when Khalid and I went back. I'm sure some of our Pakistani friends in London knew, even enjoyed pitying me as the grieving widow, clueless as to what my husband had done.

'After talking to Sharif, who got his wisdom from our darling Dolly, I have come around to how they saw it. It was one mistake a long time ago. Khalid loved me and Sharif. I know he did. But he made a mistake, and rather than destroy three lives, he bore the guilt and shame himself and allowed me and his son a life of carefree happiness. He was not a selfish man, and his memory is still in my heart. Nothing will ever change that. So I told her why it annoyed me so much to see her flirting with Joe. I was jealous, simple as that. I...I had – *have* – feelings for him, and she touching him and trying to ingratiate herself just annoyed me. I wasn't kind. Her marriage to Tariq was a bad one, and she admits it now. I think she is tired, tired of always pretending, always having to look down on others in order to elevate herself.'

Sharif looked sceptical, 'I hope you haven't said she can live here or anything, though, have you?'

Nadia smiled. 'I said I forgave her, Sharif. I didn't say I had entirely taken leave of my senses. Of course not. She could drive the Dalai Lama insane. No, she's going back to Karachi next week, just like she planned.'

Sharif sighed with relief. Carmel grabbed his hand, her glance questioning. He nodded slightly.

'Well, since we are in the business of revelations,' she said, then paused. 'I'm pregnant.'

It was Nadia and Joe's turn to be shocked.

They gently hugged Carmel and nearly squeezed the life out of Sharif. The delight in the room was palpable. Tears of joy coursed down Nadia's cheeks as she hugged her son and held her daughter-in-law's hand.

Joe texted Jen and Luke, who had come with him and were down in the lobby waiting for the all-clear to come up to see Carmel. As they entered, Joe blurted everything out, explaining the scenes of jubilation they met in what should have been a sickroom.

Everyone was talking at once, and Jen and Luke seemed amazed but pleased at both pieces of news.

Joe McDaid stood back and surveyed the various parts of his life, unfolding in ways he could never have imagined. His two daughters, both expecting babies of their own, deep in excited chat about how their children would be cousins. And his son and son-in-law teasing

Nadia about the secret romance. He began to sing, at first quietly, but eventually so everyone could hear.

'When I was just a little girl, I asked my mother, what will I be? Will I be handsome, will I be rich? Here's what she said to me.'

By the time he got to the chorus, they were all singing along gently.

'Que sera, sera, whatever will be, will be. The future's not ours to see, que sera, sera.'

THE END

I sincerely hope you enjoyed this the third and final instalment in The Carmel Sheehan Series. Feel free to join my readers club over at www.jeangrainger.com to hear about the release of new books or special offers. You'll get a free gift of a novel on ebook to welcome you. Membership is 100% free and always will be.

Jean x

ABOUT THE AUTHOR

Jean Grainger is a USA Today bestselling Irish author. She writes historical and contemporary Irish fiction and her work has very flatteringly been compared to the late great Maeve Binchy.

She lives in a two hundred year old stone cottage in County Cork with her husband Diarmuid and the youngest two of her four children. The older two show up occasionally with laundry and to raid the fridge. There are a variety of animals there too, all led by two cute but clueless micro-dogs called Scrappy and Scoobi.

[f]

ALSO BY JEAN GRAINGER

To get a free novel and to join my readers club (100% free and always will be)

Go to www.jeangrainger.com

The Tour Series

The Tour

Safe at the Edge of the World

The Story of Grenville King

The Homecoming of Bubbles O'Leary

Finding Billie Romano

Kayla's Trick

The Carmel Sheehan Story

Letters of Freedom

The Future's Not Ours To See

What Will Be

The Robinswood Story

What Once Was True

Return To Robinswood

Trials and Tribulations

The Star and the Shamrock Series

The Star and the Shamrock

The Emerald Horizon

The Hard Way Home

The World Starts Anew

The Queenstown Series

Last Port of Call

The West's Awake

The Harp and the Rose

Roaring Liberty

Standalone Books

So Much Owed

Shadow of a Century

Under Heaven's Shining Stars

Catriona's War

Sisters of the Southern Cross

Made in the USA
Coppell, TX
01 July 2022

79469890R10132